CHASING DEATH

THE SECOND DOCTOR SIX NOVEL

James Rozhon

Gotham Books
30 N Gould St.
Ste. 20820, Sheridan, WY 82801
https://gothambooksinc.com/

Phone: 1 (307) 464-7800

© 2022 James Rozhon. All rights reserved.

No part of this book may be reproduced, stored in a retrieval system, or transmitted by any means without the written permission of the author.

Published by Gotham Books (December 30, 2022)

ISBN: 979-8-88775-180-1 (sc)
ISBN: 979-8-88775-181-8 (e)

Because of the dynamic nature of the Internet, any web addresses or links contained in this book may have changed since publication and may no longer be valid.

The views expressed in this work are solely those of the author and do not necessarily reflect the views of the publisher, and the publisher hereby disclaims any responsibility for them.

Table of Contents

Chapter 1 7
Chapter 2 11
Chapter 3 17
Chapter 4 23
Chapter 5 29
Chapter 6 35
Chapter 7 39
Chapter 8 45
Chapter 9 49
Chapter 10 55
Chapter 11 61
Chapter 12 67
Chapter 13 73
Chapter 14 79
Chapter 15 83
Chapter 16 89
Chapter 17 93
Chapter 18 99
Chapter 19 105
Chapter 20 111
Chapter 21 115
Chapter 22 121
Chapter 23 127
Chapter 24 133

Chapter 25	137
Chapter 26	141
Chapter 27	145
Chapter 28	149
Chapter 29	152
Chapter 30	157
Chapter 31	165
Chapter 32	169
Chapter 33	175
Chapter 34	183
Chapter 35	189
Chapter 36	193
Chapter 37	199
Chapter 38	205
Chapter 39	209
Chapter 40	215
Chapter 41	221
Chapter 42	227
Chapter 43	233
Chapter 44	237
Epilogue	241

Chapter 1

Kalispell, Montana. That's where I live. You've probably never heard of it. But everything that was going to happen, was going to happen there. There would be side trips to be sure – including one to Portland, Maine; I was born there.

But first…

I was talking with Regina Ryan about her son, David, when my phone rang. No, not the office phone, but my cell phone. My routine is to carry it into each room, place it on the counter next to the sink and then face my patient. Had it been in my purse, I would never have known that the person calling me was my mother, Melodie Chang.

My name is Doctor Evangeline Monica Sixkiller-Collins Collins. Doctor Six, for short. Anything else confuses people, even patients.

That said, according to Regina, David's symptoms were many. Restlessness, loss of appetite, mood swings and withdrawal from their family. I could think of at least two causes that might fit his symptoms, but I'll admit that I wasn't very convinced that the one I chose fit David very well. I considered David to be bipolar. However, any further diagnostic effort on my part was foreshortened when I saw my mother's number in the display window on the ringing phone. There weren't many people whose call I would answer when I was with a patient. Mom? Oh, yes.

"A moment," I said to Regina with a smile. Then I smiled and said, "Hey. Long time. You must be busy in Congress." My mother is Melodie Chang and she is the Congressional Representative from Maine's First Congressional District.

"Alex Payne died last night," she said with as much emotion in her voice as I'd heard in a very long time.

Yes, he was *that* Alex Payne, the middle linebacker that dropped *that* pass in one of those Super Bowls and cost his team, the Patriots, the championship. Sorry, I don't follow football, so I don't know which Roman numeral he failed in. While he wasn't the reason I became a doctor – my mother was – I was the reason Alex lived as long as he did. No, that's not a brag. That's a fact. It was also eighteen years ago. Long enough to have forgotten. Important enough that I hadn't.

Alex did steroids when he played, took them for a long time. By the time he retired, he was a mess physically. Two people kept him alive. Professor Grant Waitling from San Francisco State University and Alex's wife, Ellie. Alex became Grant's first participant in a study he called Long-Term Steroid Abuse Syndrome. LTSAS. I steered Alex toward Grant and Grant laid out a regimen that Ellie made certain Alex followed. Of all the people around him who made sure that he followed the program, I credit Ellie because she devoted *them* to it.

"Oh, no," I said felling the depth of my loss. I loved that man. I was raped eighteen years ago by a lunatic and Alex kept me sane because I couldn't tell my mother for so many reasons that to enumerate now them would be pointless. However, every time I felt a twinge of the madness approaching, I sought him out and he never failed me. I can't recall the numbers of times I screamed into his chest because life had gotten too hard, too much and too stressful. He always took me home in the end and made sure I was okay before he left. It was three years before I was able to tell my mother, three years of mutual sanity. And now he was gone forever.

"The funeral is Saturday," she said as tears laced her voice. "Can you come?"

"I'll be there tomorrow. All of us will. Is that okay?"

"Yes," she said. "Evie? Thank you."

"Mom?" I said seriously. "I loved him. He meant a lot to me. I'll be there."

And that started it. Everything that followed was because I remembered the man who helped me to survive a nightmare. That memory was of a man who did everything selflessly. I have come to believe that had Alex Payne not been able to do what he did for me, that our family would have died eighteen years ago. My mother would have started a war over me, started a war that she would not have survived. It would have killed her or made life so impossible that the future of every single person in our family would have been far different than it was.

"Thank you, Baby," she said. It didn't matter that I hated it when she called me that when I was kid. It was the scene of our earliest fights. Well, mine. Mom didn't fight with me. That was another issue entirely. But now? It didn't matter. With Alex gone, the only thing left was to honor his memory.

I hugged Regina. Sue me; I hug all my patients. Even the horny teenagers. Yes, I hugged David, too.

Since it was Thursday, I asked Regina, "Can I see you again on Monday? That phone call was bad news. I've had a death in my family."

"Oh, no," Regina said with a softness I expected. Regina was one of those women who sees hope in the most hopeless situations.

I will always feel that what I said next determined everything that was going to happen. My life, which had been as quiet as a doctor would like for the past six months, was about to get interesting. My mind drifted back to a day seventeen years in my past and I mumbled, "Alex Payne? May you catch that pass in heaven."

But.

I don't like football. I know the quarterback throws the ball, but don't know why. I know the team with the most points wins. I know that a touchdown is seven points, sometimes six. Right? Well, maybe I don't know that one.

But.

When David's eyes lit up? I figured it was because he didn't have to listen to his doctor lecture him about his behavior for another four days. In a string of grand failures, that was merely another one. I didn't see it for what it was.

And I was going to pay for it.

Chapter 2

Mario was as sad as I was when I told him. Since we grew up together, he knew Alex, too. Better? He knew about football and pro sets, and wide receivers, and tight ends and defensive backs and that a touchdown was six points and that an extra point made for seven. Being my husband, he knew that I was going to take it hard. I did.

I was still crying when we touched down at the Jetport in South Portland. Travis, my son, didn't understand it. I think I embarrassed him. Madison, my daughter, held my hand as we left the terminal. She understood the emotions, but didn't understand from where they came.

Mom picked us up. Brad, my father, was with her and that was enough. Brad is my stepfather, but he is the only father I've ever known. My real father died when I was five and my memories of him are of the vague variety. Sometimes I dream of Indians, but I never know if it's him. He was half-Sioux. Mom would know but I don't burden her with my dreams. They're inconsequential. Even more so given the circumstances.

Mom was crying, too. We hugged as Brad picked up Madison. He hugged her and then knelt and hugged Travis.

"Any word on what the cause was?" I asked stupidly. Christ, I knew what killed him. Steroids killed him.

"Heart failure is what I hear," she said wiping a line of tears from her cheeks.

Mom was wearing something demure. Black and tan. Demure? Hell, depressing. Flats, a skirt over the knee and a sweater that left her shapeless. She isn't. I can remember when she used to jog all over the Prom, a crowd following her. Now? Congress has turned her into a matron. My mother, Melodie Chang, is a matron. It depressed me more than I already was.

She hooked my arm and we walked to the car that way. Dad and Mario had the luggage.

"You look like hell, Mom," I said.

"The public doesn't like their congress people to look like they're bar hopping," she said, a rally in her voice.

"Sorry," I said. "I miss him and I haven't even seen him in years." Then I asked, "How's Ellie?"

"Not good," she said.

That figured. Eleanor didn't figure to marry. Neither did Alex. Eleanor for one reason, Alex for quite another. Ellie didn't think she could attract a mate and Alex had his choice of women. Hopelessly smitten. That's how he described himself the first time he saw her. It took time, but they found each other. Committed. That's what Ellie told me when she realized how sick he was. It was easy to hope that both of them lived forever.

Mom was driving a Ford Escape, their hybrid SUV. It wasn't hard to figure out why either. While the American public can drive SUV's to their hearts content, their elected officials cannot. While they can waste oil, their elected officials must not, cannot. Maybe she's doing it because she wants to be Maine's next senator. That's possible. But I'm her daughter and I know better. She's driving that thing because it suits her. Mom never did anything she didn't want to do. And one thing she wanted was for Mario to ride back to her home in another car. Why? The Escape seats only five and there were six of us. Mario rode with Dad in his Escalade. That should have been a signal, a flare in the night. It wasn't. I was grieving Alex, and Mom's subtly evaded me.

We hadn't even left the airport parking lot when she asked, "When was the last time you heard from him?"

I sighed. "Years. I mean that literally."

She smiled – and it was still a winner. "Can you maybe be a bit more specific?"

"Wait," I said as my memory kicked in. "He was in LA when I was getting ready to move to Montana." I had, moved to Montana I mean. Kalispell to be precise. North of Flathead Lake, it's paradise unlike anything I've ever known. Even the forty below days have glory in them somewhere. But, being August, things were more perfect at home than normal.

"Did he say anything?" she asked.

This was why we were together. This conversation. This was why she drove slowly toward Portland. I knew something and being the ex-PI she was, she was going to learn what it was. The fact that I was her daughter was secondary. I was sitting on a particular nugget of information and she needed me to remember it and then relate it to her.

It was hard to remember because I placed no particular emphasis on the meeting. He was in LA on a case. He bought Mom's PI business when she went into politics. I struggled through old memories and smiled. "He was in a good mood, " I remembered. "He smiled a lot and asked me if I had nightmares anymore."

"And?" Mom asked.

"No," I said smiling at the memory of the man who kept me sane.

"Go on," she said as she waited for a stoplight. The kids were quiet.

He'd called me from LAX and Mario and I went to see him. It was brief but I would have gone to see him if the visit was to the moon. He meant that much to me. I'll say it again: that man kept me sane during a time when sanity was scarce. I smiled and said, "He asked me if I liked being a doctor."

"And?" Mom prompted again.

"I told him I loved it." That was not a lie. I do. I even love sixteen-year-old patients that grab my ass.

"Nothing else?"

We had only a few minutes before his flight was called. We spent most of that short time just chattering. No, Alex, I don't have nightmares. Yes, I love my kids. No, I don't want more. Mario? Oh, God, I love him despite that fact that he's a pig. My practice? Well, I bought one in Montana. I'm going to set it up and live there forever. That was pretty much it.

"Nothing else?" she asked like a dog chasing a bone.

"No," I said sadly. Then, "Wait a second," I added. "Does mentioning Spokane mean anything?"

Her brow furrowed and she asked, "In what context?"

"He asked me if being that close to Spokane was going to turn me into a Seahawks fan. Mom? He was a jock. I laughed and told him no." That was the truth. Football held no interest for me. Baseball either.

Page 13

Basketball either. I jog. That's my sport. Jogging because I can personalize it. But the Seahawks? I have no idea who they are and really don't care to learn.

Mom smiled, patted my leg and said, "Well, he was just being in character."

And that was it. Our conversation, the one that she maneuvered me into. She needed to know about Spokane and I gave her everything I knew about it. One sentence. I don't know who the Seahawks are being but that close to Spokane will not tempt me at all. One sentence. But it was what she was looking for.

We drove the rest of the way home and she chattered with her grandchildren as much as she did with me. When we turned onto The Promenade, I wasn't ready for the crowd. It was eight o'clock in the evening and there were hundreds of people on the wide grassy slopes of The Prom, more in her yard and dozens in the house. She drove slowly through the mass of people, parked in the driveway and led me into the house.

It wasn't the way I wanted to see my family again. And, yes, they were all there. Aunt Dora, Aunt Stacy, Uncle Albert, my sister Valerie, my brother Marty, everyone. Grandchildren, nieces, nephews, everyone was there and they all looked somber.

Mom kissed my cheek and said she'd be right back. I fell into a conversation about Alex with Aunt Tiffany. Okay, that should have been another clue. But like I said, I'm fairly clueless unless something medical is involved. I mean, Aunt Tiff got here from California *before me*. But. Like I said. Clueless.

Aunt Tiff was crying and I mean seriously. They had a history between them and she'd become a fan of his – and not because he once played football.

Then a hand grabbed mine. I looked up and saw my mother.

"Come with me," she said.

It never dawned on me to ask why. I just went with her. We went to the second floor, to her bedroom. We had to weave our way through the crowd until we were in her room. Brad was there and so was Mario. Again. Clueless. I mean, why was Mario there ahead of me? Whatever. That's what I thought. Ellie was there and so was Tiffany's husband,

Bobby Serrano. When the door closed, I turned and saw Aunt Tiff standing there. Dry-eyed. Again. Still. Clueless. The only person that wasn't part of the family was FBI agent, Barbara Reese. Pee Wee. Clueless? Still. Why? Because Pee Wee was Mom's friend and not Alex's.

Mom took my hand and positioned me in front of her closed bathroom door. I took that to mean she wanted me in a place where I couldn't bolt from the room. Well, I was ready. I wasn't going to run away. I was going to do this. I thought it was preparation for the services the next day. Well, no.

The door opened behind me, a hand covered my mouth and a voice said, "You better cry at my funeral tomorrow."

With his hand still over my mouth, I turned and saw him. Alex. Yep, *that* Alex Payne.

All that practice I had crying into his chest so no one would hear? Well, it came in handy because I started screaming. He held me in silence and I let him. There wasn't much he could ask of me that I wouldn't do.

And *that* was about to get tested.

Big time.

Chapter 3

He was absolutely beautiful. Slightly graying hair, a new beard, a body built by Ellie, hard grey eyes, but a sensuous mouth that sought only hers. He slid his arm around my waist and together we faced the room. "Mel? You got the floor," he said. Ominously, Mario and Brad guarded the door. Did he know? Well, I've been saying it. Stupid. Totally. So.

I've always known that my mother was capable of anything. For example, quite like this, she once staged her own death and came back from the dead to face her would-be executioner. Her grave, filled with one-hundred-twenty pounds of sandbags, is still in Evergreen Cemetery. Was this merely a twenty-first century reprise? Back then, the stake was a client. And now? What did Alex Payne stand to gain by staging his own death? And why was my *stupid* husband guarding the door?

I wrenched myself free from Alex and stood facing him. "Whatever it is, Alex? Just tell me. You. Not my mother. You."

Mom bowed. I glimpsed a sweeping one that came complete with her left hand arching gracefully as she dipped. "I yield the floor to the good Mr. Payne," she said with the practice of a politician. That should have been the final clue, but…I…am…a…doctor. Dammit.

He smiled in a way that proved that not only wasn't he dead, but that he'd probably never been ill. "Evie," he said the same way my mother did, with the practiced ease of endless glad-handing. "Do you know what Selective Androgen Receptor Modulators are?"

I sneered. "SARMs? Yeah, I know what they are. I might live in Montana but I'm still a good doctor. And why aren't you dead? And how did you get Aunt Tiff to cry like that?" Then I turned on my mother and snapped, "And you! I should have known you would be involved in something like this!"

Mom has a great smile and better tits. Well, she showed me the smile but kept her tits demure. "So, you'd rather that Alex was dead?"

"What is this?" I asked, my voice rising like a tide. Then I faced Alex and asked, "Is this you or her?"

"Me," he said. "Details by your mother. She had experience."

Yep. I was ready to snap. Before I did, I looked at my mother and said as neutrally as I could, "Why? Why drag me all the way to Portland when you could have just told me?"

She didn't answer. Pee Wee did. She tossed a thick manila envelope onto the bed and said, "That's why. That envelope doesn't leave my sight. You can look at it but when you're done, it goes back to me."

I don't know what history did to my mother and Pee Wee. I know that I do not have the authority to call her that. Mom does. Why is anyone's guess. But if I do? I'll probably see handcuffs. Well, shit. I'm no one but my mother's daughter. "Okay, Pee Wee. Then you tell me. Why am I here and not fucking my husband in our hot tub back home?"

Mom sputtered into laughter. "Oh, good one, Evie."

Well, Pee Wee's eyes narrowed to slits, her jaw went hard and she said with the full force of the FB and I behind her, "You watch your ass, lady. I'm the person that can make sure you spend the rest of your life standing with your back to a cell wall."

"Oh, up yours, Reese," I said going to the bed and taking the envelope. "If I was going to be arrested it wouldn't be because I called you Pee Wee, Pee Wee."

She grabbed my hand and said to my face, "Do you have any idea how many different ways I can arrest you under the articles of The Patriot Act? If I snap my fingers, you can disappear."

I snapped my fingers and said to her face, "Let me do you the favor." When nothing happened, I said, "Don't threaten me, Pee Wee. I am Melodie Chang's daughter and that has nothing to do with the fact that she's a congresswoman."

That said, I took a literal step back. I looked at everyone in the room including Alex. He moved across to where Ellie stood and hugged her. From the look on her face, she was in this with him. Whatever this was. The last person I looked at was Mario. I've known that bastard since I was five. What's that mean? He knew. The bastard knew what was going on; he was a part of it. Maybe what happened started right there.

I went to him, faced him and said because I trusted him implicitly, "Just tell me, Mario. Should I do this?"

His advice was always solid. "Look in the envelope first." That didn't change it.

"You're still a bastard," I said although my defenses lowered a bit. Look, I trust him. I always have.

He licked his lips and said, "And you're still my main momma."

I rolled my eyes and looked at Dad. "Why is it always sex with you people?"

"Because you got all the good parts," he said smiling. "But I agree with Mario. Look in the envelope. It seems the obvious next step. Or do you plan to use our hot tub?"

I leaned into Dad and said, "You're an asshole." Then into Mario and repeated, "And you're still a bastard."

The envelope was right where Pee Wee left it. As soon as I picked it up, she said, "Fingerprints. Now I can have you prosecuted for seeing its contents."

"Up yours, Reese," I snapped.

I opened the envelope and slid out its contents. Medical records, seven different sets. Well, amend that. Coroner reports, seven different sets. Each death certificate was signed by the Cumberland County Coroner, a man named John North. I sat on the bed and started reading the records and looking hard at the autopsy photos.

Snoring startled me out of my own monomania. Mario had slid to his butt against the door and fallen asleep. No, it wasn't him. Brad was on his butt as well, though he wasn't sleeping. My mother was curled up in his arms and *she* was snoring. But what were they? Those seven medical files represented the gruesome death by cancer of seven different people, all males. The youngest was fifteen and the oldest was twenty-two. In all seven cases, the toxicology screens came back clean. Well except for pot in one case and speed in another. Otherwise, none of them had anything in their system that would account for something like *that*.

And *that*? Well, the most gruesome shots of cancer I could imagine. In one case, there was an autopsy photograph of the worst case of testicular cancer I'd ever seen. And the male was seventeen.

Seventeen. Five of the other cases were variations of skin cancer. In all five cases the onset of the disease was fast and it killed the carrier within three weeks. The seventh case was esophageal cancer that spread throughout his body via the lymph nodes in the neck. It wasn't pretty. I sighed and that signaled to Alex that I was done.

"When do I meet the coroner?"

"After the service tomorrow," he said.

"And not until I'm convinced you can keep this to yourself," Pee Wee added.

A cancer that could kill in the space of three weeks was news. Worse? None of the deaths were recent. The last one happened last December. In fact, all of them died between October and December of last year. It was August, so why the delay? "Pee Wee?" I said shaking my head. "I don't think you and me are ever going to be friends." I waited a heartbeat for a reply, got none and finished with, "What do they have in common? There has to be a link between them."

Alex settled beside me. "There is. They all play football. Well, played."

"I mean a medical link. And you're not a doctor, so don't act like one."

People were waking up. At least Mom was. She yawned and Dad said something typically male coarse. I ignored him until Mario started giggling. "Mel?" he said. "I would actually pay to watch that." Then I stared at him and he rubbed his crotch and moaned.

"Why do I have to wait until tomorrow to talk to North?" I asked Reese, ignoring my husband.

"Because he's in Montreal," she answered. "He's at a convention."

Which brought me full circle. "And why am I taking part in a bogus funeral?"

"Because Alex Payne is dead. The new patient that comes to your office in Montana will be named Norman Peters."

Alex smiled and stroked his new beard. It had gray in it. "I always wanted to be called Normie."

Then I asked the big one. The Big One. "Why? And why me?" Barbara had all the information, so it was to her that I asked the question.

I didn't think that being Melodie Chang's daughter had anything to do with my inclusion on what was going to happen. *Yeah, Collins. And if you believe that, there's a bridge in New York City I'll sell you.* Look, I *wanted* to believe that being Mom's daughter had nothing to do with this. But. I was her daughter and I did have an interesting background only because that was true. Mom cheated death so many times and in so many ways when she was a practicing PI in Portland that I lost count at six. But that question? Why me? It was pointed at Barbara but everyone in the room knew that my mother was involved somehow. This had her written all over it. She was the one who never backed down, who never took no for an answer and who always got her way. Hell, most of the time it was legal. Was this? Well, with Barbara Reese and FB-Fucking-I involved, I had to assume it was. If you note a bit of anger in my voice, you're right. I was angry. Pee Wee was about to tell me why.

"Those seven people all died within ten miles of this house between October and December of last year. Then? Nothing. Something like this pops up and then goes away. People at the CDC were here in force at your mother's urging, but nothing happened. They walked away because cancer isn't a communicable disease."

I could hear it. "Until," I said.

"A kid from Flathead High School died the same way not two weeks ago."

"And no one else in the entire country?"

"No."

"Okay," I said. "I can name at least a dozen levels of military and/or government that are better qualified to do this than me. So my question stands. Why me? I'm not a cop and don't want to be one."

Barbara has a round face that she brutalizes by wearing her hair short. She looks like a bowling ball with fringe. She put her face in mine and said, "Because no one will suspect that the pansy-ass doctor from Montana is up to this. That's why, Collins. You and Norman Peters are going to catch whoever is behind this. It's ugly, deadly and aimed at kids."

And *that* put my mind back in my office, David Ryan facing me. Why? Because David Ryan is sixteen and plays *linebacker* on the high school football team. Suddenly, my objections disappeared. That monomania I mentioned earlier? Well, it extends to patients and their wellbeing. If David Ryan was at risk, I'd do anything to save him.

Everyone was looking at me. Mom was awake and focused. Jesus. She could do that better than anyone I ever met. And she was waiting for an answer with the rest of them.

I looked at Alex and growled, "I am not crying at your funeral. I'm wearing sunglasses."

Mario smiled and said, "She'll cry. Trust me."

All that was left were the details.

Yeah, the place where the devil lives.

Chapter 4

Okay. I cried at the funeral. It wasn't really hard. But the service gave me time to think about what was happening. As person after person went to the podium and spoke rapturously about a man who was not dead, the first thing that went through my mind was Barbara Reese. Why was she involved? The FBI fights crime and cancer isn't a crime. Again. Okay. I get it. Pee Wee was involved because she's my mother's friend and seven cancer deaths that took three weeks to run its course doesn't happen. Also, none of those kids had any signs of cancer. Period. Then, three months later they were all dead. And my mother is their congressperson. Again. Okay. I get it. I'm here because my mother has faith in my abilities as a doctor.

Based on our long conversation the night before, I knew that Alex was going to be the investigator in Montana. My job was going to be to provide medical support and advice for whatever he found. Yeah, the ex-football player has been an investigator for longer than he played the sport. That's the stakes for buying Mom's business.

The only person missing from the story was North – and he was under strict orders from my mother not to use his cell phone with us. Maybe Mom is paranoid, but she has the scars on her body to justify it. Still, I wanted to talk to North only because I had been assured he had some answers, medical ones.

My own testimonial was short and to the point. "Alex Payne saved my life eighteen years ago. I loved him like he was my own father." I was wearing sunglasses, but they did little to hide the tears that rolled down my face. No, since he was not dead, those were not ones of sadness. Guilt won over. I hadn't seen him or talked to him since I left Los Angeles a year ago. That seems wrong somehow. A savior should rate higher, a phone call at least.

The speech ended and we all wound up back at Mom's house on The Prom. I didn't waste any time. I went upstairs to her bedroom and North was there. Well, at least a man was. He was talking to Reese and

I'd had it with her. I interrupted her in mid-speech and said, "My name is…"

"Yes, I know," he said. "I'm aware of who you are. We need to talk."

Mom and Alex were there as well as Barbara and the coroner. I didn't have to ask: Brad and Mario were in the hallway outside the bedroom door making certain that no one got inside. Brad told him what was happening when they picked us up at the airport. The men were putting the luggage in Brad's SUV. That's when they discussed it. They talked all the way back to Mom's house. Me? I guess Mom wasn't as sure about me as she was about my husband. I'd rather not talk about how Mom felt more secure telling her brother than me because then I'd have to admit that I married my uncle – and then have to explain that they we all adopted, no blood between us. Yeah. I really don't want to explain how I've known Mario since I was five *because we grew up together.* So I won't.

"Do you know what the CSIS is?" he asked.

"Other than a series of really bad CBS television shows? No."

"Canadian intelligence," Mom interrupted.

"Well, of course," I said. "Every county coroner goes to Canada to meet with Canadian intelligence."

North was an older man. His gray hair was cut short and neat. His eyes were gray. Maybe that was apt, too. But his hands were large and strong. I notice such things about doctors because we hold so much in them.

"I met with two intelligence officers. A man named Paul Fields and a woman named Deborah Hollis. Well, Fields was an officer, but Hollis was a doctor."

"Fields was no more than thirty, short and stocky?" Mom asked. "And Hollis was thin, taller than him and tended to lisp?"

He smiled. "Yes."

"Just checking. Go on."

"There have been no similar deaths in Canada," he said to her. Then to me, "You've read the autopsy reports?"

"Yes," I said. "You read the toxicology reports?"

"Several times."

"Then you know that they ingested nothing toxic – or that they at least had clean drug screens?"

"Yes. I also know that there are several ways to mask symptoms."

"Yes, then you know that one of them had been using drugs to mask his pot use."

"Yes." Before he could go to the next item on his list, I asked, "And how does a buffoon like Alex Payne know the term 'SARM' and what does that have to do with those seven bodies?"

Alex smiled. "Buffoon?"

I smiled back. "I didn't think you could spell 'bozo'."

"SARMs are the only thing any of us could see that might cause something like this. They bypass toxicology reports and that makes them primary focuses for bodybuilders and people who compete in sports. But a side-effect was cancer. It fits but they found nothing on their side of the border."

Pee Wee sighed and said, "Yeah. Same here."

"And why weren't you in Canada with Doctor North?" I asked her.

The answer was left for Mom. She stared at Pee Wee for a long moment and then looked toward the French doors and the ocean beyond them. Without being told that she was going to get up, walk to them, open them and stand staring, she did. I can remember countless times when I was kid that I'd see her do this: stare at Casco Bay as though something about the scene mesmerized her. As she stood staring at the deep blue water of the bay, my mind rolled back through all the years I spent here. Yes, I battled her. Many times. I wanted her to challenge me and in the end, she did. She pushed me to become a doctor, much like Alex pushed me to remain lucid. Now, both of them were asking me for help and I was playing the role of spoiled brat.

I got up and went to the open doors where she stood. "Mom? I'll do my part. I'm sorry I've been so difficult."

She's kept her hair as black as midnight and as long as it always was. Draped over left shoulder, she had a lot of holier-than-thou people moralizing against her. Well, most of them don't live in her district because she's carried it by 3-to-1 margins in each of the last three elections. She'll be the next senator from Maine because she's going to run in the next election and she's going to win.

"Baby?" she said as she stared at the deep blue water. "Doctor North told me that the average survival rate for metastatic melanoma is eight months. Is that right?"

"Yes. But it's also true that skin cancer is very treatable."

"If caught early."

I knew more about skin cancer than she did, but I also knew that it was rare for cancer to metastasize at that rate. The tumors I saw in the photographs given to me by Barbara were gruesome. In one photo? There was a tumor in the small of the back that measured two feet long and half that wide. According to the report, it developed almost overnight and wasn't the only tumor he had. All I said was, "Yes, that's true," because it was. "I'll help Alex in whatever way I can."

"Alex is dead," she said sadly. "You must mean Norman."

But there was more in her voice other than Alex Payne. I'd been seeing symptoms in my mother since I was seven. I was convinced once that she was dying because she was taking aspirin. I cried, wailed, begged and pleaded for her to stop. Then I got a phone call from my Great Uncle Sydney. He was my grandfather's brother. Doctor Morganstern. He invited me to stop by his office after school. Coincidentally, Mom picked me up that day and took me there. He dropped all of his appointments and talked to me for an hour. Considering my own hourly rate, I know what it cost him. But he smiled and showed me proof that my mother wasn't going to die of aspirin poisoning. He even gave me the book that proved it. And, yes, I used it to prove to my mother that she was dying because she ate *bran flakes*. Yes, I've been seeing symptoms in her eyes for the vast majority of my life. But this, *this*, was different. This was sadness that had little to do with medicine. "What is it, Mom?"

There were tears in her eyes. One broke free and rolled down her cheek. "I didn't want this for you," she said to me. "I know that you're a doctor and that's all you've ever wanted to be. But I'm sorry I got you involved."

Which summoned the face of David Ryan back home in Kalispell. Was he the ninth victim? That was hard to say because the symptoms the first seven showed were all over the map. Doctor North had visited the family doctor in each case. And there were no commonalities. Which meant that David Ryan, if he was a victim of this, had maybe two or three weeks left to live unless I could figure out what was killing young football players from Maine to Montana.

"Mom? I swear I'll find out."

And that put us in each other's arms, both of us crying. We hugged and then she said, "And you can't tell anyone. Mario knows because I trust him."

"And you can trust me, too," I said.

"Thank you, Evangeline," she said as she wiped tears from her eyes.

Evangeline. I missed it entirely. Maybe it is the curse of human beings to forget. Maybe it my curse. But I missed it. What did I miss?

Mom had a habit of using my given name when she had something serious to tell me. As a kid, I dreaded it. As an adult, I'd forgotten it. Okay, you can say that she'd already given me something serious. Seven dead football players in Maine and an eighth back home in Montana. You could say that and it would be true. However. Yeah, however. Let's just leave it there, okay?

However.

Chapter 5

We flew back to Montana Sunday morning. Mario knew better than to talk about it, but I didn't. I figured in general terms, it was okay. As soon as I used Alex's name, Mario turned to me in my seat and put his face in mine. That's enough, Evie," he said with enough venom in his voice that I got the message. "It's not enough you fucked him? You have to throw his name in my face, too?" Well, both of us know I did *not* fuck Alex. He was telling me to shut up and I understood. I bit his ear. Then I kissed him.

Montana is home now. Yes, I grew up in Portland in that house, but I became an adult in Montana. The issues that make that true all happened six months ago. The winter of my soul became the summer of my heart. Was going to anyway. But as we got off the small plane and headed for home, my mind was already on David Ryan and his symptoms.

As soon as we got settled at home, I kissed Mario and told him, "I have to go to the office."

"Need us?" he asked.

"No," I said hugging him. "Just looking for a phone number."

"You be careful," he said stroking my cheek.

I hugged him again and said, "I was horrid to them, to Mom, Pee Wee and even Alex."

I love his smile because he puts so much into it. The one he showed just then was perfect. "You know? Your mother has absolute faith in you. She told me that whatever this is, that you can figure it out. She didn't take offense to you, wasn't angry or anything other than completely trustful of your talents."

"I need to stay in touch with them."

"True," he said. "But if that crap lands here in Montana, then you'll be busier than normal." Then he held my face in his hands and said, "And both of us have the greatest faith in you. You're a good doctor and you'll figure this out."

A medical mystery. That's what I thought I had on my hands. It went no farther than eight kids who caught the same disease two thousand miles apart. That was my starting point. There was something in their environment that held common cause with cancer. All I had to do was figure out what it was. And my mother's place in this was to keep a lid on what might become a general panic if people found out what was happening.

"And if it goes beyond me?" I asked.

"Then you'll know who to ask," he answered, my face still in his hands.

There were three oncologists within walking distance of my office down on Windward Way. One of them, Doctor Ward Davis, has had lunch with me several times. He's trying to start an affair, but I've been blunt with him: I'd rather have my guts ripped out with pinking shears than sneak around behind Mario's back. However, he's a very good doctor and he'd be the one I'd consult with if the time ever comes.

Anyway, Mario kissed me again and hugged before I left.

I drive a silver Toyota Highlander only because it's a hybrid. Okay, that makes me a lot like my mother. She can blame constituents for her hybrid. Me? I like the way the damn thing looks. Gas mileage is entirely secondary.

My office isn't far from my home; a bit more than two miles. It didn't take long to pull into a parking space in front of it. Given that Mom said to be circumspect, careful and deliberate, I looked at the area, at the parking lot, at the medical center lot across the street and saw nothing and no one. It reinforced that all I had on my hands was a medical mystery – and that was something I could solve. All I needed to do was concentrate on the problem.

I unlocked the door, opened it, flipped on the lights and went back to my office. Nothing was amiss. All the monitors were off and that was by design. Liz Dempsey, the office manager, made certain of that before she left. I logged onto the system and found Regina Ryan's name, address and phone number. Then I called her.

She was surprised to hear from me. Well, wouldn't you be if your doctor called you on a Sunday night and offered to come to your home?

That kind of surprised. I told her I wanted to see David because our appointment had been cut short on Friday.

"But we have an appointment tomorrow," she said.

"It's important," I said not trying to hide it.

"Well, okay," she said. "He's out with the horses, but I'll call him inside. Okay?"

"I'll be there in ten minutes."

"Is he okay?"

"That's what I'm going to find out," I replied as truthfully as possible. Then I asked, "You live on Valley View Drive?"

"Yes, Doctor. We're the last house on the road. You know it?"

"Yes. Like I said, I'll be there in ten minutes."

"Well, thank you."

I gathered up everything I was going to need and left the office. Blood is what I needed most. I needed to see what sort of drugs, if any, David was using and then verify it with a drug test. But I needed to check for lesions on his body, stuff that was either cancer or could become cancer.

Valley View Drive is on the south side of town and runs along the hills that lead up to Foy Lake. It's entirely rural down there. The hills are to the west and flat farm land runs all the way to the nearest subdivision to the east. All that meant was that Regina Ryan had a nice and fairly secluded home.

I was thinking about David as I drove. Worse, I was convincing myself that his symptoms did not match those of the sevens victims back in Maine. If those kids were the victims of a SARM-styled drug, then David was the victim of a steroid-styled drug. That was my first intention with a blood sample. I wanted to rule out steroids as a cause for his symptoms. Everything else flowed from that point.

I turned onto Meridian Road and drove through a nice neighborhood. The road turned to the right and became Foys Lake Road. The houses became fewer. Their number shrank even more as I made a right onto Valley View Drive. I wasn't thinking about where I was or who might be following me. I was still thinking about David Ryan and his symptoms. The road turned left and became Sunnyside Drive. Valley View picked up again as a right turn.

The area was wholly rural now. There was one last knot of houses where Valley View ran in a straight line for a nearly a mile before ending in a meadow of tall grass.

It was still daylight, nearly six-thirty. Like Maine, daylight lingers here. It wouldn't be fully dark for hours yet. While I wasn't thinking about the daylight hours, the person who was following me was. He didn't want to be seen but had little choice but to be there. Who? Well, I couldn't say because I was driving south along the road, not even bothering to check my rearview mirror. I was wondering what drugs were going to come back from the David's tox screen.

His appearance didn't impress itself on me until he closed the distance between us and flipped on his high beams. Their brightness blinded me for a moment and I winced and tried to shield my eyes from them. Then he rammed the back of the car and I had a fight on my hands to keep control of it. Through the glare, I was able to see him drop back, positioning himself for another run at me. I hit the gas.

There wasn't much road left. Maybe half a mile. The nearest house was at the end, Regina's. I heard his engine roar and braced myself for another impact. I took the time to swat the rearview mirror. Its reflection went elsewhere. That's when the engine noise got worse. I heard a crash and only knew it wasn't me. That was good because I had hit the accelerator and was gaining speed. I took another swatch of time to look behind me. The car that was following me had veered off the road and was leaving a trail through the meadow that led to the rail line off to the west. Despite the alarm bells in my head and the adrenalin rush that was starting to induce panic, I slowed to a stop.

Another car pulled up behind me, one that I recognized. It was Mario.

I opened my car door and rushed to him. He was out of his car and we met between them.

"What are you doing here? Where are my children? What's going on? Are you okay? Oh, lord, tell me to shut up and hold me," I said in a long string of run-ons that had me shaking.

He slid his arms around me, smiled and said, "I know how you get when a patient is involved, so I followed you."

Everything that my mother told me before I left Portland hung in the air like so many foul fragrances. Above all? Be careful. As I hugged my husband, I asked the one question that was left when everything else was eliminated. "Am I fit to do this, Mario?"

He held me at arm's length and his look was serious. "Jesus, yes," he said. "I don't know any doctor that could do this except you. Why do you ask?"

I swept my arm at the field and said, "This. The first time I leave my office, I'm followed and threatened. Worse? I didn't even know it! And headlights? It's daylight! You would think I would have noticed!"

"Are you afraid?" he asked.

"No!" I practically scream at him. "But you would think…"

And the fool kissed me. It has always been that way between us. I feel safer when he's around – safer even when the threats aren't as apparent as they were that night. Everything began to dissipate around me as he held me and kissed me. Finally, he said, "That's why I'm here. Your mother said to make sure nothing happened to you. She didn't need to threaten me either. You're my life, Evie."

"So…"

"I'll be following you a lot for a while. You just figure out what's happening to those kids."

"And if something happens to you?" I asked.

"You can blame Alex…I mean Normie…because we'll be together a lot."

"And the kids?"

"Cayn's with them."

Cayn Wyatt was a good man. They were safe.

I kissed him again, looked at the slight dent in my bumper and then got back into the car and drove down to Regina Ryan's home. Before I ever got there, I saw David standing next to the garage. If he hadn't seen what just happened, then he was blind. And I knew he wasn't. Still, it never dawned on me to worry about him.

That was still in the future.

Chapter 6

Horse pens surrounded the garage. I could see four horses grazing in the grass. David stood next to the garage staring at me as I parked on the driveway behind a nice Dodge pickup. I smiled at him as I got out of my car. He licked his lips and turned to look at where Mario stood on the roadside not fifty yards from the house. Nervous. That's how I'd describe him. He turned his head back to me and said, "Hey, Doctor Six. Why are you here?"

"You, David. You're why I'm here. Is your mother home? Your father?"

He shrugged. "Sure. In the house."

"Can we go inside? I'd like to look at you, but want your parents involved."

He shrugged again. Then he turned and looked at Mario. "Why was Coach Horn doing that stuff down there?" he asked.

"What stuff?" I asked knowing full well the stuff he was talking about.

"With his car. That was him, Coach Horn. Why was he doing that?"

I don't think about stuff like that. I think about people like David and whether or not they're suffering from steroid abuse. I think he is. But he'd just stepped into an affair started by my mother – and I respect her judgment. I took a deep breath, turned and looked at Mario. I gave him a thumb's up and he returned it.

"How do you know it was him?" I asked.

He snickered. "Been in that damned thing a dozen times. He takes us for pizza sometimes after practice."

"It's August, David. There is no practice."

"Played JV last year. He was the coach on that team. He got promoted this year and he's kept in touch with all of us, not just me. So, why? That looked nasty. And who's the asshole watching you?"

That brought a smile. "The asshole is my husband."

He turned back to me and said, "I could fuck you up before he could get here."

Well, *that* brought a laugh. "David? Trust me here. No, you couldn't. And that's just one more reason I think you're shooting 'roids. You turn into your basic creep who thinks everyone else is an adversary. I'm not. I'm not a woman either. I'm a doctor who can put you safely on your ass if you try anything stupid."

"Safely?" he asked with a smile that looked too much like a leer.

"Without injury," I replied, my own smile looking like a genuine one. Well, I hoped. "Now? Can we go inside and see your parents?"

Without waiting for an answer, I turned and headed toward the house. I rang the doorbell, but David just reached past me and opened the door. Pushing me with his shoulder, I entered and he said, "Mom? The doctor's here." Then he pinched my ass and crossed the room.

Regina was all smiles. Trailing her was her husband, a man I knew only as Bernie. He had a full beard that was deeply red and a face that matched it. A candidate for a heart attack? I wondered. Regina extended her hand and said, "Imagine a doctor making a house call."

Okay. I'm a doctor. Do you know how many times I've a heard a version of that? Well, Regina seemed nice, so I just smiled and said, "Well, I'm here because I think I owe David a better visit than what I gave him last Friday. I'd like you, Mrs. Ryan, to observe while I examine David."

"What's wrong with him?" she asked like every mother would. His father said nothing, just watched.

I smiled and said, "That's what I'm here to learn. Until I examine him? I don't know. We need a room with a door. That's all."

"Our bedroom," Bernie said, his voice deep and mysterious.

"Good enough," I responded.

David tried to lag, but I was behind him. I hooked his arm, smiled at him and said, "Relax. This time a phone call won't distract me." Considering that I thought he'd recognize Alex's name, I added, "I owe Alex Payne more than that. He lived clean the last twenty years of his life and I swore I would help others the same way he did."

He didn't say anything, but he didn't struggle either.

I could smell dinner. Something with a roast. I smiled at Regina and said, "I interrupted dinner. I apologize."

Bernie said with his deep voice, "Go on Regina. You take care of that and I'll stay with the doctor."

She nodded but said to David, "And you be nice to her. She's here to help."

As she left the room, I said to David, "Strip down to your underwear." I needed to examine his skin, all of it. When I was done examining the skin that showed, I was going to examine the skin that didn't.

"Go on," Bernie said. "Just do whatever she says."

Bernie Ryan is a big man. Period. Maybe six-three, I would be surprised if he was less than three hundred pounds. If I needed a better reason to suspect that David Ryan was using steroids than his father, I couldn't see what it could be. Bernie Ryan was massive. Even the words he spoke sounded like capital letters. Again, I wasn't surprised when David started to remove his clothes.

It allowed me to concentrate on my visit. I started slowly checking the skin on his neck, arms and face – all the places that would be in the sunshine. Skin cancer has many causes and two of them were obvious. David and Bernie both had red hair and men with red hair and fair skin are more susceptible to skin cancer than those that don't. Also, men are more susceptible than women. Why? Men tend to be outside more than more than women. That puts them at greater risk. All that said, I checked David carefully, even under his hairline. Still, I saw nothing that looked like skin cancer and nothing that might blossom into it.

"Your underwear, David," I said. Then to his father, "It's necessary."

"Do it," Bernie said, again speaking in capital letters.

Well, other than David's embarrassment, I found nothing. He felt better when I checked his butt. When I was done, I told him to get dressed while I readied a syringe to take a blood sample.

"Why are you going to take blood?" Bernie asked.

"Because I'm thorough, Mr. Ryan. Or do you not agree with your wife as to David's symptoms? He could be using steroids. This will tend to answer where or not he is."

He nodded, but said nothing other than, "Okay."

David managed to get back into his underwear and his pants by the time I was ready to get my sample. From the look in his eyes, I'd say he wasn't happy about doing it, but wasn't prepared to argue with his father. That made my job easier. I took the sample and stored it. It wasn't going to degrade by the time I got it back to the office.

Because David was a minor, I couldn't ask his father to leave the room. I wasn't going to either because my questions were general enough that I didn't think Bernie would get suspicious.

"Do you agree with what your mother told me last Friday?"

"Well, yeah," he said with a shrug. "I guess."

"Up front, David. Are you taking anything?"

"No."

"Anything you want to tell me?"

"Nah, I'll do better. It's nothing more than a girl anyway."

There were so many things wrong in that room that I'm *still* surprised I didn't see even one. For one, I'd forgotten that David pinched my ass. As evidence, I can't imagine a more obvious red flag. For another, he'd given me the name of the person that rammed my car. And another, thrown just enough fuel on the fire that his name was going to stay active for a while. Unfortunately, there was one thing he couldn't tell me. And what was that?

I'd taken blood from the wrong person.

Think about it.

Chapter 7

Alex…um, *Normie*…was the third person waiting outside my office when Liz Dempsey opened the door at nine o'clock Monday morning. The first one was Bill Henery. He was there for a follow-up to a kidney stone operation. The second person was Katie Osbach. There's nothing wrong with her that a good diet won't solve, but try telling that to her. She insists that she has everything from salmonella to Ebola but her weight is going to kill her. She already has signs of diabetes and is on every medication I can legally prescribe for her. My guess is that she's going to badger my PA to start looking for one of those mysteriously missing ailments. No, she's overweight – and not just by a little. The last time she stepped on a scale, she weighed in at three hundred fifteen pounds – and she's five-two. Worse? She used to weigh more than that. As a symptom for diabetes, weight loss is high on that list. I'm beginning to believe that my office is nothing more than part of her social life.

I heard Flo Pillow, my receptionist, start to tell Alex…um, Normie…that while we accepted walk-in patients that it might be a while before he would be seen.

Well, no. Bill was ready with his urine strainers and the specimen jar I gave him and Katie was going to get a very firm but professional order to start the diet she'd been given. I smiled at Flo and said, "Tell the gentleman that it might be twenty minutes before I see him. And put him in room three."

He was holding a package of cigarettes and I was going to go all medical on him when I saw him. Smoking? And with his history of heart disease? I didn't care what his name was, I was going to rip off his head and spit down his neck.

Bill's appointment was easy. He passed the stone fragments and had them in the specimen jar. I made certain he was okay and he left happy. Katie didn't. She told me that she had symptoms for kidney failure. I told her that her symptoms fit diabetes and that was more likely. She refused treatment, advice and left. Before she walked out, I pleaded with her to go to another doctor, to the ER across the street, to anyone that could help her. She grumbled and said something like, "All doctors are quacks." That meant she'd been to all of them. Maybe she'll wind up in Billings pleading with those doctors. My guess? She'd go into diabetic shock and die before she actually listened to anyone.

That left Alex…um, Normie.

He'd filled out the new patient forms and was waiting *patiently*, his package of cigarettes in his hand. I closed the door behind me and then snapped, "Cigarettes? You're smoking now?"

He smiled and held up the package. "Your receptionist's phone is bugged. I'd like you to take this thing back to your office." He tipped the end of the pack to me and I saw a black gadget stuffed inside a Camel cigarette wrapper. "Hold the package within six feet of the phone and if the red LED lights up, then your phone is bugged. Then do it to every phone in the office. I think you'll find they're all bugged."

When I hesitated and did nothing more than stare at the package, he smiled and pushed me toward the door. "Go on, girl. Then we have to talk."

I stared at the box and replied, "Yeah, we do. Stuff is happening."

I left the exam room and went back to my office. The light blinked when I held the box over the phone. It bothered me because a bugged phone was not something I ever thought about. Holding the package against my leg, I went to every phone in the office and the light blinked on all of them.

My first question to him was, "How do I remove them?"

"You don't. Knowing about them and not tipping your hand is a point for us." Then his face went serious and he asked, "And what happened?"

I shrugged it off by saying, "A guy I know only as Coach Horn of Flathead High School rammed my car last night. If Mario hadn't been there? I would have had to prove that Melodie Chang is my mother."

I expected something other than a pencil and notebook. He noted my reply and said, "Anything else?"

"Yeah. What's Pee Wee's place in this? This has my mother written all over it. Why is she necessary?"

"She got North in front of the Canadians. That's her place in this. Otherwise? It would have been you and me, kid."

"And why do the Canadians need to be involved?"

"Because if the cause of those seven deaths is in Canada, they need to be in the loop. That's why."

"And that's the job of the CIA, not the FBI. Why her?"

"Because your mother trusts Pee Wee," he said with the smallest hint of a smile. "Unlike some people I know."

He was wearing photo-gray sunglasses and wearing a cowboy hat. The only reason I recognized him at all was because I'd recognize him anywhere, wearing anything. Our history is too long, too deep and too meaningful to give any other answer. But he was right. I don't like Pee Wee and that prejudiced my answer. Objectively, someone like her was necessary, especially if this was criminal. But was it? Well, considering that slight dent in my bumper, I'd have to say yes.

"Sorry," I said. "I'll be more professional from now on." I took a deep breath, stared at his nearly-chart and said, "The eighth victim? The one here in Kalispell? I contacted the county coroner and I have an appointment with him this evening, dinner actually. I want to see those records and compare them to the ones from Portland."

He interrupted. "That's fine, but you can't tell him about those cases. As far as you know? That one is all there is and your interest is because the death is so anomalous."

"Anomalous?" I smiled. "That's a pretty big word for a football player."

He smiled back. "I'm a PI, just like your mother was. You can only underestimate us at your own peril."

"Well, I need another answer other than that death was anomalous. The coroner in Flathead County is also the county sheriff and he'll be suspicious. It's his job."

"Evie?" he said, his smile gone. "Whatever answer you give him will be fine. Just keep this issue in Kalispell and nowhere else. Also? If you ever contact me with your cell phone, I'll personally stuff you into the nearest garbage pile. No cell phones, no phone contact at all."

I'm not stupid. I know that cell phones are devices that are abysmally insecure. Unsecure? Whatever. I know that it is easy to intercept a cell phone signal because they are little more than portable radio stations and the nature of radio stations are to be heard. So, that led me to ask, "Then how do I contact you?"

"You don't. I contact you."

"How?" I said leaning across the space that separated us.

"Your home is on the north end of Stillwater Loop and is the only one on the inside of it. Just below your home is a dirt road that leads down to Mario's school. There's a telephone pole at that junction." He reached into his windbreaker and handed me a red square of paper. "If I need to see you? This will be stapled to the pole down there. When you see it? Drive to the cemetery that's on the other side of the river from your home. I'll be there. In fact? Meet me there tomorrow morning when you're on your way to your office. I want to know about the eighth case."

Well, while all this was very clock-and-dagger, my last concern was him. "Dammit, Normie…Alex…you're running a slight fever and your blood pressure is slightly elevated. Considering I know your medical history like I know no one else's, that's wrong. I'm going to take a sample of your blood and find out what's going on."

I take a history of everyone that visits me. Period. There are no exceptions. That means I see fewer patients than most doctors do. I don't need the money. I was rich before I started studying medicine, still am and my kids will inherit a shitload of it when I die. I do this because of people like Alex, people that need a doctor and not someone who jams as many patients into his schedule so he meets some sort of minimum, or who sees dollars in all those names. In fact, I knew my next patient wasn't due for another ten minutes, so I had time to spend here. What surprised me was his reply.

He stood and said, "No you're not. I'm not the issue here. The kid in that morgue is the issue."

"And I won't tolerate you in a morgue, Alex Payne. Roll up your damned sleeve and let me do this."

Well, the fool hugged me and said to my ear, "I'm fine. Don't worry about me. Just let me work."

My position? "I'm the doctor and you aren't fine until I say so."

"Evie? Please. Don't worry. Just find out what killed all those kids. If I need you? I know where you are."

I didn't like it. Not at all. I'm the one who started studying medicine because I was convinced my mother was going to die unless I did. That worry got transferred to everyone in my family – and I considered Alex Payne to be one of my uncles. Don't worry about him? Like there was any chance that was going to happen.

But.

He's one of those Manly Men. You know. The type that damns the torpedoes and faces death with a smirk? You know. Stupid. One of those. I know him well enough, though, to know that my opinion of his life won't stop him from doing what he thinks is best. I didn't think I had to worry about him. Well, in short?

No.

I was going to find myself in a load of trouble before the next two days were out. And Alex? Well, let's leave it at this: my fear that someone in my family was going to need me to study medicine? There were two people in my life that were going to need me – and he was just one of them. The other?

Please, please, please don't ask.

I don't think I could stand failure in that case.

Okay?

Chapter 8

The county coroner/assistant sheriff is a man named Allen Hastings. That's all I know about him, his name. He's been on the job for four months and was appointed by the county council to fill an opening created by me six months ago. You heard that right. I created the opening at the county by a case I inherited six months ago. The previous sheriff/coroner was a slime by the name of Livingston. While I have no desire to recount *that* story, I can simply say that the bastard *really* deserved it.

Hastings met Mario and I at Sonny's just before seven o'clock Monday night. Sonny's is a restaurant/bar. I like the restaurant. My experience with the bar is so slight that I have no opinion of it other than the big screen TV behind the bar looks interesting even if all they ever broadcast are Jazz, Seahawks and Mariners games. Cayn had the kids at home. Mario was there to watch my flanks. That's how he put it. Then he started laughing and couldn't stop until I smacked him. Then he said, "I'm serious. I'm going to watch your flanks." Then I smacked him again and said, "Just mine. No one else's."

Hastings turned out to be younger than I thought he'd be. I judged him to be maybe thirty-five. His hair was militarily short – hell, Nazi short – and his smile looked like it had been dipped in formaldehyde before he used it. Of course, maybe he knew it was me and maybe he knew my past with is office. That could be. Still, I smiled.

"Mr. Hastings," I said with a handshake as we met him at the bar.

"Doctor Sixkiller-Collins," he said with practiced deliberation. Then he shook Mario's hand and said, "And you are?"

"Mario," he replied. "Assistant hubcap."

"My husband," I said with a smile. "He thinks he has to be interesting when all I want is for him to be invisible," I said with my best withering glare that was directed at Mario.

"Well, a drink?" Hastings said. "Coke, beer, something stronger?"

"With dinner," I said. "We have things to discuss and I'm sure you want to know what they are."

A hostess from the restaurant seated us near windows that looked out on the parking lot. I like the restaurant despite the view. A drug store, a video store, a realtor and the restaurant. Not glamorous. It's at the intersection of Main and Idaho Streets. Main Street is Highway 93 and it goes north all the way to Canada and south to where it connects to Interstate 90. If you guessed I was sitting at the crossroads of whatever was happening in Kalispell, Montana, you guessed right. The road – 93 – was the funnel through which the deal was going – and I had no idea. Yet.

I was there only to get Hastings to tell me about the eighth victim. I knew everything about the other seven. I wanted nothing more than to compare the symptoms of this guy with the other seven. Also, I wanted to know who his doctor had been. There was an oncologist in the mix somewhere, too. All I wanted was information that I could study and pass along to Alex…um…Normie.

"How do I address you?" I asked. "Doctor Hastings? Mr. Hastings? Officer Hastings?"

"Al," he said. Then he smiled. "You can call me Al."

Okay. That was a practiced line, but he seemed nice nonetheless. I replied, "Then I'm Evie and he's Mario."

A waitress came by and took our drink orders. A beer for Al, a Coke for me and water for Mario. He considered that he was working. Me, too. Al? Well, maybe he was relaxing.

"Al?" I said getting right to the point. "I've heard that there has been a rather gruesome cancer death recently. If so, did you do an autopsy? If you did, what can you tell me about the death. I've heard it was an aggressive form of cancer and I need to be up-to-speed on such stuff." That was as blunt as I could be.

He sighed, blowing a long stream of air between his puffed cheeks. "Yeah. Danny Hardiman. From first diagnosis to death was seventeen days. He spent the last week of his life in an isolation room over in the hospital."

"From fear of contagion? And it was cancer? That doesn't follow."

He shrugged. "It was just fear. No one could account for it, so that was the precaution they took. I heard this from his doctor."

"His name?"

"Bender. John Bender."

I nodded. I knew John socially, that's all. "And his opinion?"

Al shrugged again. "That it's a virulent form of cancer and that it didn't respond to treatment. Danny was comatose for the last three days."

"When did he die?"

"Today's Monday? Last Tuesday."

And my mother already knew about it. There had to be a pipeline back to her, but for the life of me, I couldn't see it. Not that it mattered. I was more concerned about how cancer killed someone in seventeen days. "Are there any records I can see? I understand patient confidentiality, but this is extraordinary."

"If Danny's parents don't object, I don't see why you wouldn't be able to see them. I'll call Doctor Bender and Danny's parents and let you know."

"Thank you," I said and meant it.

I took that to mean *tomorrow,* that he'd call them tomorrow. Instead, he pulled out his cell phone and called someone, Danny's parents I assumed. That's where I would start, with the parents. He talked with someone very sympathetically. From the conversation, I'd say with Danny's mother. Then he smiled and said, "You're sure, Dyan? It might be late. Well, okay. And thank you."

Dyan turned out to be Dyan Hardiman, Danny's mother. She agreed to sign a form that would enable Doctor Bender to turn over Danny's records to us. That made dinner a lot more enjoyable. After Livingston, I was going to cultivate the county sheriff's office like it was a rare flower.

Luckily for me, Al Hastings was a good man and he started to describe what he saw of Danny's Hardiman's body to me. It was as disturbing as the other seven. If anything, the course of the disease progressed faster in Danny than in the others. Technically, the shortest span of time from where the disease was first diagnosed to the time of death in the other seven was twenty days. One went twenty-six. That Danny went only seventeen could have meant anything, but I wasn't prepared to dismiss it. Instead, I was going to compare whatever notes Doctor Bender had with the ones I got from Maine.

Hastings paid for dinner, but only after I insisted that the next one was on me, us. He told us that Dyan and Fred Hardiman lived on Route 2 on the west side of town. "Follow me. It shouldn't take too long."

We headed west route 2. Ashley Creek roughly parallels the road on the south side. Thick trees line its route like a picket fence. There were fields growing something between the road and the creek, but I didn't know what it was.

Dyan Hardiman's home was on the south side of the road. Tan and chocolate brown, it sat alone. The nearest house was at Dern Road, maybe a half mile farther on.

Hastings pulled into the driveway and we parked behind him. There was a pickup in the dirt next to the driveway and a Ford Explorer next to where Hastings parked. It made sense that they were home. It was almost eight o'clock. This far north, there was still a lot of daylight. It was like home, in Maine.

Our collective mood was upbeat as we went to the door. Hastings knocked and we waited. And waited. Nothing happened, no one answered. He knocked again and shouted, "Dyan? It's Al Hastings." Nothing. Worse? The door opened slightly as he knocked. To that point, none of us were concerned.

That changed as soon as Al pushed open the door. Or tried to.

Chapter 9

Al had to lean into it as he pushed the door. Calling out, "Dyan? Fred? It's Al Hastings," he stopped as soon as he saw an arm, Dyan's. Then he slipped into the room without disturbing anything more than he already had. I looked at Mario and we exchanged knowing glances. He knew; so did I.

When I heard Hasting hurry away from the door, I slipped into the living room and saw a woman laying face-up on the floor. She was on her back, her arms splayed. Most of the top of her head was missing; a huge spray of blood was against the back of the door. Hastings was in the doorway between the living room and the kitchen crouching over a male form, his head likewise missing.

That's when I noticed it; a pink backpack sitting on the couch. "Mario?" I said quietly. "Find her." He nodded and moved down a hallway to my right.

I moved to where Hastings was staring at what was left of Fred Hardiman. "You realize it took a fairly large-sized caliber weapon to do this."

"Yeah," he said. "One shot to each of them. I figure Dyan was trying to get out the door. Fred was probably shot first." That's when he said it. "He could still be here."

And Mario was looking for a girl.

He looked into the kitchen. "The back door is open. He's probably outside, probably gone."

"There's a girl somewhere. Could she have done it?"

"Janice? She's nine."

"Still…"

"Where's Mario?"

"Looking for her."

He stood over the mess that was Fred Hardiman and called 911. His report was short, professional and meant to be that way. Then he said quietly, "Follow me."

My worry went through the roof. I wanted to scream but knew better. I expected to hear another gunshot. I grew a bit stronger when I didn't. Also, that was the first moment that I realized Al Hastings was carrying a gun and had been all night. He reached into his coat, pulled it out and held it against his right leg. What kind of a gun was it? The kind that kills you when you pull the trigger. Look, I have no idea about guns. None. All I know is that it was a pistol. Beyond that? No idea. I followed him.

He peered around the corner of the doorway where Fred lay. I assume he saw nothing because he slipped into the living room. I followed. Maybe he wanted me in the kitchen, but Mario was my husband. I was going to go to wherever he was. Period. That was not negotiable.

There was a dining room off to our left, a nice place where the family could gather and talk while they shared a meal. But there would be no more meals around that table. I glanced at it one more time only to convince myself that no one was there. No one was. We crept along the wall, avoiding nice furniture as we went. Hastings still had his gun against his leg. Me? I was crouching behind him because I wanted to be invisible. I've seen too many gunshot wounds. Call it a macabre benefit of working in Compton, California, before I moved here. I didn't want to become another victim of one.

We heard whispering coming from one of the bedrooms down the hall. I wanted to tell Hastings that it was Mario, but I couldn't. It was faint, indistinct and faraway. For all I knew? It was the killer and he was toying with Janice, Mario dead at his feet. But wouldn't I have heard a gunshot? Well, what do they call them? Quieters? Silencers? Something like that? Wouldn't that make sense in a place like this?

Hastings turned to me and whispered, "Wait for the police in the kitchen."

I shook my head no and mouthed, "Mario."

He frowned but wasn't in a position to do anything about my decision.

Also, the whispering had stopped.

Either Mario was dead at the hands of the killer or...and I couldn't finish the thought. Beyond Mario was nothing. I've known him since I was four. I've tried to find other men, other answers, but I learned a long time ago that he's my answer. If he's dead because I didn't think, then I killed him.

Hastings crept along the wall. There were four doorways along it, two on either side of the hallway. The first one would be a bathroom. That was on the right. The one beyond that would be Dyan and Fred's bedroom. My guess? Danny's was at the left end of the hallway and Janice's the first one on the left.

Hastings' gun came up.

I can't emphasize this enough. I was scared, worried and so nervous that it was possible whoever was down there could hear me breathing. Still, I had enough foresight to stay behind Hastings. *Come on, Mario. Say something. Do something. Don't be a dead jackass. Be alive and be mine.*

The whispering started again. It sounded male, but I couldn't tell for certain. I wanted to scream out Mario's name, but didn't. Hastings edged farther down the hallway, then signaled that he was moving to the other side. He did and I followed. That made the whispering more distinct and more localized. It was coming from the bedroom, from the one I assumed was Jan's. Hastings held up his hand and made a motion that I assumed meant he was going inside.

I heard sirens in the distance. Did it matter if gunfire erupted *now*?

It was obvious that he was going to rush into the room. I had no idea what that meant. Would he go in shooting? Would he say something first? Were there others in other rooms that would hear?

Well, crap.

Mario rendered all if moot when he came out with a girl in his arms. He saw Hastings and his gun and said, "Thanks for the vote of confidence." Then to me, "She needs help."

Psychogenic shock. Emotional trauma. Catatonia. Call it what you will, but the girl was totally nonresponsive. I looked back down the hallway to where her father lay dead without much of a head and said to him, "Back in her bedroom. She doesn't need to see this." Then to Hastings, "Make sure they know I'm in here. I don't want to become a victim of a mistaken gunshot."

"Will do," he said and moved off.

"Lay her on the bed," I said.

He did and moved away so that I could see her.

Blond and blue-eyed, she might survive to become a cutie. Of course, severe trauma has many consequences, not the least are the ones that become self-destructive. Drug use, promiscuity and a host of other behaviors result from issues like this one. I turned to Mario and said, "You keep them out of here with their goddamned guns. I see one gun and it's no hot tub for you, buster."

"Ooh, motivation," he said and moved out of the room.

That left Janice Hardiman alone with me. I smiled down at her. It wasn't hard to do. She was in deep pain and a smiling face was the least I could do. I took her right hand in mine and said, "I'm going to help you, Janice. Don't worry." I needed drugs, probably Xanax before that promise was going to be real. Which meant she had to be transported to the medical center as soon as possible. I kissed her forehead, maintained a wide smile and said, "My name is Doctor Six and I'll right back. Don't go away."

I got up and the last thing I expected to happen did. She spoke.

"Doctor Six?" she said weakly.

I knelt, smiled and said, "Yes, honey?"

She's small for nine. But then, maybe I'm used to seeing Maddy, who's tall for seven. No matter. Janice had my attention. I held her hand and maintained my best smile. Sometimes it's all the therapy we have.

Her eyes began to fill with tears, her face began to crease with fear and sorrow and she wailed, "They said you were going to find out what killed Danny and then…"

That was all she managed. My job wasn't to finish her sentence. My job was to make certain she was healthy and she wasn't. Her tears got hysterical. I sat back down and picked her up in my arms. Holding her wasn't hard.

Movement in the doorway betrayed Mario.

"Janice, honey?" I said to her. "I need to talk to the nice man. I promise I won't go away. Okay?" She nodded against my chest, but said nothing.

I kissed her forehead and went to where Mario was guarding the doorway. "Find an EMT and make it soon. I figure we have half an hour before serious psychosis sets in."

"You got it," he said and walked toward a knot of brown-suited cops who were talking to Hastings.

Take her mind off of what she saw and heard. That was what I was telling myself. I looked at her and she was as near to a complete breakdown as anyone I'd seen in a very long time. I went back to where she lay on the bed, sat down next to her and took her hand in mine. I kept my smile active as I said, "I'm going to take care of you, Janice, honey. Don't worry about anything."

"My Mommy…"

"Wants you to be okay," I said, my active smile becoming more so. In truth, I wanted to keep that news from her as long as possible. But how? The police weren't going to move the bodies and there was no way out of the house that would guarantee she wouldn't see one or the other of them. Grasping for any line, I looked at the window and decided, *that's where she's going out. I won't allow her to see her parents that way.*

Al Hastings appeared where Mario was standing. They talked quietly and then Al came into the room.

"Honey?" I said to Janice. "I have to talk to the nice man. Okay?"

She didn't reply. Instead, she was staring at the cop who stood talking with Mario in the doorway. I looked at the cop and looked at Janice and all I could see was a terrified little girl. That's where my concentration went. I looked back at Hastings and said, "I want her taken out the bedroom window. You understand why?"

"Yes," he said looking at Janice.

"Now. She needs a hospital, treatment and attention."

"There's an ambulance on the way. You open that window and we'll be ready."

Mario said something to the cop and then turned back to me and said, "I'll open the window. You take care of Janice."

But Janice was catatonic again. Her mouth was open as though to scream and drool rolled down her cheek. I wiped the drool and closed her mouth. She was slipping away from me.

Then I heard the approaching siren. I picked up her hand and it was limp. She'd gone away and I wondered if she would ever come back. *Janice Hardiman? You're my patient now and I swear that you'll get the best care I can give you.* That was my mantra to every patient I ever saw. To that point, I didn't think Janice was anything special. But she was going to be a deal breaker.

For someone.

Chapter 10

Mario went outside while I stayed inside to supervise the EMTs getting Janice through the window. No one had a problem, she got through and I rode in the ambulance to the medical center with her. Mario followed.

The tech was a guy named Robert-not-Bobby Jenkins. As much as I wanted him to give Janice something for her condition, I knew he wasn't carrying anything that could help. All he could do was monitor her vitals and worry like I was already doing. Luckily, nowhere in Kalispell, Montana is very far from the medical center. We got there within ten minutes and they rushed her into the ER.

Wanda Lansing, my best friend, is an ER nurse and she was on duty that night. I was glad to see her, but then I've never assumed anyone I met in an ER to be anything other than qualified. Still, I smiled at her and said, "You still in our poker game?"

"Not if you're wearing that damned playboy bunny costume, I'm not."

Yeah, I do. I mean wear a playboy bunny outfit when Mario sits down to play poker with the gang. I don't play. I drift among the players and make sure they have all the snacks they want. I even dip when I think it might benefit Mario. And, yes, you can call that cheating. Mario doesn't mind and neither does Wanda. We all have fun and the stakes are never more than pennies.

"Well, Mario is the judge on whether or not I'll wear it."

She rolled her eyes and groaned. "Damn, Evie. No one in town can compete with you when you dress like that." Then she got back to business and said, "Whatcha got?"

It was busy for a Monday night in the ER. All the beds were full and there were others waiting outside. The doctors – as usual – were running at full speed. My memories of Compton were still fresh enough that I could empathize with them.

"Nine-year-old female. I think she saw her parents being murdered. It wasn't pretty and I'd describe her condition as emotional trauma."

She turned and barked something at a doctor, at Doctor Kristen Tice. I like Kris because she's as thorough as I'd like to think I am. I watched as Wanda relayed Janice's condition to her. She put her fingers at her neck, then her wrist, then her ankle. Pulse. She was doing nothing more than making sure Janice's pulse was consistent. It seemed to be. Janice was getting worse if my judgment meant anything.

"She spoke at home. Since then? She's been getting worse."

Kristen turned to Wanda and gave an order for a sedative. She was doing what I would do. A sedative would calm her, make her condition less serious and even allow Janice to talk to us without sliding into an abyss of fear, pain and horror. I think Kris has a smile that I'd call infectious. You know, the type of person who you want to have smile at you. It's powerful, engaging and unique to her. When she smiled at Janice? I felt that the healing process had finally begun.

"Can you tell me your name?" she asked.

Between the mixture of her smile and the sedative – Xanax – Janice's eyes fluttered and she looked up at the doctor. "Um, Jan?" she said.

"Well, hi there. My name is Kris. Doctor Six and I are going to take care of you. Is that okay?" She turned to another nurse and said something about the on-staff psychologist. The nurse acknowledged the order and found the nearest phone.

So far, everything was going as I would have wanted it to go. Janice was receiving the care she needed and the people giving it to her were qualified to do it. I turned and saw Al Hastings talking to a doctor. I said to Kris, "I'll be right back."

"Yeah, just don't be wearing a playboy bunny outfit or the nursing staff will have you committed for observation."

"Promise," I said smiling back.

"Does that mean yes or no?"

"Yes," I said smiling back at her enigmatically.

"Just go," she said and turned back to Janice.

Hastings was in the middle of the ER talking to a doctor whose name I didn't know. A uniformed deputy was with them. Hastings looked calm, but the officer looked wary. "Can I talk to you, Mr. Hastings?" I asked.

"What happened to 'Al'?" he asked.

"Depends on your answer to what I'm going to say."

"Well, go ahead."

"I want to reiterate. No cops are going to talk to Janice Hardiman until I say she's mentally prepared for it. She isn't. Understood?"

He shrugged and said, "Sure. Her parents aren't going anywhere. As long as you assure me that she's being taken care of and that eventually we'll get a chance to talk to her, I'll make sure she's gets the time and space she needs."

"That's all well and good, but that crime happened within the city limits and means you don't have jurisdiction. Chief Adams does. Will he see it the same way you do?"

The person I referred to as Chief Adams was a bowling ball named Roy. He was the Chief of Police of Kalispell and the murders of Janice's parents were his responsibility. I didn't know him at all, just his name and title from pictures I'd seen in various places.

A motion at the ER doors caused Hastings to say, "And there he is now. You can ask him yourself."

I excused myself and walked directly to where Adams was barking orders like he was Patton. I didn't know the underling but the man was absorbing everything he was being told with rapturous eyes. He would do whatever he was told – and do it with a gusto I have always found sickening. If told to get physical, he would use those instructions liberally and not care if the bruises showed.

"Chief Adams?" I said, interrupting a long string of commands.

Both men looked irritated at me.

"Yes?" he said, his eyes showing his displeasure.

"Chief? My name is Doctor Collins and Janice Hardiman is my patient."

His eyes rolled and he said, "Oh, God. The lesbian."

Anger welled up from a deep place and began to break free. The only reason I didn't say anything was the underling. He leaned into his boss and said, "Um, Chief? That's the other broad. The one down there."

Broad? We're broads? Okay, Kris is a lesbian, *but so what?* Cayn is homosexual and *I play poker with him while wearing a playboy bunny costume!* Okay, okay. It doesn't work on him. It works on Wanda and I have no idea why. But broads? I leaned into him as much as the underling did and said, "The lesbian and I are going to monitor Janice Hardiman's condition and you will not be allowed near her until either one of us says so. Am I clear?"

It was all bluff and I knew it. Worse, Adams knew it, too. If he insisted on barging into where Janice was lying, he could undo anything we might be able to accomplish for her. His belligerence would cause an untold amount of damage that Janice might not be able to recover from. Okay, bad English. Deal with it.

I knew my hands were full when he said as though I was one of his underlings, "I'll talk to her whenever I'm good and ready. Am *I* clear?"

Well, more flies with honey, you know? I retreated mentally and offered, "Look, she's had a trauma. Can you give her a little time before you start asking her questions that might trigger a relapse?"

"How much time? There's a killer out there."

My first inclination was to say, "As long as it takes." But that was going to lead to a conflict I didn't think I could win. So, even though I wanted to be…well…my mother…I was Evie Collins, doctor, and that meant my bargaining position was a lot less than hers. With Janice Hardiman's wellbeing the foremost thing in my mind, I said, "I realize that, but she wasn't hurt in the attack. It mighty mean she wasn't a target – or didn't see what happened. Look, Chief Adams, can we do this tomorrow? That will give her an entire day to rest and for the medication to take effect. Please? It's for her sake."

Adams rumbled like Mt. St. Helens as he considered my request. His underling stood ready to do whatever he was told. Period. Start a war. Spread a rumor. Arrest someone. You name it. But the Chief said slowly and with a warning in his voice, "Tomorrow, Doctor. I'll be here tomorrow, twenty-four hours from now and that kid better be ready to talk to me."

"Thank you," I replied with what I hoped was a magnanimous voice.

He turned and left, his underling following like a baby duckling at his feet. It felt like a victory, like watching a cure happen. But I knew otherwise. Janice was going to have to get the most restful sleep of her young life before tomorrow. Considering her condition, I didn't think things were going to end well for her. Adams was going to treat her like a criminal and I couldn't see her reacting well to that sort of pressure.

I went back to where Kris was talking and smiling with Janice. Another person was there, a man named Arthur Berrington. He was the on-staff psychologist. His voice was warm ,reassuring and hopeful. And that's how *I* heard it. I could only hope that Janice heard it the same way.

"Kris?" I murmured to her. "I need to go out and see Mario. I'll be right back."

"Sure."

He was in the waiting room and doing it patiently. He smiled when he saw me and asked, "How is she?"

"Shaky," I said.

That's when things took an ugly turn. Was I expecting it? No. Emphatically no. What was it? Well, he looked away, looked toward the ER doors and said, "She'll freak when they talk to her."

"Well, yeah," I said. "I think her condition is fragile at best."

He nodded. And that's when it happened. That's when I realized that things were going to get a lot worse than they already were. He nodded, shrugged and said, "And a cop killed her parents. When I saw her reaction to the deputy? Well, you saw it."

It was worse than a nightmare. It was a waking dream which could easily kill her. But see it? No, I hadn't. I was worried about Janice and nothing more. I stared at Mario uncomprehendingly and finally said, "What?"

"You didn't see it? When she saw that cop? Her condition worsened and didn't improve until he left. I saw Adams leave. He didn't see her, did he?"

"No," I said feeling numb.

He put his hands on my biceps. "Evie? You can't let a uniformed cop near her. I'm not a doctor and I can see it. She'll freak out and no one will ever find out what she knows."

I can't stress this enough. I'm not a cop, have no wish to be one, no wish to act like one and no skills to pretend like I'm one. I'm doing the one thing I love and that's practicing medicine. To that end, I looked at him with a desperation I hadn't felt since I was…sixteen. I was being raped again and the only person who could save me was…Alex. "You find Alex," I said. "You bring him to our house and you tell him I'm not playing spy with him. He needs to find out what happened to Janice's parents and he needs to do it by tomorrow night. Please, Mario? Please find him and tell him?"

Mario is the most competent human being I know. Throughout our long history together, I have wanted him to fail many times for no other reason than to convince myself he's as human as I am. Oh, I know. He is. But now? I was counting on him to be a bit more than human. I was counting on him to find a man who did not want to be found.

He smiled. "Hot tub if I do?"

"Twice a day and four times on Sunday," I said hugging him.

"Consider it done."

We kissed, then he left.

What was going to follow was going to fall directly on me. My entire life as I lived it to that point was going to haunt me. Does that make it wrong? Does that make my choices and how I got here to be something to regret? No. Why? Because what happened was going to fall on me – and I've been living my life for this moment because *I always knew it was going to happen.*

Chapter 11

Janice finally fell into an exhausted sleep just before midnight. I was with her the entire time and I managed to get her to talk a little. I studiously avoided what happened in her home because my professional opinion was that she wasn't strong enough mentally to withstand questions as to what happened there. Fortunately, Doctor Berrington agreed with my assessment. While his questions were designed to get her grounded again, mine were designed to get her comfortable. He would ask, "Do you need anything? Water? Dinner?" I'd ask, "You have the prettiest dimples I've ever seen. You should smile more because they make you look pretty." Between us, I think we comforted her and enabled her to sleep. Yeah, despite the Xanax, she fought sleep as she held my hand tightly in hers. I counted it as a victory when she finally drifted off.

I shook Berrington's hand and he promised to keep me in the loop as far as Janice was concerned. I thanked him and tried to leave.

Yep. Wanda and Kris stopped me. Both of them had their arms folded over their chests. Wanda gave voice to their displeasure. "Kris comes to the next poker game and she wears the bunny costume. You have to play."

I smirked and said, "Her? No one would notice."

"Precisely," Kris said. "But then, my date might."

"Not her," I said eyeing Wanda.

"Nope. You'll meet her when the game starts."

I hugged both of them and said, "I'll call you when the next game is on."

"How's Janice?" Kris asked. Wanda looked sadly sympathetic.

"Given time, she might be okay. My fear is that Adams will lean on her and send her back into catatonia."

"Does she know anything?" Wanda asked.

That was just it. I talked to Mario before he left to find Alex and he said yes. "Babe? The way I see it? She saw something because I found her doll in the hallway. She was sitting on the bed in plain sight when I entered the room. Scared? Well, that was my first impression and my last one, too."

Despite myself, I asked warily, "Why isn't she dead then?"

"It's possible you saved her life just by showing up when you did."

"Then why aren't we dead?" I asked. It seemed the most logical question to ask.

"Because Hastings had a gun? And he would have recognized them if they were indeed cops?"

All that made sense but then I had no idea. I'm not a cop. I'm a doctor who only wanted to save a little girl from a lifetime of terror. But to answer Kris's question? I sighed and said, "Yeah. I think she saw who did it. Mario was there and he told me what he saw. If it all adds up? Someone is going to try to kill that kid to keep her quiet. I hope the police in this town are up to the job."

"Well, we're up to ours," Kris said. "And I know you are, too. You have to assume they are as well."

It all made sense. I thought about it and knew that even if it wasn't, that there was nothing I could do about it. I hugged them again and headed home.

It isn't far from the medical center to our neighborhood. Given what I knew and had determined, I expected something to happen on the way home. I turned right out of the parking onto Highway 93. I'm not usually paranoid, but I'd plead guilty that night. Every car I saw was a potential enemy. I can't number the thousands of times I looked in the rearview mirror when a pair of headlights popped into view. I wanted to be aware of my surroundings – and all I managed to accomplish was a gurgling stomach by the time I drove the two or three miles home. Mario was there and so was another car. Alex, I assumed.

Mario was still awake when I walked in. He was sitting on the couch talking with Alex. Sorry, Alex. I'm never going to get the hang of calling him Normie.

Mario bounced off the couch and hugged me. As he did, he whispered, "Take a good look at him."

I hugged him tighter and whispered, "Specifically?"

"You're the doctor. Just watch him."

"And how are my beautiful kids?" I asked him.

"Sleeping beautifully," he answered taking a chair adjacent to the couch.

The first clue I had that something was wrong with Alex was his entire demeanor. I can't imagine sharing a secret about Alex with Mario and him not knowing it. That was the Alex I remembered. The one that was sitting on my couch had his head down as though tired. It signaled a man who did not pay attention to his surroundings and that was not the man I knew as Alex Payne. He always maintained that a middle linebacker – and I *still* don't know what that is – was the smartest person on the field. His contention was that the middle linebacker had to know what everyone on defense was doing – and on offense, too. Then he had to react to whatever the conditions on the field were and destroy whatever play the offense was running. He said to me more than once, "Every play is search and destroy."

I settled onto the couch next to him and hugged him. He seemed lethargic. "Are you okay?" I asked like a doctor might.

"Just tired. Jet lag, I guess."

Well, that was horse pooey.

He coughed slightly. Then took a deep breath. I didn't like what I was seeing. Call it intuition. Call medical training. Call it a lucky guess, but I wasn't going to bed until he convinced me that he was okay. "How long have you had that cough?"

He smiled and it looked tried. "Playing doctor with the person who's going to be running all over northern Montana, huh?"

He coughed again.

"Just tell me."

Then he took another deep breath.

It might not have been enough for other doctors to know what was happening to him, but I've known every line of his medical file for the last eighteen years. I know that he hasn't eaten red meat in all that time and that he exercises regularly. I know he watches his fats, his cholesterol and I know that because Ellie tells me. She's always known how precarious his health can be if allowed to go unchecked.

I'll give him this: he tried to rally. Anyone else might not have caught it. His smile was the same one he gave me eighteen years ago, the one that reassured me and allowed me to believe that the world wasn't as ugly as I thought it had become. When he said, "I have my nitro, Evie," I knew that he was hiding it from me.

"How bad is it?" I said, putting my hand on his arm.

He put his left hand over my right one. "Do you think I'd come here to do this if I wasn't able?"

"Yes," I said. He would.

"And leave Ellie?"

Damn. Trumped.

He has loved Ellie since he first saw her over twenty years ago. In a world that gave football players of his stature anyone they wanted, he loved her. She wasn't statuesque, svelte or glamorous. She considered herself dowdy, as plain as vanilla ice cream and felt she would never find a man to marry. Then he asked her and told her what was wrong with him. Their lives have been rigidly guided by her ever since. She adheres to the same diet he does. There were only two ways he could be here and in this condition and for Ellie not to know. One, the symptoms were new. I doubted that. Two, he avoided Ellie and did not allow her to notice. That was doubtful, too. Still, if there was a third alternative, I didn't see it.

"Alex, dammit? You're going to be in my office tomorrow morning whether you like it or not. Heart disease is nothing to laugh at."

"Or what? You'll hold your breath and turn purple? You know as well as I do that someone out there is going to try to kill that little girl. You save her mental health and I'll save the rest. The police can run around and do their bit, but I already know more than they do."

"How?" I asked.

"Him," he answered nodding at Mario. "Police, or people dressed like them, are responsible. Is any of that connected to those eight cases of cancer? I don't know, but that's why I'm here. I'll follow the physical leads while you follow the medical ones. You be as thorough as you always were and so will I."

Lord, I did not like it. He was not one hundred percent, was in fact a long way from it, but he wasn't going to allow me to touch him until he knew what was happening. He'd played football while injured. That figured. He told me a lot of players did. That figured, too. But as someone whose primary concerns were a quantum difference than a team trainer, I allowed him to judge his own condition.

"Well, while you're running around, here's a name. Coach Horn. He tried to ram my car Sunday when I went out to see a kid named David Ryan. Mario managed to save my lumpy ass, but that's where it stalled. David saw the incident and recognized Horn's car. He asked me why it happened and I had nothing to tell him. You find out about Horn if you're going to be doing stupid man stuff."

"Stupid man stuff?"

"Yes!" I said hotly. "You need a doctor and we both know it! And Ellie? How do I tell her that the next funeral will be real?"

I was looking for symptoms on his face, but he was always pretty good at hiding them. But heart failure? That was one problem he couldn't hide. He sighed and said, "A lot is riding on this, Evie. More than you know. Can we compromise? If I think I need help, I'll go to your office."

I closed my eyes and shook my head. "I'll be in the medical center. And then? Talking to a doctor named Bender."

"Your cute PA will help me," he said smiling. Then he took my chin in his hand and said, "Please? I know my condition as well as you do. Let me do this as long as I can. After that? I'm all yours."

I smirked. "Norman. What sort of name is that for an All-Pro linebacker?"

"You still don't know what a linebacker is, do you?"

Despite my mood, I started laughing. "You won't hold that against me?"

And he hugged me. One of my problems? I didn't know whether or not it would be the last hug I'd ever get from him. Or. Yeah, or what other issues were more important than his life. The biggest problem were the issues swirling around those eight deaths. I didn't know them all and neither did he. I don't think anyone did – at least on this side of the border. However, by this time tomorrow, everything was going to fall into my lap. Whether or not I wanted it to, whether or not I was ready, even whether or not I was willing. Worse? As bad as it was going to get? It was going to be worse than I imagined. Somewhere down the road, I

was going to be asked to do the impossible. Literally. I was going to be asked to do something no one else had ever done.
    Or else.
    You figure it out.

Chapter 12

Alex was gone before I woke the next morning – and I woke early. I had five hours of sleep and felt like I was an on-call resident back in LA. Cayn Wyatt was still sleeping – and I didn't even know it until Travis walked in, yawned and said, "Cool. Cayn is still here. We can go into the woods." Maddy followed him, yawned and said, "Well, I'm not going in there." Mario walked in, smiled and said, "See what happens when Mom wakes up early? The house has to know what she's doing today."

"I'm going down to the office and ask Norma to see my patents today. Then I'm going to the hospital to see Janice and her doctor."

"Who is?" Mario asking leadingly.

"A man named John Bender. Don't know much about him. Met him once, but it was brief and we didn't get much of a chance to talk."

"Well, go," he said.

"Gotta kiss my kids first," I said kneeling for them. Maddy is always first. She wormed her way past her brother and threw herself at me. I think I had a good mother. She taught me how to raise kids because my childhood – my rape notwithstanding – was idyllic. All she ever wanted from me was to talk to her. There weren't even any restrictions on subject matter – or language either. I can't say I cursed in front of her on a regular basis, but I can remember saying things that were designed to get a reaction from her. I did, but her response usually came with a smile and a calm admonition to use better language. In the end? I came to see that the way I was raised was perfect. Compared to kids I knew? My childhood was as close to perfect as people can get. In that sense, it wasn't hard to hide my rape from her. It would have destroyed her, the family and everything she ever worked for. When I finally told her? I rolled my eyes and said, "Oh, God, yes, Mom. I was raped. Yadda yadda. Uncle Alex helped and we survived. Didn't think you were ready to handle it, so we did it together."

Alex got the brunt of mom's wrath. She punched him every time she saw him for a year. Once? He rolled up his sleeve and showed me the bruises. Naturally, I worried about him and them. That is until I saw him carry her through the office door one day. *Then* she punched him. He even rolled up his sleeve for her. Her only words? "It better not happen again, Payne." Good memories, those.

As Maddy stood there with her arms around me, I asked, "Any news today?"

She smiled and giggled. "No, mommy. But I promise to tell you if I ever get pregnant." She's eight. We've been having that exchange for at least four months now. It started when she asked me with casual bluntness, "Where do babies come from and don't say from your stomach either."

That guaranteed a visit to the medical dictionary. I showed her the entire sequence of a pregnancy. I'll give her this: she listened with rapt attention and then said, "Travis said the mommy eats him."

I smiled. "Well, now you know that's not true."

"Mom?" she said looking up at me.

"Yes?"

"Ew."

That led to a continuing joke between us. "Pregnant yet?"

"No, Mom." We smiled at each other as she added, "And I haven't eaten any babies lately either."

That led Travis to ask, "When do I get to find out how it's done?"

"Mom?" Maddy said. "He'll faint."

"As soon as things quiet down a bit. Soon, okay?"

"Can Dad do it?"

"Your father doesn't know where babies come from," I said smiling at both of them.

"So I can watch when you show him?" Mario asked.

"Any time, big guy," I said.

For the record? With Mario Collins as his father, there was no way Travis didn't already know where babies came from. The only reason this started was neither of us thought Maddy was curious yet. That she was only served to teach us a lesson we thought we already knew: they're ready long before you think they are. Me? I already knew when

I was her age. You'd have thought I would have known better. We all hugged.

I drove to the office first. Norma, my PA, was already there reviewing patient files. I sighed as I sat down next to her.

"Just say it," she said.

"Can you?"

"Is this about Janice Hardiman?"

"Yeah."

"Then, yes. I can cover your patients all week."

"Thanks," I said breathing a sigh of relief.

"One condition," she answered with a straight face.

"And that is?"

"I get invited to your next poker party as a bunny."

"What am I going to tell Kris Tice? She asked, too."

She shrugged. "Not my problem. Deal?"

We shook. "Deal."

She giggled. "This is going to be so cool."

"I can't wait to tell Kris," I said miserably.

"Oh, relax, Evie. Or who do you think told me about the game?"

It took a moment, but then I gasped. "You and Kris?" I said with wide eyes.

She smiled and said, "Yeah. I like her a lot."

I waggled my fingers between us and said, "But that means..."

Her face turned bright red. "Yep. Does that mean I can't work for you anymore?"

I frowned and spat, "No! but I thought you were..."

She smiled and said, "So did I. Then I met her. Wow. Bells. Fireworks. You name it. The rumor is that you're going to let her know when the next game is being held." Her smile got wider. "You could just tell me."

"Sure," I said. Then I caught myself and said, "We had a patient named Norman Peters in here a couple of days ago. If he comes back? Bill him to me. I'll take care of it."

She frowned and said, "And what do I tell Mario?"

I frowned back. "That I'm paying for his bills. Why?"

"Well, how do you know Alex Payne?"

I whispered. "You know?"

She whispered back. "Yes and so does everyone else. Flo is beside herself. She wants to take him home tonight and tie him to her bed. And Liz? I actually caught her in the bathroom with her pants around her ankles. And don't bother trying to deny that it's him. The most famous middle linebacker in NFL history and you try to shove Norman Peters down our throat. Now, why is he here causing mass hysteria among your staff? And if you say you're meeting him in a motel room later, we're all going to follow you and get our turn." Then she turned her head and said, "And there's an envelope from Al Hastings on your desk."

The eighth victim. I looked back at my office and then at her. *Well, why not? Maybe she'll see something that I didn't.* "Wait here," I said and walked back to my office. I grabbed the envelope, opened it and confirmed that it was everything Hastings had on the victim, plus case notes from Danny Hardiman's doctor, John Bender. The notes on the other seven victims were in my briefcase. I opened it, took the files and brought them back to where Norma sat. I dropped everything in front of her and said, "This is why he's here."

"Short version," she said.

"Cancers that kill the victim within seventeen days of initial detection. All young, all football players, all from the Portland, Maine, area except one from Flathead High School."

"Tox screens?"

"All clear except some pot and minor stuff."

"No steroids?"

"No."

She fingered the files and said, "I'll take a look over lunch."

"Red," I said.

"Excuse me?"

"You're not invited under any conditions unless the costume is red." Mine is green.

She smirked. "Done."

We hugged and I left for the hospital. It's not far; just across the street, in fact. Still, I got in my car and drove to a spot as near to the ER as I could find. Janice was most likely in a private room, but I wanted to talk to the ER doctors to see what had been done for her. I was greeted by everyone that wasn't busy with a patient. I approached the nurses station and smiled at a girl I knew only as Sophie. "Hi, girl. Are either Wanda or Doctor Tice on duty?"

"Nope. Both come in later," she said as she frantically typed at a keyboard.

"Who's on?"

"Hammerhead."

That would be Doctor Frank Hammer. I nodded and asked, "Is Janice Hardiman still down here?"

Sophie's fingers blazed across the keyboard as she said, "No. She was transferred upstairs." Then they landed on Janice's file and I got her room number.

"Thanks," I said.

As I was leaving the counter, she said, "Oh, this came for you." She read the label on the envelope and said, "A blood test for a David Ryan." Then she handed it to me.

"Thanks, Sophie. I owe you one."

That sent me in search of Doctor Hammer. He has no sense of humor and would not understand the need for a poker game and the accompanying playboy bunnies. Let me put it this way: I like the way the game blows off steam in a harmless way. Considering the pressures that were mounting, I was already looking forward to our next game. And, yes. Now I had to learn how to play poker.

I found him with a male patient. He was prescribing something for him. He gave him the instructions for the prescription and asked if he had any questions. Having none, Hammer turned and asked me, "And how can I help you Mrs. Bunny?"

I moaned, put my face in my hands and said, "Does everyone know?"

"Since you told Kris? Yes. Everyone knows. And I want in."

"She's a lesbian."

"You aren't."

"And I won't be wearing a playboy bunny suit."

"And why would I care? The rumor is that you're playing poker. The rumor also is that you're not very good. Hence? I want in."

"Let me talk to my husband," I said miserably.

"This is about the Hardiman girl, isn't it?"

"Yes. Who's been with her, what's her condition and has Adams gotten to her?"

"Berrington is with her, has been all night. She slept and seems to be reacting well to her medication. And no, no cops have been near her, although there is one on the floor up there. He's been under strict orders not to let her see him."

"Thanks, Doctor," I said.

When I turned to leave, he said, "Doctor? Would you consider playing for something other than pennies?"

"No," I replied and left.

The poker games were supposed to be fun. Suddenly, everyone had their own take on the game and wanted to change it. I was upset when I got off the elevator on the second floor. My heart began to melt toward the little girl with the blue eyes and blond hair. Why? Because there were media vans in the parking lot, one of them from CNN. Trust them. She'll probably be on their network *au nauseum* from now on. Maybe that's why the mnemonic for their network is Contains No News.

I saw two people on the floor that didn't belong there. One was the cop Hammer referred to. The other was Cayn Wyatt, Mario's partner. They run a school from a house on Highway 92. They started with four kids. Travis, Maddy and their best friends Woody and Josie. Six months after they started the school, there are twenty-seven kids and two part-time aides. Better yet? It's all licensed, legal and fun.

But, now. I could disregard the cop. But Cayn? I would have never guessed why he was there. Never in a million years.

If he wasn't gay? Nah. Mario is too cool.

But thanks, Cayn. You just made this a lot easier.

Chapter 13

The cop was keeping Cayn in the hallway. I brushed off the cop and took Cayn into Janice's room with me. Berrington was there and that made me feel a lot better because Janice wasn't alone.

When I first saw her, I was surprised she knew my name. But Cayn? She actually smiled and shouted, "Uncle Cayn!"

Well, I knew better. Cayn wasn't related to the Hardiman's, either of them. I knew Cayn had no siblings. But considering that I married my uncle, a man I was not biologically related to, I could cut Cayn and Janice a lot of slack. I felt even better when she jumped into his arms and let him hug her.

I grew worried when Janice broke down and started crying. Berrington merely shook his head no. He was smiling when he did it. Cayn, who is a big man, put her back down in her bed, but did not stop hugging her. It seemed to last forever until Cayn asked with Janice's arms still around him, "And how's my little princess this morning? Did they give you ice cream? Ice cream is the best medicine in the whole wide world."

The next moment broke my heart. Cayn laid her on the bed, unwrapped himself from her and smiled widely. Janice looked up at him and cried, "Uncle Cayn? They...they...they killed..." and that was as far as she got.

Cayn picked her up again and held her as she screamed. Berrington came around to my side of the bed and whispered, "She hasn't reacted all night. She slept without medication, but I took it as a sign of withdrawal. Until right now? I would have said her future was grim. But he's had a breakthrough all by himself."

"And now?" I said.

"We work with her."

"Can she withstand it?"

"That's up to your friend. Can he stay?"

Cayn turned to us and said, "Yes. Mario and the aides are covering the school. I'll be here from now on."

Janice was bubbling, crying and doing all of it hard. Cayn held her as she did and Berrington made no move to stop them. A nurse came to the door, but Berrington shook his head at her, too. The nurse left.

I need to reiterate why I was here. I don't care about the legal issues concerning her parents and why they died. Well, murdered. Janice Hardiman was my issue. She was. I was going to be here until I was certain she was going to survive reasonably intact. I assumed a state agency would handle her case and that her welfare would be their first concern. I never counted on Cayn smiling down at her and saying, "Sweetie? I need to talk to the doctor for a second. Okay?"

"Okay, Uncle Cayn."

He winked at her and said, "I'll be right back." Then he tickled her chin and said, "Don't you go away."

She giggled and said, "Okay. I'll wait for you." He began to stand, began to face me and Janice tugged his sleeve. "Uncle Cayn?" she said uncertainly. "Is Doctor Six a nice lady?"

His voice betrayed his emotions toward me. "Oh, my goodness, yes," he said enthusiastically. "She even has two kids of her own. Would you like to meet them?" He wrapped his huge arm around my shoulder and said, "I'd marry her but that doody-head Mario already did."

Her smile was tentative. Maybe she was going to make up her own mind about me. With Cayn's arm still around my shoulder, I smiled at her and said, "Janice, honey? I'd like to help you get better." I saw a lot of gunshot victims in Compton. A good part of them were kids, some as young as Janice. One thing they all shared was the horror of what happened to them. While Janice hadn't been shot, she was a victim nonetheless because her entire family was dead except her. What was going to happened to her? Was that nameless state organization going to help her or become another obstacle to her? Well, Cayn settled all of that.

"Please, Evie," he said pulling me away from the bed. "I need to say this right now."

We were standing by the door. "I'm going to file adoption papers. No one is going to take her away from me."

"Have you talked with Berrington about it?"

"Yeah, and he's encouraging me. There's no law in Montana that says I can't, so I'm going to adopt her and take care of her forever."

Jesus, I hugged him. "That's great, Cayn. If you need any character witnesses, just let me know. I can't think of anyone that would make a better father than you." Then I asked, "But where and why does she know you?"

Cayn has a red beard that will go slowly gray as he grows older because he won't cut it. He trims it and that's it. Why is that pertinent? Because Janice played with it when he held her. She smiled at him, pulled his beard and he let her. they were comfortable together.

"Fred and I went to school together. We were best friends growing up. We had a bad falling out when I outed myself. We didn't talk for years." He turned and looked at Janice. "It's hard to believe they're all dead. Danny was a shock, but now Dyan and Fred, too?" His gaze returned to me and he said, "I went to their house one night about five years ago. I pounded on their door until Fred answered. Then I hugged him before he could say anything. I told him we were friends and my sexual orientation had nothing to do with that. Dyan pulled me into the house and we talked until two in the morning. Janice was three or four then. God, but I took a liking to that kid. She started calling me Uncle Cayn after a while. It wasn't hard to love her. And Danny? I played basketball with him on their driveway." His voice lowered even more when he said, "I swear I'm going to get her through this. Then I'm going to protect her for the rest of her life."

That boded well for me. I was worried about her, too, but Cayn was making Janice his mission. That was going to free me to read Danny Hardiman's autopsy file. But I wanted to talk to her first. I wanted to be assured that she was okay *now*. I know that Adams and his ilk will get their time with her, but I still considered her to be my patient even though Doctor Bender nominally was.

We went back to her bed again and I smiled down at her. "Sweetie?" I said with the same voice my mother used to use when she called me, "baby". Yeah, I hated it and I imagine Janice doesn't like it either. *Use her name, stupid.* "Um, Janice…"

"My mom used to call me Jan," she said. "Can you do that?"

Chastised by a nine-year-old. Ouch. It wasn't hard to smile at her and said, "Sure. I can call you Jan. You can call me Evie."

"That's a pretty name," she said almost sadly. "Not like mine."

My smile got wider. "When I was your age? I asked my mother if she could call me Stephanie because I thought Evie sounded like a baby name." I thought my middle name – Monica – was worse. I was convinced my mother hated me because she picked the two worst names in the English language and then stuck me with them. I almost stopped wanting to be a doctor because I was convinced no one would ever go to one named *Evie*. I took her hand and said, "Trust me. Jan or Janice is a good name." Then I asked the one question I came her to ask. "How are you this morning. Are you up to visitors?"

"Will Uncle Cayn be here?"

"Yes," he said. "All day."

"Then I can see them."

"Including the police?" I asked.

Her hand tightened in mine. "Only if Uncle Cayn is here. Can you be here, too?"

I looked at him and said, "I need to see Doctor Bender, so I'll be gone for a while. If Adams or any other cop shows up while I'm gone? Call me and I'll come right back." Then I looked at Janice and asked, "Is that okay? I'll be here as soon as Uncle Cayn calls me."

"Well," she said looking up at Cayn. "Okay."

I hugged Cayn and then leaned down and hugged Janice, too. "I'll be here, Jan," I said to her. "All Uncle Cayn needs to do is call me."

God, she was shaky. And I mean that in every sense I can. Her eyes darted back and forth between us, her hands shook, she had perspiration on her forehead and if she closed her eyes, she'd probably see that night all over again. She'd probably see it for the rest of her life. It wasn't hard to make that promise to her. To Cayn I said, "I mean it. You call me and I'll be here."

"Will do. You go and do whatever you need to do."

Still, I felt like I was deserting her when I left the room. Yes, I could call Doctor Bender, but I wanted an eyes-only view of his files – if he would let me see them. I wanted to compare Danny Hardiman's case to that of David Ryan. But first, I had to pull out David's blood test and look at it.

I got out of the elevator went to a chair in the waiting room and took the test results out of the envelope. It wasn't hard to see. I sighed, folded up the paper and sat for a long moment. David's result was fairly clear. That result also put him outside the parameters of the eight cancer victims. Why? Because David was using HGH, human growth hormone. Steroids, in other words. If the pattern held, David was safe. I still felt that way when I went to see Doctor Bender. But, things change.

They were about to.

Real fast.

Chapter 14

Doctor John Bender's office was down the street from mine. I'd never been there and couldn't imagine needing to. Well, all that was different now. I needed to see him, needed him to be yielding concerning his files and was prepared to be sweeter than a Cadbury bar to a diabetic.

The first thing I noticed about his office was that it was structurally identical to mine. While I'd made changes to the interior, his was still in its original configuration. I went to the window – I have a counter – and asked the girl who sat there, "Can I see Doctor Bender? My name is Doctor Sixkiller-Collins." I handed her a business card.

She looked at it, then me and asked, "You're just down the street, right?"

"Yes."

"Give me a second," she said and disappeared down a hallway.

His waiting room had nine people in it, two of them of them were children under the age of three. As I was waiting, the office door opened and two more people came into the office. That meant there were eleven people in it. I probably don't make as much as Bender does because I don't cram as many patients into my schedule as he does. It makes my affiliations with the medical groups interesting, but I think my lawyers are at least a match for theirs, maybe better. No, I'm not worried about getting blackballed by medical groups. If anything, I have more time with my patients and can give a better diagnosis as a result. Bender was practicing medicine in the fashion it is practiced in this country.

The receptionist came back, opened the inner office door and said, "Come on back, doctor."

His staff looked competent, and that's all I suppose any doctor can ask for. There were three rooms on the right side of the hallway and two of them were closed with a patient file waiting in the holder attached to the door. That meant he had two clients waiting for him. We've had meetings in my office. I've asked for input from my staff about patients and how long they should wait. We try to limit them to one at a time.

Ideally, no one should be waiting for me. I don't know why, but his arrangement bothered me.

Bender was sitting behind his desk in his office. He smiled at the girl and said, "Thank you, Judy."

John Bender was as old as my father. Well, Brad Chang. Brad isn't my biological father, but he married Mom when I was four. He's the only father I know. Bender was his age, in his fifties. Brad's thick black hair is flecked with gray; Bender's was similarly speckled. Like Brad, Bender looked to be in shape. Any further similarities I was going to find would only happen when we started having a conversation. Brad can talk about anything – including the color of the drapes in their Portland home. He's a writer and a good one. My most fervent wish was going to be that Bender was as good a doctor as Brad was a writer. If so, my job here was going to be easier than otherwise.

"Doctor Bender?" I started as I stood in front of his desk.. "Did you have a patient named Danny Hardiman?"

He bit his lower lip and said, "Yes." Then he indicated the chair in front of his desk and said evenly, "Please, have a seat."

He was wearing The Doctor's Uniform. White lab coat with a pen sticking out of its pocket, a stethoscope wrapped around his neck and a red power tie knotted tightly at his throat. I wear clothes that are appropriate for the season. For August? A light sweater and black pants. Yes, I felt distinctly underdressed as I faced him.

He asked, "Why do you ask about him?"

"I'd like to inquire about his death. I've heard he died of a rare and very virulent form of skin cancer. Is that true?"

I already knew it to be true. All I was giving him was a chance to be honest.

"Danny Hardiman is deceased. I can verify that much. The cause of death is not something I can pursue, however."

"I talked with Al Hastings," I said. "I even got his autopsy notes. Doctor Bender? This could be serious."

"What is your interest in his case?" he asked neutrally.

"To find out what killed him."

"And how did you learn of it. Hastings didn't volunteer it. Danny Hardiman's death was the most carefully guarded secret in Montana, if not the country."

"Does it matter how I heard? Hastings was very helpful. I merely wish to know if there are any details of which you are aware, but he was not."

"I cannot divulge anything in Danny Hardiman's file," he said, his hands resting calmly on the desk. "Please. I hope you understand."

"I don't," I answered as civilly as I could. "Cancer that spreads that quickly and kills that fast is unknown in this country." I was asked by my mother not to mention the other seven cases. By phrasing my answer in that fashion, I was hoping he would spill something that he was not supposed to know.

His eyes got distant. If he wasn't thinking about his patient, I'd eat as many cow chips as Mario could find. It was that obvious. He began to fidget, too. Finally, he looked at me and said, "I've never seen anything like it. Nothing we did stopped it. No treatment we used was effective. It was virulent, necrotizing and spread so fast that it was almost as though you could watch it spread in real time."

"You know his parents are dead."

"Yes. I'm going to the hospital tonight to see Jan."

"You realize that I've already seen the files you gave to Hastings?"

He drummed his fingers on the desktop and avoided looking at me. He bit his lip again and slowly reached down to his right. I heard a drawer open. He extracted a file from the drawer, laid it on the desk and said, "I need to use the bathroom. Please excuse me." And he walked out of the office and closed the door.

Okay, he was giving me free reign to look at Danny Hardiman's file. Not knowing how long that reign would last, I took the file and wanted to cross off one item from the list of things that could have done this. Necrotizing fasciitis can kill even faster than this cancer did. Its mechanism works beneath the skin and comes in two types. The first is caused by anaerobic bacteria. The second is caused by group A streptococci and can be called synergistic gangrene. I was looking for any references to those two conditions. I found nothing. What I did find were three biopsies of the cancers. All were positive just like the seven cases in Maine. It was definitely cancer and not another disease of the skin.

I put the file back on his side of the desk and waited. It didn't take long. He came in, sat down and said, "Where were we? I believe I was apologizing for my position?"

"Yes, we were," I said holding my hand out across the desk. "I understand your position and I sympathize with it."

He paused before he took my hand, but he shook it in the end. "I hope this doesn't preclude us from being colleagues," he said.

Without a smile, I said, "I can think of three reasons why it might, but not one of them ever will." If he didn't catch my reference to the three tests he did on Danny Hardiman, then I wasn't sure I wanted to be his colleague.

In the same fashion, he replied, "Very well. I have patients waiting. I hope you understand."

"I do."

I left with more knowledge than I came with. There are bacterial strains that kill faster than this disease did, but nothing that grabs public attention quite the way cancer does. Its victim gets public sympathy and support. If the victims dies? They get respect and admiration for battling something that is both unseen and deadly. Any other disease merely gets you a sympathetic nod and the feeling that you were merely the victim of a bad break. Cancer gives you the image that you fought a good fight against long odds and lost admirably.

I couldn't know, not then, that the image of sympathetic death was not what was happening here. Someone was going to a lot of trouble of create a disease that would kill its host and generate antipathy. The operative word in this case was kill. Someone was creating a disease that would garner its victim widespread notice, but would still do its job and kill its host. Upon that, they were counting. And they were almost ready to loose it upon the one person that had always been their target.

As I left Bender's office, I couldn't know that the world of medicine was about to draw me into it farther and more personally than I ever dreamed. And I'm already a doctor.

Yeah, it never dawned on me either.

Chapter 15

My next visit was to David Ryan. I wanted to confront him about the reasons he was taking HGH. I was still nervous about Alex's condition, but I knew that he was more aware of it than I was. With Ellie as his wife, no one in North America was more aware of his physical condition than either of them. I had to assume he would get help when he needed it. But Alex was the reason I went out to see David and his mother. If I could save David from a lifetime of health concerns on the scale Alex had them, I'd consider myself successful.

The drive to his home was stressful only because of my previous trip to it. For that reason, I kept my eyes on the rearview mirror as much as on the road. Honestly? Had I seen anything suspicious, I don't know what I would have done. While I'm grateful for everything Alex did to help me to become as competent as I am in personal defense, I never expect it. I expect sickness and ill-health, expect symptoms and disease, expect diagnoses and the ravages of time. I have trained myself to learn these things. I have lived my life to help the sick and the infirm. I don't expect things to jump out at me, at least not from the physical world. I expect maladies to come from physiology and not from the roadside. I train for one; try to react to the other.

So, I was nervous while I drove. I kept rehearsing things in my mind. *If someone tries to drive me off the road, I'll swerve, brake and turn around. I'll call Mario. I'll call 911.* Nerves began to get the best of me as I turned onto Valley View Drive. This was where it happened. Well, up ahead maybe. I gripped and re-gripped the steering wheel as I drove toward the Ryan home that was at the end of the road. The hills to right led up to Foy Lake. The plains below me on the left led down to a housing tract. If trouble came, it would come from the hills and woods above me.

The urge to hit the accelerator and speed down the road was immense. The only reason I didn't were the people who lived along the road. I had to be careful because someone might step into it. It meant being watchful and alert.

And nothing happened.

The Ryan house was on the left; the open fields rolled out below it. The horse pens surrounded the garage, the horses grazing in the grass. I saw normalcy, peace and quiet.

The pickup was gone, but Regina's Subaru Outback was in the driveway. I parked behind it and checked the area for trouble. All I saw were horses and a cluster of houses back up the road. If anyone was there, I didn't see him.

I grabbed my medical bag, got out and continued to scan the area. I stopped at the back end of my Highlander and scanned the trees and bushes across the road. Nothing. No one. I took a deep a breath and went to the front door and rang their innocuous door bell. No one answered. I looked back at the Outback and wondered if it was normal for them to go places in Bernie's pickup. That could explain why the Outback was still in the driveway; no one was answering the door. I rang the doorbell again and then knocked impulsively on the door. Unexpectedly, it opened.

I heard nothing from inside the house. I called out, "Hello?" and pushed the door with the knuckle of my right hand. I was prepared to apologize. The door had opened no more than six inches when I said it again, "Hello?" Still nothing and no one answered. I pushed the door open even further and looked at the living room just inside the door. Everything was calm and quiet.

A part of me wanted to notice how interesting the carpeting was compared to the only piece of furniture I could see. The carpeting was rust-colored, while the cabinet just inside the door – probably one that housed a TV of some sort – was mahogany. But it didn't matter. I tried to visualize someone sleeping on the couch. "Hello? Is anyone home?" I called out again. There was still no answer. *Just close the door and leave. They're not home.*

I grabbed the doorknob and started to pull it shut. But the whole thing seemed so preposterous that I pushed open the door all the way and yelled, "Regina! It's Doctor Six!" There was no answer, not at first.

Then I heard a groan and that was enough. I entered the house and called out, "Regina! It's Doctor Six!"

A big screen TV was just inside the door. It was easy to ignore until the screen shattered and blew outward. *What?* I ducked away from flying glass only to hear an odd noise on the wall opposite from the TV set. There was a small hole in the wall above a chocolate-colored couch. *What the hell?* Then someone tackled me and screamed in my ear, "Someone is shooting at you!"

Mario.

Another shot hit the floor where I'd been standing. I smacked him and screamed, "Someone's in here, you fool!"

He pulled me toward a hallway off to the left and said, "And you won't be any help if you're dead!"

Another shot hit the sofa.

"Are you okay?" he asked, worry written all over his face.

"No, Regina..."

He put his hands on either side of my face and said, "Were you hit?"

I put my forehead to his and said, "No, but one of us is about to be!"

Another shot hit the wall near the hallway.

From somewhere in the house, I heard the same moan. Neither male nor female, it was simply the voice of someone in pain.

He kissed me, smiled and said, "You'll excuse me? I have to go take care of a sniper."

I grabbed his arm and said, "911?"

He smiled and said, "Already done. I have to go neutralize Bernie before they get here or he might actually hit someone who's trying to help."

The moan sounded like Regina. If I had to put a name to it, hers was the one I'd use. "Look, dude. He has a gun."

His smile got wider. "Wow. And you actually realize it."

"Mario..."

He kissed me. "Oh, don't worry. I'll drive up into the hills, chase him down, then hogtie him."

It's beginning to dawn on me that he might get killed whenever he does something like this. Maybe it doesn't worry him, but I'm beginning to wonder how many more chances he has before his luck changes. With my hand still on his arm, I stared at him for a moment, then said, "Look. You don't have to go. I'll need help anyway and you already called 911. Let them handle it."

Someone – Regina, I thought - moaned again. Mario kissed my nose and said, "I can hear your stomach rumbling. Go take of her. I'll make sure that Bernie Ryan leaves you alone long enough to handle whatever crisis you find."

"Mario," I said, my voice full of worry. "It's dangerous. And how do you know it's him?"

"I saw him running across the road as you drove up. That's why he didn't shoot at you while you were knocking on the door. He was getting into position. A minute later and we wouldn't be having this discussion." He touched my cheek and said, "Please, don't worry about me. I'll be fine. You go take care of whoever is back there. Okay?"

Six months ago, I would have already been in there. Instead of worrying about him and his safety, I would have put myself in harm's way by ignoring those same bullets. In truth? I wanted to run back there and do whatever I could to help whoever it was. But I needed him to know how important he was to me. "Mario? I can't do this without you. Please?"

He kissed me again. "Do you hear it?"

"Hear what?" I said studying his beautiful face.

"No gun shots."

I blinked, listened briefly and said, "But, how?"

"Alex." He kissed me again and said, "Gotta go."

I wrapped my arms around his neck and kissed him as thoroughly as I could. "I love you," I said when it was over. "More ever day."

He put his hand to my cheek and said, "Indescribable. Luscious. Unforgettable. Sweet. Mesmerizing. All these things, Evie. All these things and more."

He turned and ran off.

And me? I was left with more than enough to do this. Far more than enough. There was a time – six months ago – that I don't think I was a very good wife, mother and companion for Mario and my children. I've tried so hard ever since then. I've tried to be better, more considerate and more alive for them. The playboy bunny costume is nothing more than a symptom of my commitment to them. And, no, the kids are not home during the poker game. They have friends and they both do sleepovers on those nights. That's another symptom. I grew up with friends, lots of friends, and I want them to make the effort I did. I won't choose their friends, but I will guide them in the right places.

What's all that mean? This: I'm trying to change my life. I'm trying to show them that they count. I'm trying to show them that I don't live my life in a vacuum. There was a time when I don't think I could have said that. On top of being a bad wife, mother and companion, I was probably a bad doctor, too. I can't say the balancing act I'm doing isn't stressful. It is. But it's heavenly stress. My kids smile at me more often, talk to me, ask me questions and I take the time to help them. All of them. People I meet get my full attention, not the version where I was still diagnosing my last patient. If you find yourself in front of me? You get my best effort. Mario is convinced and my kids seem that way, too.

While I wanted to stay and savor his touch, I knew my next patient was just around the corner in the kitchen. I hurried to her and found quite something else. There were two of them. Regina was struggling, trying to get to her feet while blood rushed from a hole in her chest. The object of her struggle was in the middle of the kitchen floor. From his position, I'd say he was trying to get out the back door. Who was it?

David, Regina's son. There was a hole in his neck, but not much blood. Regina, on the other hand, was trailing a line of blood as she dragged herself across the floor.

"Down," I said to her. "If I don't stop the bleeding, you'll die before you reach him."

"David," she said, struggling to say his name.

"Isn't bleeding the way you are. I have to get your bleeding under control and then I'll work on David."

I glanced at the boy and he wasn't moving. But there was little blood. Either he was already dead, or his wound wasn't as serious as

Regina's. In a sense, Regina got lucky in that there was no exit wound. Had there been, the bleeding would have been much worse than it was.

    I opened my bag, pulled out a compress, slapped it against my thigh, then pressed it over the wound. It wasn't what I wanted to use, but it was all I had. It was of the type that grew cold when activated. It would help to stop the bleeding. I leaned on it, changed it, but kept my eye on David. He still hadn't moved. Regina was talking, or trying. She wasn't making much sense. Slowly, when the bleeding slowed and stopped, I went to David and was reassured by a pulse.

    Then I heard sirens.

    Both of them were alive.

    Well, technically.

Chapter 16

The Ryan household turned into official chaos. Chief Adams was there and that made me feel better because that meant he wasn't harassing Janet Hardiman. The EMT's that showed up were Russ Quailes and Deidre Tomasi. I didn't know any of the cops except Adams.

I assisted Russ and Deidre while Adams hovered above us like a bad memory. While Regina looked better, David was still unresponsive. His pupils dilated nicely when I flashed a light in his eyes, but he was otherwise unresponsive to every tactile stimulus. The longer I watched him and helped Russ and Deidre, the more worried I got over his condition. I didn't like his blood pressure, his heart rate or anything I saw. I wanted – needed – diagnosing tools to help me ascertain what was happening to him.

A second ambulance showed up. Tom and Richie. They transported Regina – quite against her will I might add – while Russ and Deidre transported David. Russ asked, "You need a ride?"

"No. I'll meet you there."

"Cool," he said and slid David into the back of the ambulance.

They raced away while I watched the area across the road. Adams came up to me as I stood watching. "I figure the shots came from over there," he said.

I shrugged. "Whatever." I was watching the second ambulance race up Valley View Drive.

"Who do the tracks belong to?" he asked.

I looked across the road. A dual set of tire tracks tore through the underbrush and headed up the hill toward the lake above. I shrugged. "Mario, my husband. He thinks Bernie Ryan did this. He says he saw him cross the road and head into the hills."

Adams turned and yelled at someone behind him. A cop came running and Adams pointed across the road. "Bernie Ryan's up there! Organize a search party. Move!"

I put my hand on his arm. "Um, Mario's up there? You mind telling him that?"

'The doc's husband is up there, Denny! Don't just shoot anyone you see!"

"Yes, sir," the cop said. I don't know if Denny was an important cop or just another underling. It made no difference to me. I wanted both Mario and Alex safe – and that was all. They could play cops and robbers for the rest of the day if it made them happy as long as they didn't shoot either of them.

The cop ran off.

"You need me for anything?" I asked Adams.

"You're kidding, right? There are more holes in that house than in Swiss cheese and you want to know if you can go? No, Mrs. Collins," he said calmly and ruthlessly. "You're going to answer every question that Detective Carson asks you. Do I make myself clear?"

I shrugged again. "I suppose I'm going to have to jump through your hoops before I can go to the hospital."

"That's exactly right," he said with some spite and anger in his voice.

I wasn't surprised that of the Kalispell PD's two detectives, I got Detective Paul Carson. I know the other one. Norm Houser is a regular at our poker games. If Wanda stops coming, Norm will stop, too. Then we're going to have to scour every motel room from here to Canada because those two people are going to wind up in bed some day. That's why I got Carson. Norm is "prejudiced" since he takes part in our poker games. Anyway, Carson's older than the Black Hills and just as rugged.

I spent the next hour with Carson and repeated my story seven times. The last two repetitions were recited verbatim, the same way and without any vocal inflections that might have helped him. Also, he asked seven different ways if I either saw or knew from firsthand experience that Bernie took those shots at me, at the house and whether he shot his wife and son. I answered him the same way every time. "No," I replied to his unspoken and prodding insistence that I was holding something back.

Carson finally nodded and walked away. Adams came back in his stead. "Will either of them live?" he asked.

"Regina? Probably. David? Don't know. He was unresponsive the entire time I was with him. I don't like it."

"Is that queer on duty in the ER?"

"You mean Doctor Tice?"

"Yeah, her. The queer."

"No idea. I'll let her know that you were thinking about her if I run into her."

"Well, if you see her, then tell her I expect that boy to be lucid and talking like there was a pull tab in his back."

I shook my head and said, "Sure. I'll let her know."

"Thanks," he said and waddled off.

It hadn't dawned on me until Mario pointed it out that there had been no more shots. To be sure, I wasn't as worried of those shots as I was about Regina. Then when I saw David, my worries about a shooter up in the hills became nonexistent. Now, as I stood at the rear of my Highlander, I couldn't help but wonder what had happened in those hills across the street from where I stood. Mario hinted that Alex was up there. I knew his condition was marginal at best, but I also knew I wasn't going to convince him to do anything he wasn't already prepared to do. *You know he has a heart condition. You know he needs attention. You should have told Mario, you fool. You should have said something.* It would have been easy to berate myself endlessly – especially if anything happened to either of them – but my thoughts went to David.

I've seen my share of gunshot wounds. They bleed profusely. Considering the shot that hit David was in the neck, the floor around where he lay should have been a pool of blood and it wasn't. The only way that could be was if the bullet didn't hit a vital area, blood vessels and such. But his condition – totally unresponsive – suggested just the opposite. It suggested a wound that hit something vital. It suggested that he was in danger and I couldn't place that with how I saw his physical condition.

It's easy to discount the daylight in Kalispell. It was the same back home in Portland. Only in LA did I notice that there was less daylight in the summer. I had friends and coworkers that told me they never thought about it – and considering my monomania with medicine, they wondered how I did. Now? As I stood thinking about David Ryan, my subconscious was looking at every square inch of those bushes and trees. I knew there was a lake up there, Lake Foy. But between here and there was nothing but a million places from where Bernie could spring his trap on Mario and Alex. *You should have said something. They wouldn't be up there now.* Of course, the other side of that argument was that Bernie Ryan would still be shooting at me. And truthfully? I'd rather Bernie being be shooting at me than them. Maybe that makes me a selfish bitch that I don't want to live without Mario, but would condemn him to live without me. Maybe the best answer is for all of us to survive whatever this is.

I reached for my car keys and decided to find out what was wrong with David Ryan. Still, I paused for a long moment and scanned the hills across the street. Police officers and a few volunteers were moving up the hillside. I swallowed hard because America is a land of shoot first and worry later. *Mario? Please. Don't die now. We've come so far in just a short time.* Well, I have. Mario's belief tended to the sort that we got what we needed. If he was convinced that I needed to be alone, then he'd let them kill him. *You're being stupid, Collins. He'll come back. He always does.*

I got into the driver's seat and tried to concentrate on David. My mind wouldn't focus, so I got out of the car and stood by the door looking up into those hills. Then my phone rang.

"Hey," he said. "Don't worry about me. I'm fine. Go worry about David Ryan. He needs you."

"But the cops are up in the hills and they might mistake you."

He said, "Hang on a second. The next voice you hear will be Officer Douglas." I heard the static of a phone being passed to another person when suddenly a voice said, "Your husband is fine, Doctor."

That made things easier to bear. I smiled when Mario said, "Go, girl. David needs you more than I do."

"Thanks, babe. I was worried."

Unspoken in that conversation was any mention of Alex Payne. I assumed they were together and that Alex was as fine as Mario sounded.

But. Yeah. But. You know what the word assume means.

Don't make me say it. It hurts too much.

Chapter 17

Kris was on duty and she allowed me into the ER. Wanda was there, too, and that meant I had allies. Well, friends. They walked with me back to where David's condition was being assessed. Kris said, "We're getting a CT scan of the wound. We're working on it stat, but it can't be soon enough for me." David was being wheeled out of the ER. His eyes were closed. He looked asleep.

"What's your preliminary assessment?"

"Too soon to say, Evie."

"Come on, Kris," I prodded her. "Give me something. There was practically no blood."

She turned on me and gave me the Dr. Tice stare. "You know about gunshot wounds. That shot should have splattered half the house with blood and the EMT's said there wasn't any. My fear is simple. Where did all that blood go?"

My thoughts exactly. Blood, like water, follows the gravity well once it gets outside the circulatory system. If any blood vessels were severed, then the blood in his veins and arteries went *somewhere.* But where? Yeah, I had the same worries she did.

"How's Regina? What's her condition?"

"Stable. She'll recover."

"Can I see her?"

"Sure."

We went to a bed as far from the nurses station as you could get. Regina was being hydrated but nothing more. Her eyes, which I never thought of as haunted before, looked that way now. I supposed I would be that way if someone shot me.

"Doctor Six!" she said as though I had the answer to a great mystery. "How's David?"

Kris whispered, "I'm going to go check on the results. I might be gone for a while."

I smiled. "You do that. I'll be here with Regina."

For some reason, my thoughts immediately went to Janice Hardiman. I had to find time, take time, to go up and see her. But why did my mind flit from one to the other?

I smiled down at her. "Dr. Tice is going to check on him right now. But you? How do you feel?" She should feel as though she'd been hit by a truck. That was the physics of a gunshot wound. It burns, knocks you down and lays you out. Your survival depends on the skill and/or luck of the shooter. In her case? She got lucky, but it still hurt.

She grimaced and proved her humanity to me. The wound was above her right breast. How it missed the ribcage, I couldn't possibly guess. Or any of the veins and arteries that run through the chest and arms. If ever there was an immaculate bullet, Regina Ryan got hit by it. "I'm fine. I need to see David."

"He's having a CT scan right now. He'll be back in a moment."

"Then?"

I smiled because it's a good tool to use. Long practice has taught me that smiles get more mileage than anything else. "Let us figure out his condition first." Then I forced my smile wider and asked, "Okay?" I was as worried about David as Kris was.

She turned her head and looked at the wall. Then she said, "You want to know who did it."

"No," I replied honestly. "I don't care who did it. I'm not a cop and have no desire to be one."

"It wasn't Bernie. I know that's what you think."

I took her hand smiled and said, "If Adams shows up here and asks? Tell him. My only interest is what's best for you and getting you healthy."

She sank lower into her pillow, bit her lower lip and said, "He'll kill me if I say anything."

It sounded as though she was speaking more to herself than to me, so I merely watched. Then I said, "Rest. I'll go check on David."

Wanda was at the nurses station looking at a chart. I came up next to her and said, "Hey, girlfriend. Hear anything about David Ryan?"

She stared straight ahead and said, "I think I'm going to fuck Norm Houser to death."

"Wanda?" I said to her. "Please concentrate."

She clasped her hands together, leaned over the counter and said as she squinted at the opposite wall, "Yes. Very definitely. I'm going to fuck him to death." Then she nodded, bit her lip and said, "Jesus."

"Smitten, huh?"

"Nah. It's just physical."

"Ryan? David?"

She nodded down the hall. "Kris is down in radiology. Ask her."

I bumped her shoulder, laughed and said, "You be cool."

She grinned and said, "I am water in his glass, ice cubes in his drink. Putty in his hands."

"Can you manage to hold yourself together long enough to finish your shift?"

She bumped me back. "Just go."

I headed out of the ER toward radiology and stopped when I saw Kris leave the CT room. She was wearing her most severe doctor face. As badly as I wanted to read something into it, I couldn't. She was probably cataloguing everything she saw on the scan and trying to find an answer.

She's slender in all the places where women want to be that way. Throw in her nice blond hair and she should be on a beach in California somewhere instead of in an ER in Kalispell, Montana. It doesn't help that she moves effortlessly. I know she drives men crazy and that she says she can't help it. "I walk that way," she says with clear irritation in her voice. "If I ever get implants? Then I'll be guilty of what you're only implying." She's cute that way. Fortunately, she's all doctor and doesn't want to be known as a tease. There are at least two EMT drivers, an orderly and a cop that want a weekend in Las Vegas with her.

"Hey, Kris," I said greeting her in the hallway. "You've been with David Ryan?"

When she paused, I knew everything she was going to say and none of it was good. "Evie?" she said severely. "The report I got said that he had visual reflexes, that his pupillary response was good. True?"

"Yes."

"Well, now? Not even oculocephalic reflex is present." She hooked my arm and said, "Come on. You need to see this."

We went into a room where orderlies were moving David back to the ER. I didn't know that. It was what Kris said. "They're taking him back to the ER and not admitting him."

That stopped me. "That can only mean…"

"…that he's dead. Yes, Evie. David Ryan is brain dead and you need to see why."

I thought she was going to show me a scan of his brain. Instead, she showed me a scan of David's chest cavity. "All through here?" she said. "Blood is collecting around his lung, heart and even as low as his kidneys. The reason?" She indicated an area in David's neck. "This is where all the blood went. All the vertebral arteries were cut by the bullet. Since the blood had to go somewhere, it flowed down the neck, into the chest cavity and began pooling everywhere. How long has it been since you found him?"

I looked at my watch and said, "Maybe three hours."

"With no blood in the brain? What do you think his chances were?"

Was that why there was still a pulse? His heart kept beating because…why? It didn't make a lot of sense. *The accelerans and vagus nerves send impulses from the brain that control heartbeat. But, the heart can continue to beat even if the brain is dead by the S-A nodes in the right atrium. Is that why I got a pulse? It was laboring to continue beating in the absence of stimuli from the brain?* I put my finger on the tear in the artery and knew she was right. David was dead and probably died as I was tending to his mother. Could I have prevented his death? I don't see how.

"Have you declared?"

"No. I'm on my way down there to do that now."

"Can I do it? Regina is my patient."

"Yeah. I'll need a favor, though."

"Name it."

"Keep him alive until I talk to Regina. I want to let her decide whether to donate his organs."

Her smile was weak. "Well, that's already being done. But, sure."

The walk back to the ER was a sad one. Kris put her arm around my shoulder and said quietly, "It's never easy."

"Yeah," I said.

We entered the ER together and I went straight to Regina's bed. She looked nervous. Nothing else describes her. Her eyes looked haunted and her face looked haggard and drawn. Did she know David's condition? Was she lying to me about Bernie? Would she protect him if she thought he killed their son? Once again, however, I realized I didn't care about who did what. I'd lost one patient, but saved another. Did one balance the other? No, of course not. I wouldn't trade Travis for Maddy. Or vice versa either. Or Mario for Alex, or my mother for my aunt. Each life was precious, unique and special. My job, the one I have dedicated myself to since I was seven, was to care for those lives, nurture them and return them to their families. If I got too far involved in their lives, I'd never find the strength to save even one because a single failure would drain me of any reason to keep trying.

"Hi, Regina," I said to her.

"What's wrong?" she said through horrified eyes.

I took her hands because I didn't want her to hurt herself when I told her. It was bad enough what she was going to hear. Even inadvertent harm was too much, though. I needed her to survive this for her own sake. "It's David," I said. "We lost him." I've learned not to beat around the bush in these cases. It hurts everyone.

But she tried. She tried to yank her hands out of mine but I held them as tightly as I could. I leaned over her and said, "Regina? I'm sorry."

David Ryan had been my patient for no more than three months. I knew that he was a patient of John Bender's before he started seeing me. Logically, that can only have been because Regina wanted me to be his doctor. The issue of why had never been a problem, but now I wondered. Janice Hardiman's family and now Regina Ryan's and both of them were patients of John Bender? Did one have anything to do with the other? Yeah, and me the person who claimed not to want to be a cop – or to think like one. I shrugged it off and concentrated on Regina.

She leaned into me and began to clutch my hands as though she was drowning. Trust me, I knew why. She had one child - David – and now he was gone. I'd be this way if even one of my kids died. It wasn't hard to be empathetic and sympathetic.

There would come a point when she would want to know what killed him. Medically, it was simple. He bled to death. Realistically, I don't think anything could have saved him. Three minutes without blood and you're never coming back. Your life will unravel worse than a ball of yarn being chased by a cat. And in that case, the cat is death.

I sat with her for another hour. She cried and I let her. It was better to cry here than anywhere else. Alone? Oh, no. I don't think I could allow that. When she asked how did her son die? I told her the literal truth. "David bled to death inside his body. An artery in his neck, two actually, were severed by the gunshot. Even had I diagnosed the wound correctly, he would have died before help arrived."

That was enough to make her lay quietly on the bed. As tears rolled down her cheeks, she said with a choked voice, "Then he was murdered."

Yes, I agreed with her. And then didn't think about it anymore.

The issue was simple: it wasn't the first instance of murder I'd seen in the past two days and it wasn't going to be the last. But who was the last person on the list?

I could not have guessed it in my wildest dreams.

Or yours.

Or. Put it this way: what issue would push a father to murder his own son and try to kill his wife? Yeah. Think about that.

Chapter 18

Janice Hardiman was sitting in Cayn's lap when I got to her room. She was crying and Cayn was holding her protectively. With her arms around his neck, she was saying as she cried, "I don't want to go, Uncle Cayn. I wanna stay with you. Please? Please don't send me away."

Yep. There was a social worker in the room with a cop. I groaned inwardly because it seemed that cops were one of Janice's hot points. Cayn stood, Janice still wrapped around him and came across the room and kissed my cheek. "Hi," he said. "Gotta slight problem. I'm trying to convince them that Janice would be better off in my custody than in the state's, but the lady here doesn't agree." Janice continued to cry. Cayn held her easily as she clung to him.

I hugged both Cayn and Janice. Then I looked at the social worker and extended my hand to her. "My name is Doctor Sixkiller-Collins Collins." I don't use my full name very often. When I do, it's to make a point.

"Doreen Wallace," she said evenly. She was an older woman, plump and matronly. She wasn't smiling and I doubted my ability to make a point with her. Still, I was going to try.

"Ms. Wallace," I said as happily as the occasion allowed. "I know Mr. Wyatt to be a good man. I think Janice's welfare would be well-placed with him."

"The law is quite specific," she said. "Janice will be placed in a temporary shelter until what is in her best welfare can be ascertained."

Yep, spoken like a lawyer. My winning smile wasn't going to make a dent in her highly polished veneer. Knowing that, I said, "Have you ever heard of The Van Landingham School in Portland, Maine?" It was all or nothing. The school is run by my Aunt Dora. They take in runaways, victims of abuse and so many others that don't fit into any category that I still wonder how they succeed.

"Yes," she said bluntly, her eyes narrowing on mine. "It's an interesting place. I've been there."

"And?"

"What's your connection to it?"

"Dora O'Leary is my aunt. I'd hate to see Janice wind up there when there is a good place here in Montana for her."

"And you can vouch that Mr. Wyatt can provide Janice with a good home?"

"Not only can I vouch, but I can guarantee. Mr. Wyatt and my husband, Mario Collins, run The Other Place, a school in town. Janice would get protection, a good education and a future."

Her jaw set firmly. She'd reached a decision. "Excuse me," she said and walked into the hall.

"What is this, Doc?"

I smiled at Janice and said, "You really want to go with Cayn?"

She nodded and said, "Uh huh." Then she hugged Cayn tighter and he held her that much firmer.

"Well, I think you're going to get your way."

"Really?" Cayn said. "No joke?"

"No joke."

"What's that school you mentioned back in Maine?"

"The best thing to ever happen to kids," I replied. "In fact, you need to go there. I'm surprised Mario hasn't mentioned it."

"He did. I didn't believe him."

"Well do. Then go down to Old Port on a Saturday night and listen to her sing. It will change your life."

Aunt Dora has an amazing voice. I can remember a time from when I was a kid. She was the victim of a savage beating that almost killed her. Her head took most of the damage and the fear was that she wouldn't be able to sing again. I was there the night she came to our dinner table, clasped her hands tightly together in front of her and started singing, "Isn't It A Pity." It's her signature song because she believes everything George Harrison wrote. Mom cried because her voice was as perfect as it had ever been. Hearing that, people usually want to know why she runs an obscure school in Portland, Maine, rather than singing professionally. Aunt Dora's answer is usually blunt and to the point. "These kids need me more than you need to be entertained." Sweet, elegant and final. That's Aunt Dora.

The door opened and Doreen Wallace came back into the room. Her face was still harshly neutral when she reached for Cayn's hand and said, "There will be a formal hearing in a couple months and an inspection of your home. Be everything the doctor said you were or Janice will go to a shelter at that point."

"What's happening, Uncle Cayn?" Janice asked, her voice full of fear and pain.

He hugged her tighter and said, "We're going home, my little angel."

She hugged him even tighter and cried on his shoulder. He held her in his arms and tears rolled down his cheeks as he did. "Thank you, Doc," he said. "Thank you from the bottom of my heart."

I kissed his cheek and said, "Well, dude? Keep your house clean and throw away the beer bottles, you hear?"

Both of us laughed and Janice kept her grip on Cayn.

Doreen Wallace shook his hand as Cayn balanced Janice easily. She left and the cop followed her.

Cayn closed his eyes, sighed and went to the bed. Laying Janice in it, he said, "I have to talk to the doctor and then we'll go home. Okay, Jan, honey?"

"Okay, Uncle Cayn," she said hopefully.

As I stood watching her, it was easy to see that she was putting all of her trust, hope and energy into him. Her eyes begged for him to help her, to love her and to keep her safe. Knowing Cayn, I don't think that will be a problem. But there was a problem and I thought it was obvious even before he said, "Outside?"

"Sure," I replied.

He smiled at Janice and we stepped into the hallway outside her room. It was quiet and meant to be that way. A nurse walked down the hall, smiled at us and disappeared into a room.

"Jan told me that a cop killed her parents. She described the uniform of a county sheriff."

"So, tell Adams," I said.

"Another cop? Look, Evie. I don't trust any of them and that has everything to do with that little girl in there."

"So, what can I do?" I said.

"Let Mario help me. We work well together and I think we could catch this guy."

"He doesn't need my permission, Cayn." Then I shook my head and said, "I'm his wife, not his mother."

"Will you have a problem with it?"

His question brought to mind everything that happened at Regina Ryan's home. There were several fingers being pointed at Bernie Ryan. Was he guilty of all this? Since I'd already told Detective Carson everything that I knew, everything that happened and even conjectured Bernie's name, there was nothing more I needed to do. "No," I said as my worry for my husband notched upward.

"Why are you lying to me," he said. "You don't want Mario in this, do you?"

I sighed, smiled and tried to put a good face on my worry. "Cayn? He'll do whatever is right. That much I know."

"That doesn't answer the question."

I remembered my mothers' admonition. *Don't talk about Alex, don't act like he's there. Just do your job.* Well, the issue here was simple. If I told Cayn that he could work with Mario, then he'd meet Alex at some point. Normally, I wouldn't challenge that arrangement at all. But Alex was not well. My fear for him was his heart. He had all the symptoms of heart failure and I was afraid for him. So, in this case, if I sent Cayn to Mario and told him to help, then I'd be guaranteeing that Mario had help. *Because you aren't going to let this go, are you? They took a shot at me and that means you'll run yourself ragged trying to protect me.* While *that* was true, also true was the fact that Alex would go ballistic if I was wrong about his condition. He'd pillory me and I'd never hear the end of it. I smiled. *Yeah, you brute. You'd be mad, but you'd be around my little finger, too.* No, Alex Payne was unable to get angry with me.

"Yeah," I said smiling. "You call Mario and tell him I said that it was okay."

He looked back at the room and said, "She'll be here for the night. Then no one will ever hurt her again."

We walked back into her room and her face lit up. I had no doubt she would have some long nights in her near future, but her life was

assured. Unfortunately, there were several lives in the balance when I left there. No, Janice Hardiman would be fine. But there were others whose lives were going to be in the balance and I was going to be the one who tipped them into life or death. Who? Don't ask.
    Please.

Chapter 19

I expected someone to catch me in the parking lot before I could get to my car. No one did. I locked the doors for no good reason I could see but still felt better about it. I took a deep breath and looked at my office across the street. Liz and Norma would still be there working to close all the files. Liz was relentless in her work. How many times have I seen her go without dinner because she was working late? If nothing else, I had to go over there and make sure they all went home.

It was sliding toward late evening when I parked in the space in front of my office. As I thought, both Liz and Norma were still there finishing the day's work. It was close to seven-thirty and they were still there. I hugged both of them and Liz asked, "How's Janice?"

"With Cayn. He's getting temporary custody but I think she's in for a rough time. She saw her parents killed and that's going to cause a trauma no matter how much Cayn loves her."

"That's true," Norma said sadly. "Can we help? Can I?"

As much as I wanted to ask them to see her, I said, "I don't figure to be here very much for the next few days. I'd rather that you kept the office going. Is that okay?"

She smiled. "Can we do both?"

"Sure," I said smiling back at them.

They gathered up their stuff and left. I went back to my office and say down just as my cell phone rang. It was Mario.

"Dude," I said.

"You alone?"

"Yeah. Why?"

"It's Alex. I was hoping you could talk sense to him. We'll be there in a few minutes."

There were so many questions I wanted to ask, but he'd already hung up. I stashed the phone back in my purse and hurried to the front door. I threw it open just as Mario pulled into a parking space in front of the office. He didn't have to say it: Alex was in trouble.

Mario had to open the door for him, and then Alex practically fell out of Mario's Hummer. I rushed to where Mario was struggling to keep Alex on his feet. I draped his right arm over my shoulder while Mario got under his left. From the way Alex was panting, coughing and struggling for each breath, I'd say he was experiencing heart failure. "He's talking crazy, girl," Mario said.

"No…no…no," Alex said and then fell into a coughing fit that almost caused us to lose control of him.

"He keeps talking about Josh and Kristi and how he can't fail them."

"They…they…need me," he wheezed.

Mario pushed open the office door and we sat him in a chair in the waiting room. I wasn't worried about him running off but I still said, "Wait here with him. I'll be right back."

I could have taken his pulse with my fingers, but I wanted to listen to his heart. I raced into my office grabbed a stethoscope and went back to where Alex was gasping for every breath. He was on the verge of passing out when I place the cup his chest. As I thought, his heart was racing and beating erratically. By racing, his heart was trying to provide blood to parts of the body that probably wasn't getting it. He was also most likely suffering from systolic heart failure.

I knelt in front of him, looked at his face and saw pain, confusion and death. Alex Payne was going to die and this time it wasn't going to be a side show effort to make my mother happy. He was going to die – unless I could arrange a heart transplant.

"We're taking him to the ER, dude."

"Good."

With what energy he had left, Alex started thrashing with an uncoordinated effort to throw us off. It wasn't hard to pin his arms. As a sign, that was a bad one. He should have been able to throw us both across the room. Instead, we hefted him between us and steered him back toward the door. Getting him into the passenger seat of the Hummer wasn't a whole lot of fun, but we managed. Then I ran back to the office, grabbed my stuff, locked the door behind me and got into the back seat behind Mario. I wanted to able to see Alex and that made it possible.

He dropped into unconsciousness before we got to the ER – and that was just across the street. I pressed my fingers to his neck and felt a weak and very erratic pulse. When Mario pulled into the lot by the ER door, I got out, opened Alex's door and felt for the same pulse at his ankles. If anything, it was weaker. That meant his veins were getting thinner as the heart pumped less and less blood to the body.

When Mario came to the my side, I asked, "If you're here and Cayn is with Janice, then who has our kids?"

"Holley," he said. Then he helped me get Alex out of the Hummer. Holley Kellogg was an aide at the school. She was younger than me and twice as energetic. I worried about drugs for a while, but she trumped me by offering a blood test. I took it, checked for everything I could and then told her, "According to your blood test, your mother isn't."

She huffed. "Well, of course of not. I'm adopted."

I smiled. "And how would I know that without your mother's blood?"

"Brat," she said, smacking my arm. Yeah, I like Holley. She has a bedroom in our home and has started back to Flathead Community College and is studying pharmacy technology.

As we struggled, it became obvious that Alex was no help. We were going to need a gurney.

"Stay here. I'll get help."

I don't know everyone in the hospital; six months isn't enough time. I knew enough of them, however, to get a team together with a gurney. Two male orderlies rushed out to the Hummer and together with Mario, got Alex onto it and into the ER.

They got oxygen onto him quickly when I told him that he showed all the signs of heart failure. My first issue was when someone asked, "Who is he? What's his name?" The kneejerk reaction was, "His name is Alex Payne. He's a friend of mine." But the cautionary warning used by my mother echoed lively in my mind. *Don't. Just don't.* That meant his name was, "Norman Peters. I knew him from Portland."

The next surprise I got was when I checked his wallet and it agreed with me. His name, according to the information in it, was Norman Peters. Moreover, his address was listed as a place in Spokane,

Washington. There were even credit cards that agreed with that assessment. It bothered me on several levels, not the least of which was the time involved to do all this.

The ER doctor was a man named Quinn Riley. He was a robust Irishman from Alabama. Yeah, yeah. I know. Huh? Quinn's father emigrated to the US after World War II. Quinn was born in Tuscaloosa and spoke a variety of English that I would describe as fascinating. He could a speak a language that would make him positively indecipherable, or he could speak like the President. When he saw me? I got the indecipherable version that I believe included the word "boobs", but it might have been bus or margarita. I mean, Quinn can be quite impenetrable. It was only when he said, "Heart failure," that I got the decipherable version.

My basic instinct was to say, "I'll be responsible for him." My basic intellect said, "Yeah? And then how do you explain why?" That meant I had little choice but to hope and assume that he had some sort of medical insurance in that phony persona he brought with him to Montana.

A team of ER people went to work on him – whatever his name and ability to pay might have been. I was a tagalong and they allowed it. Well, Quinn did. I followed what they were doing and even understood it when Quinn put in a call for a trauma surgeon. While a failing heart wasn't the definition most people think of when they hear the word trauma, it was the best answer Kalispell could provide. That was going to be Doctor Aidan Hall. Doctor Hall was a qualified surgeon but I wondered if he'd ever participated in a heart transplant.

I heard Doctor Riley order a BNP test. That was a test that measured amounts of a protein called B Natriuretic Peptide in the blood. That protein was secreted by a failing heart. I knew of the test and even ordered a few. But I had never operated on a person with a failing heart – and that was what I saw on the table here. Doctor Riley was going to tell me that Alex was in full-blown heart failure. And then what? Could Hall perform the surgery? Was a donor heart even available? If you guessed I did not like the situation, then you guessed right. The only viable solution for him was to transport him to a city with better facilities. Maybe Salt Lake City or Spokane. God, I needed to call Ellie.

Riley told me that they were going to do an EKG in addition to the blood sample. That was cautionary, but good thinking. I nodded and said, "I have to go find my husband."

"We'll be done with the tests before you get back. Then we'll do a cardiac MRI just to be sure."

"Thanks, Aidan."

Mario was in the waiting room talking on his cell phone. He said something quickly and then bounced to his feet. "How is he?" he asked nervously.

"Not good. I have to call Ellie," I said craning my neck back to the ER. Then I turned to him and said, "Okay. What did he say? And what happened in those damned hills?"

There were maybe a dozen people in the ER, two with small children in their laps. He looked at them and murmured, "Not here." He grabbed my arm and led me outside the ER doors to the parking lot beyond. Scanning the lot for anyone who might be able to hear and finding no one, he said, "He saw Coach Horn up there with the gun that killed both Dyan and Fred. But there was another person and he didn't know who it was."

"Dude?" I said with worry in my voice. "He could have seen Santa Claus up there and he wouldn't have been in a condition to tell the difference. His brain isn't getting enough blood either. And don't tell me you didn't notice his symptoms up there."

"He got so much worse as time passed. Jesus, Evie, I think he was masking his symptoms, too."

"I need to call Ellie," I said.

"Yeah," he agreed. 'You want me to do it?"

"No, it's okay. I can answer her questions better than you could."

He nodded in agreement. It was nearly ten o'clock back in Portland and I wondered if it was right to do this to her at the end of her day. *If it was Mario?* Yeah. I needed to call her right now.

I dialed and didn't know that the message I was going to pass to her was going to be worse than the one I thought I was going to deliver to her when I dialed.

Much worse.

Chapter 20

The phone rang twice before Ellie answered it. I've known her only since Alex got serious with her many years ago. She described herself as not self-conscious of her weight, but resigned to it. She was a reporter for the *Press Herald* in Portland when he met her. When he asked her to dinner, she was insulted because she thought he was making fun of her. Why? Because Alex Payne was a famous football player and could have any woman he wanted and here he was asking a chubby woman for a date. That encounter has passed into the realm of fantasy because when you hear them recount it, Ellie was leading him on and Alex was on his knees begging. Eventually, she relented and he took her to dinner where he related his condition to her. Essentially, he was describing this moment, the one when his steroid-filled past would cause one of his organs to fail. It didn't have to be his heart; it merely was.

"Hi, Evie," she said, her voice happy and alive – even at the hour. "What's up?"

Mannerisms. It's odd how married folks begin to absorb their mates habits. "What's up?" was one Alex used on me whenever I'd go to him in pain, confusion and guilt over a crime of which I was a victim and not a perpetrator. Now his wife was using the same opening. It wouldn't surprise me if they jumped up, bumped their chests, then their asses and ended it in a high-five.

Resorting to what people have said is my cut-to-the-chase manner of relaying bad news, I said, "It's Alex. You need to come here as soon as possible. I think he's in heart failure."

She gasped and said, "Oh, God, no."

"Ellie? I think it's serious. Do whatever you can on your end, but be here. Just seeing you will help him."

The last time I was in Portland, Mario and I had dinner with them. The moment that Ellie was living through right now, Alex said he thought would have happened years ago, that he would already be dead.

Then he turned to her, kissed her and said, "Ellie Madsen Payne has saved my worthless life."

She's done an amazing job balancing what he eats with an exercise program that works. Better still? She eats the same menu and even accompanies him when he's exercising. The chubby girl from Bangor, Maine, is no longer chubby. If Alex dies? She will, too. To me, it's bloody obvious.

I saw the ER doors blow open and a male orderly came rushing out. He scanned the waiting room, saw me and came to where I was sitting. "Doctor Six?" he said. "Doctor Riley told me to tell you. The patient is in full cardiac arrest."

Ellie heard it and screamed.

"Ellie!" I screamed into the phone. "Is anyone with you!"

I don't know what happened on her end, but I heard soft muffled sounds before a male voice said, "This is Josh Payne."

"Josh? Evie. You know from…"

"…Montana. Yeah. Melodie's daughter. What's wrong?"

"Your father is here in the hospital and he's in cardiac arrest. You need to get your mother here as fast as possible."

Josh and Kristi, theirs kids, were adopted after their parents were murdered years ago. Josh is a tough kid – and that was true before he met Alex at the family cabin in upstate Maine. They'd been dropped into Moosehead Lake in what their captors thought was a sealed bag. Josh ripped it open and took his sister to the shore near their cabin. He lived there with her for the better part of a day when Alex showed up in the middle of a funk. Ellie's funk. He was convinced she didn't love him and went up there to think. And found a family, one that included Ellie Madsen. And now, a part of it was in deep trouble.

"We'll be there. Mom has your number. We'll call you when we're in town."

"Josh? I can't stress this enough. If you want to see him alive, then you hurry. And still, there are no promises. Your father is very ill."

His voice reflected all the stress such a moment would engender. "Evie? Doctor? We'll be there. All of us."

"At our house," I said. "We have room."

"I'll call. Bye."

I disconnected from him and tried to see how it must have been with them and couldn't. True, I lost my father when I young, but I was too young to remember him. That was Brian Sixkiller. Yes, I feel and felt sad that I couldn't recall his voice, his face or anything about him. But Brad Chang? My mother? A brother or a sister? Those people are etched in my mind as though on the finest glass. To lose one of them would be devastating *just like Josh and Ellie must be feeling.* So, yes. In that sense, it wasn't hard. If it was my mother? I don't know how I would react to it. Okay, I'll have to cross that Rubicon some day, but not now. That enabled me to reserve all my empathy for Ellie, Josh and Kristi. Their names might not be Collins, but they're family nonetheless.

God, I needed a hug. I turned to Mario and he threw his arms around me.

"That obvious, huh?" I said, close to tears.

"It always has been," he said gently.

"Alex is going to die, babe," I said. There. I'd said it. Alex Payne was going to die because…*wait.* My mind didn't exactly go blank. But everything else did. My husband, the man who may well have been my right hand, vanished for a moment. I was thinking of something so grotesque that it was possible I'd crossed a line somewhere.

When the world flashed back in, Mario smiled and said, "Damn, I like watching that."

"Um., what?"

"The way you make connections. The way you think." Then he raised his hands and said, "Don't worry. I know you're going back inside, so I'll go home. Just don't tell me the lesbian doctor won't give you a ride when you're done."

I kissed him and stuck. I mean, it felt like that. My mind was going a million miles an hour, and when I leaned into him to give him a gentle kiss goodbye, I couldn't take myself away from him. I slowly wrapped my arms around his neck and sank like a stone into him. Nothing else existed, especially my preoccupation with madness. It always happens this way. I'm four years old again and this terrible *boy* walks into my home and steals my heart. Truth? Without Mario, I'd be just another rich kid smoking dope and having casual sex with anyone that caught my eye. When he walked in? My life changed and has been changing ever since. He makes me better simply by being alive.

There's a story in the family that Grandpa bought him from a crack whore for three hundred sixty-two dollars. I didn't believe it – and not because I didn't know what a crack whore was. I believed it when Grandpa smiled and said, "Evie? It was all the money I had that day. If I'd eaten lunch before I went to her apartment? He'd be worth that much less. Well, DPS made it legal, but Mario still prides himself on the bargain Grandpa got that day. It didn't dawn on me until years later what he meant by that, but when I saw it, I smacked him on the arm and called him a "doofus". Well, he isn't a doofus anymore. Indeed, there was going to be a time in the near future when he was going to save a life – and I'm the doctor in the family. When that time came? There was going to be nothing he could ask of me that I'd ever deny him. Nothing.

All that was in the future. When he said, "Go. I can see it already. You've got a way to save Alex. You go do that and I'll save Holly from our kids."

I wanted to kiss him again but he me pushed toward the ER.

There was a time coming in the near future when my life was going to be in his hands. Luckily, he is the most able human being I have ever met.

Someone out there was counting on me.

And it wasn't Alex.

Chapter 21

Technically, David Ryan was still alive. That was the first thing I checked before deciding that my version of madness was worth exposing to the world. Then I found Doctor Riley and cornered him at the nurse's station.

"Is David Ryan a suitable heart donor for Norman Peters?" That was as blunt as I could make it.

"No idea without a blood test. But what would the people on the waiting list say if David's heart went to a guy who wasn't on it?"

The ER was getting busy. Nurses darted around like trout after worms. An intern followed a gurney to a waiting bed. The noise level was bearable because despite the chaos, an ER is usually quiet. All that contributed to Quinn feeling the need to get involved.

I looked around for an empty office. One was right behind him. I pushed him toward it and said, "I need five minutes. Then I'll leave."

It was hard to admit that I'd just condemned Alex Payne to five minutes of life and no more. If I couldn't convince Quinn, then Alex was dead. *Calm down. You're a professional and Alex is a patient that you can help. If it looks like you're campaigning for him, then he will have every right to stand on protocol and give David's heart to whoever needed it the longest.* So saying, I took a deep breath, closed the office door behind me and said, "Did you look closely at Howard Peters?" If you guessed I was about to reveal Alex's identity, then you guessed right.

"Enough to monitor his condition," Quinn responded with a shrug of his massive shoulders.

"Are you a football fan?"

He frowned at me. "Look, Evie. Why don't you just say it?"

"Norman Peters' real name is Alex Payne." When Quinn's eyes focused narrowly on me, I smiled and said, "Yeah, *that* Alex Payne."

"I saw his funeral on TV not a week or two ago. *That* Alex Payne is dead."

"Alex Payne's death was faked because of a cancer outbreak in Portland, Maine. He's working for the government to find out where the disease is coming from and why. There were seven cases of skin cancer back there. All seven died within two weeks of being diagnosed. Then, one case appeared here in Kalispell. Danny Hardiman died the same way those other seven did. In each case, it was kid between fifteen and twenty-two. Danny was sixteen when he died. More? All of those eight kids were football players. Three played college, the other five were high schoolers. Alex was here because my mother, Congresswoman Chang from Maine, asked him to find out what was going on. You can't let him die. He's working for us, Quinn. You and me and our kids."

He leaned down and said almost angrily, "And how many times have I heard you say that you're a doctor and not a cop, *doctor*? My job, in this case, is to follow the protocols and give David Ryan's heart to the name that most matches it. You hear me?"

It wasn't what I wanted to hear. When he tried to push his way past me, I put my hand in the middle of his chest and said, "What would it take? What would I have to do? Please, Quinn. If David Ryan's heart can save him, we would doing more good than if we saved a bookkeeper in Sheboygan."

I didn't know whose office we were in. Man or woman, all those details escaped me. All I knew was that Quinn moved past me, pulled the blinds closed and locked the door, then said, "Drop your pants and lean over the desk."

For a moment, for a split second, I betrayed Mario by thinking about it. Then, total disgust and revulsion set in and snorted, "Up yours, Aidan. I'll find an administrator who can make the same decision without having to lock myself in an office with him."

Then he started laughing and said, "Oh, Jesus, Evie. I thought you were really going to do it."

Well, I smacked him. And not on the arm either. I smacked him so that he had to duck. "You ass," I said chasing him to the door. "The only thing you're ever going to do with my ass is kiss it."

"You drop 'em and I'll kiss it," he said smiling.

I pushed him toward the door and said, "Go on, you ass."

He draped his arm over my shoulder and said, "You should become an ER doctor. We'd have fun."

"I have a practice that I like. And how about we go and talk to Regina Ryan?"

"Let's," he said, unlocking and opening the door.

As we left that total anonymous office, I couldn't wait to talk to whoever made the decisions about transplants. A phone rang somewhere as we entered onto the floor. Ringing telephones aren't a distraction in an ER. The one I heard just then became immediately subliminal. Quinn and I went to the bed where Regina was tossing and turning. Well, maybe not. I do *not* think it's possible to toss and turn with an IV spike in your arm and a heart monitor above your head beeping its insistent rhythm.

We were just about to talk to her when his name was called on the hospital loudspeakers. "Doctor Riley to the nurses station." Then it repeated and he winced. Still, it was something that had happened a million times before, so he wasn't really worried or bothered by the page.

That left me with Regina. I stood at her bedside and tears began to roll from her eyes.

"You want me to say my son is dead," she cried.

I saw Travis in his place. I put myself in her position and it *still* didn't compute. I had another child, a daughter. David was her only child and he was brain dead, if not officially and legally that way. Worse? Her husband was missing. Bernie hadn't been seen since the shooting at his home. If someone was seen in the hills across the street from their home, it would be logical that it would be him. And the tragedy swirling around Regina got worse when I replied, "Yes. David is beyond help and you can save a life by donating his heart."

She leaned up toward me on her elbows and said with bulging veins in her neck, "You're a terrible doctor! You should be saving his life and instead you want to murder him!"

It wasn't hard to commiserate with her. By everything that I'd heard, her husband killed her son and then shot her, too. By all accounts, she was alone. By insisting that David was alive, she had someone in her life besides a deranged husband that had murder on his mind.

"Have you seen him?" I asked gently.

"He's sleeping," she said anxiously. "Or in a coma! He'll wake up! You'll see!"

"Did the doctor explain his condition and show you his EEG? Was the monitor flatlined?" She was about to lose control. It was obvious she didn't want to admit her son was dead. Instead of just letting her rant, scream and vent at me, I took her hand asked, "Was it, Regina? Was it flatlined? Did the doctor get any reaction from his pupils? Were they reactive to the light at all?" Then I smiled and tried to make her see the ugly truth behind David's condition. "I can't imagine losing a child because I have two, but you're not gaining anything by denying what is true and obvious to the medical staff here. Please, Regina. Mourn over him, cry over him, bury him, but let his last act be to help another person live. It's the right thing to do."

She squeezed my hand and the fight flowed out of her. "There's a rumor that there's a little girl that can identify the person that killed her parents. Is that true?"

"Janice Hardiman. Yes, I believe so."

"And you think…"

"…nothing, Regina. I keep telling everyone. I'm not a cop. I'm a doctor. Chief Adams is in charge of thinking about this case."

She looked up at me and repeated. "And you think Bernie killed them?"

It wasn't hard to tell the truth. "I didn't see anything at that house. I was trying to help them. Janice was hiding in a bedroom. It's possible she's alive at all because I showed up with my husband and scared away whoever did it."

She sighed and tears flowed freely down her face. I noted, however, that she did not let go of my hand. "You aren't being very honest, doctor."

"Do you want me to say that I think Bernie did it?"

Her eyes riveted mine. "Yes. Just say it. Just say that my husband killed his son, two other people and then tried to kill me. Just say it."

"I can't, Regina. I don't know. But do you want David to live in that world? Do you want him to live in a world where he knows his father wants him dead?"

And that was enough for her. She rolled onto her side as far as the IV would allow and cried into my extended hand. Then she moaned, "Yes. Okay. You can have his organs."

As a mother, it was hard to watch her cry for *that* reason. She was saying goodbye to only person left to her. It was obvious that she believed Bernie did this to them. Me? I can't say I didn't care, but there was nothing I could do about it. Regina Ryan was my concern, just like Janice Hardiman was. With that in mind, I said to her as gently as I could, "Regina? I'm still your doctor if you wish. Call me and I'll help. There are lots of places and people that will help you get through this. But call me?"

"I need to see him before you do anything," she said somewhat nonresponsive.

"That can be arranged," I said and turned to start making those arrangements.

I ran into Quinn Riley who was coming back to her bed. He looked grim in a way only doctors can be. "I need to talk, Doctor Collins."

He escorted me to the nurse's station and said, "That page was from an FBI agent named Barbara Reese. She said that David Ryan's organs are going to Norman Peters. Everything that will make that legal is already in motion." Then he looked at the various other stations, leaned into me and said, "And you know that man. What the hell is this, Evie? Doctor Hall has already been notified. He's already assembling a transplant team."

What could I tell him? The truth? That my mother was a congresswoman with a ghastly problem on her hands? That Barbara Reese was a friend of hers? That the entire fucking United States government was now bending to her will just like the city of Portland did when I was a kid? Could I tell him all that? Well, crap. I already did. He already knew that Alex Payne's alter ego was one named Norman Peters.

"Quinn?" I said as truthfully as I dared. "It's like I said. They're trying to find out what this cancer is to get a handle on it."

And that's when he ratcheted the whole affair up a notch. "And cancer isn't infectious."

Okay, I know. I *know*. But the disease doesn't progress that fast. Two weeks? How many thousands of people will die while laboratories try to figure this out? And me? What did they want from me? Well, in short? They were going to ask me to cure cancer.

No, really. They were.

And Alex didn't have cancer and they were going to go all out to save his life. Why? Because Alex had a name stuck in his brain, one that was going to fall on me to figure its relation to this affair. Yeah, me, the doctor, the person who said she wasn't a cop was going to start acting like one.

Quite against her will, I might add.

And then?

Oh, god, no. Please.

Chapter 22

One condition that Pee Wee made in getting David Ryan's heart was that I'd have no part in the operation to transfer it to Alex. They forced me to leave and Kris took me home. My mood was ugly and stayed that way when she said, "Red. I'm thinking of a red playboy bunny costume. Whatcha think?"

I growled, "Black. Everyone should wear black." Then I threw open the car door and tried to leave in a huff.

She was smiling. "Ooh, black. Black satin. A black satin Playboy Bunny outfit in front of all you heteros. She stuck her hand out toward me and said, "Done. Just let me know how soon I need to get one."

I let all my anger dissipate, took her hand and said, "Well, it won't have any effect on me, but the men? You'll be the hit of the party. I'll let you know when it's on."

"Evie?" she said smiling. "Let it go. David Ryan is saving a life and that's all we can be asked to do. Don't be angry that your family had something to do with who, how and why. Just accept that a very famous football player came back from the dead." Then she laughed and said, "Twice."

I reach into the car and hugged her. "Sorry for being a bitch."

"No, the bitch is going to be wearing black satin. Thanks for the idea."

She waited to leave until I was safely inside my home. Yep, my family was still awake. The first one to hit me was Maddy. I dropped my bag, my purse and caught in flight. "Mommy! Mommy! You know what a Cooper's Hawk does? He doesn't bite them and kill them, he holds them under the water until they drown. And he's big! And he's gray and brown and we saw one field trip today!"

Birds. Ornithology. I had to look up the word a few months ago when it became only bloody obvious that my daughter liked birds of all types. We went to Yellowstone a few months ago and she saw her first Eagle. She identified it as a Golden Eagle and I can't really argue with her because she was right. Well, according to Mario. She chattered on about all the things she knew about them and started to repeat it. As much as I wanted to scream, I kept seeing my mother in my mind's eye and she was smirking at me. *What goes around, comes around, little girl.* That was my mother and what I imagined she would say right about now. I was always studying something to do with medicine and now I had a daughter that not knew Cooper's Hawks existed but knew what color they were and how they killed their prey. It wasn't hard to hug her and say, "Wow, I didn't know that."

"And you know what else? Girl Cooper's Hawks are bigger than boy ones!" Then she gave her best imitation of the family Evil Eye to her brother Travis.

"Yeah," he said. "And no stupid bird can hit a three-run homer in the bottom of the ninth and beat the Giants."

It was baseball season and he was telling me that one of his Dodgers hit a home run in tonight's game. I guessed the only name I knew. "Matt Kemp?"

"James Loney," he returned with the eyes of an expert.

Holley picked up my stuff and carried it into the living room. Maddy was still in my arms chattering about hawks and wingspans and how far they can fly and the extent of their territory's and such. Given my own monomaniacal past concerning medicine, I could see a trip to a bookstore so that she could buy a new one. She already had a large library of books in her bedroom. While other kids were busy waiting for the next great movie, Madison was waiting for her next bird species to make an impression on her.

"And we need a parakeet!" she said, her voice tinged with disgust that we didn't already have one.

Mario just made it worse. "We could get a parrot and then teach it to talk."

Maddy's eyes grew large and she shrieked, "Yeah! And I could get him to say, 'Travis is a dummy! Travis is a dummy!'"

Travis put his hands in his armpits and retorted with a voice that sounded as though he was on helium and spat, "Maddy is stupid! Maddy is stupid!"

Holley had settled, her legs curled under her, in a chair near the fireplace. You'd swear that she was a blood relative with her thick, black hair and easy smile. "Travis?" she said sounding a bit too much like his mother. "Tell her."

Maddy giggled and sing-songed, "Travis is in trouble, Travis is in trouble."

Mario was trying not to laugh and that made Maddy giggle hysterically.

"Okay, what happened?" I said to him.

"Nothing," he grumped.

"Travis?" Holley said and nothing more.

Maddy started it again and I said with my best faux-stern smile intact, "Okay, now let him tell the story."

"I broke something," he said miserably.

Since Mario was still trying not to laugh, I took that as a blatant attempt to get me to see the humor in whatever he broke. I frowned at him. That made his laughter overt and his face turned red. Then I looked at Travis and decided that it wasn't a catastrophe. "Okay, what did you break?"

"Your nightstand," he said miserably.

Mario got up and put himself next to him, draped his arm around his shoulder and said, "Don't worry. No one will know."

He pointed his finger at his sister and wailed, "She'll tell everyone!"

Trying to keep a straight face, Mario said to Maddy, "And that trip to the bookstore? What happens when you tell Becky? Or anyone else? No trip to the bookstore and no more trips to Yellowstone."

She stuck out her bottom lip, crossed her arms *just* like I do and grumped, "Okay. I won't tell anyone."

Maddy slipped from my lap and crossed to the couch to where Mario sat with Travis. I got up, sat next to him, took his hand and said, "It's just a nightstand. We can get another one."

Maddy laughed. Holley didn't, but wanted to. It was only obvious.

Mario said to him, "Whisper it in her ear."

Travis has the same impenetrable look that Mario has. While Mario perfected it years ago, Travis is still working out the finer details of his. Meaning, that while he wanted to look benignly neutral and above the crass details of the incident, that he was entirely embarrassed by them. He looked mortified when he whispered in my left ear, "I was wearing your high heels when I fell."

The mother inside me wanted to scream, rant and rave at him for being so stupid. The daughter in me remembered the first time I discovered Grandma's closet. The neighborhood joke was that my mother was the neighborhood bitch, but that my grandmother was the neighborhood Klingon because she had platform boots that guaranteed she was the tallest person on Munjoy Hill. The first time I put on a pair of her thigh boots? Oh, god. I started laughing.

"Ah, the Klingon memory," Mario said.

"Yeah," I replied.

"Hey, Travis," he said to his son. "Wanna see a picture of Mom?"

"Um, okay," he said uncertainly.

When Mario pulled out his wallet, I said, "You carry it?"

"Of course. You never know when you might need to blackmail your wife."

Then he open the picture compartment and showed Travis two pictures of me that were taken when I was eight. One was me in my grandmother's thigh boots, boots that went all the way over my hips and made navigation precarious at best. I don't know who took the picture, only that Mario didn't. Trust me here; I know that one. The second picture showed me with a broken arm after I fell down the stairs wearing them. I wore that cast for seven weeks and hated every minute of it.

"And all you did was break her nightstand," Mario said. "She broke her arm."

"Was Grandma mad?"

I smiled. "She was upset that I broke my arm, but not mad that I'd raided her closet. We became real close after that."

Maddy crowded in to see the pictures and so did Holley. We all laughed and decided that what Travis did was in the best tradition of adventurous kids everywhere. But. Travis hadn't really did the one thing that would have convinced me that Travis was in this escapade by himself. He hadn't feigned humiliation for wearing my shoes. The rat. Mario, I mean. This had him written all over it.

I smiled at Travis and said, "You aren't embarrassed because you were wearing shoes made for a woman?"

He swallowed hard and looked at his father.

"Oh, you rat," I said to him. "This is you trying to get me to wear heels."

"Dad?" he said. "Am I off the hook?"

"You are," he said smiling.

Holley laughed and said, "Are you two always like this?"

I rolled my eyes and said, "Great. Now I have to wear them to work."

Mario high-fived Travis and said, "Son? I just doubled your reward."

"I'm really sorry about the nightstand, Dad. I didn't mean to."

"Doesn't matter. I'll give your mother my nightstand and do without. Ain't that big a deal."

Well, not so fast. Maddy was *pissed*. She jumped up, put her hands on her almost nonexistent hips and squealed, "You mean Dad was behind this?"

"Yep," he said. "I think Mom looks hot in heels and this was a way to get her attention on them."

She pointed her index finger at him and said as her voice broke, "You should love Mom without heels!"

"I do," he said smiling at her. "This is different." Then he closed his eyes and said, "I love you mother but she's hot when she wears heels."

And *that* ended a stressful day. Maddy was furious because her father put her brother up to wearing the heels. It was supposed to be done in front of me, but he spoiled his part by falling on my nightstand. The doctor in me had to make certain he was okay and I found what I expected to find; he was embarrassed about the heels and not willing to complain about anything as insignificant as pain. It took a lot of poking and prodding before he started to giggle and said, "I'm okay, Mom. It's your nightstand that isn't."

Well, the day ended with me in bed – wearing those damned high heels. Mario went to sleep happy and so did I. Very. Mmm. Trust me. But that day was the last nice one I was going to have for the foreseeable future. Why? Well, let me put it this way: it all started the next morning.

Someone was leaning on the doorbell. And not just someone.

A very particular someone.

Chapter 23

Someone was about to get the full force of my anger. The doorbell had been ringing continuously for five minutes by the time I reached the door. I threw it open and was about the screech my displeasure when I saw, "Mom!" Behind her were Ellie, Josh, Kristi and their kids.

Yes, it was my mother, Congresswoman Melodie Chang of Maine's first congressional district. Her greeting brought me up to speed. She hugged me and said, "Thankfully, Alex is okay. He has a new heart and everything seems to be working."

I looked outside and grumped, "I'm surprised Pee Wee isn't attached to your ass, Mom."

Mom smirked and changed the subject. She was *very* good at it, too. "I see you had an interesting night even if Alex didn't."

Damn. I was wearing the heels. I put them on unconsciously when I went to answer the door. I kicked them off and hugged her. "This is a surprise. I expected Ellie and her family, not you."

Seeing Ellie made me curious about what my mother said. As I led them into the living room, Mario came down the stairs and said, "Hey, sis? Or is it grandma? Or what?" My mother is Mario's brother. Yeah, yeah. Don't make me go through it again. The most interesting thing about their relationship is what it does to the family tree. Among people that know us? No one brings up the subject of children who are at once sons and daughters as well as nieces and nephews. Among people that don't? It's none of their business because, like I've been saying for my entire freaking life, *there is no blood between us.*

Anyway. Ellie looked deathly worried. I wondered if they went to the hospital before they came here. Well, there's one way to tell. "Have you seen him?" I asked them, all of them.

Ellie looked scared. "He seemed so small. He never seemed that way before."

Well, that answered the question.

They all looked tired. Thankfully, we've had the house redesigned after Mom, Aunt Tiff and her entire family showed up here last February. They stayed at Big Mountain, a ski resort just north of our home. I swore that would never happen again, so we added an entire third floor to our home and populated it with plush bedding, a game room and all the oddments that kids would find necessary. Yep, empty. Not a soul for six months. That doesn't count the three times that Travis counted taking friends up there as "camping out". Maddy won't go up there without either Mario or me. Now? Lord, I was glad we did all that work.

Josh is married to a lady named Dyan and they have a son, Alex, Jr. Kristi is going to school at UM at Orono. Okay, okay. The University of Maine at Orono. She's studying psychology because, "Our family shouldn't work at all and it does. Creeps me out and I need to know why we work so well." So far? No answers.

They call Alex, Jr, APayne because they say he is. Well, Josh smiles when he says it. Dyan smacks him. I guess she learned the family mannerism quickly. Josh always ducks when she does it. I like Dyan.

Little Alex fell asleep on the couch. The commotion downstairs only guaranteed that Travis and Maddy were awake and curious about everyone downstairs. Maddy saw Mom and streaked to her like a lightning bolt. "Grandma!" she shrieked. Mom caught her and said, "And how's my little Eskimo?"

"Oh, grandma," Maddy smiled. "I'm not an Eskimo, I'm a…a…an…ornithologist."

"Very good," Mom smiled at her. "You like pigs, then?"

"Birds, silly," Maddy cried triumphant over her grandmother once again.

Mom turned to Travis and said, "Willie McCovey hit .270 in his career and hit five-hundred-twenty-one home runs. Can James Loney claim that?"

Travis squinted and said, "Yeah, Sandy Koufax went twenty-seven and nine in his last year with the Dodgers. And McCovey couldn't touch him. Neither could the rest of the stinkin' Giants."

And Mom's a Red Sox fan.

Still, they hugged and Travis even smiled. Having a grandma that could talk baseball was cool. UC. Ultimate Cool as Travis would say.

"How's Dad?" I asked.

She rolled her eyes and said, "The bastard's on tour again."

"Which book?"

"Wages of Prosperity," she said with a smile. Mom loves Brad and is proud of him. He was a struggling author when they first met. He says that there was a time when she was his only fan. Then she'd smile and say, "Well, your mom and my mom were fans before I figured it all out." My grandmother, Nikki Sixkiller-Collins, gave him his first break. She was a world-class artist and she reissued a book of New England art history with text added by him. She put his name on the cover right under hers and that made his future. They toured together and when she and grandpa were murdered, he was instrumental in finding the killers. Well, Alex and him did. I can't stress this enough: Alex Payne is responsible for any success I garner for myself. Without his selfless devotion to me and what happened to me when I was sixteen, I wouldn't be here. Period. And Mario? There would have been nothing he could have done to help me. Alex was responsible for my mental health and everything that implies.

Mario brought in coffee for everyone before I even knew he'd gone to make any. He put a tray of cups and a pitcher of coffee on the table in front of where Mom sat. Everyone started grabbing cups and pouring their own. Except Mom. She was looking into the beyond. That's the only way I can describe it. She'd seen Alex. I think that was obvious, but there was something else on her mind.

"Baby?" she said, blinking at last.

I laughed because that name – baby – was the subject of our first arguments. I hated being called that and, in retrospect anyway, I think she tried to stop but obviously never succeeded. I smiled and said, "Yes, Mommy dearest?"

She put her left hand to her mouth and said, "Oh, god. I'm still doing it." Then she looked at me and said, "I'm really sorry, Evie. I don't try to do it on purpose."

Well, all those battles are behind me. "It's okay, Mom. Really. But what? I know you're thinking about Alex."

The whole room fell silent. Mario settled in next to me and I absently took his hand in mine. Mom had this reputation when she was younger for putting together disparate pieces of information and finding relevant connections between them. If I had to guess, that's what she was doing now. Her face was blank, but her eyes showed an intenseness that I recognized from years of growing up looking at it. Mario knew it, too. He remained as silent as I did. We would know in good time what was on her mind.

Finally, she blinked, looked at me and said, "You need to be at the hospital when he regains consciousness."

"No problem," I replied. "And why?"

Mario squeezed my hand and whispered, "Here it comes."

Mom nodded directly at him, at Mario. "You've been his right-hand man. Right?"

Mario nodded and said, "Yeah."

"And yet, you don't know what he's been doing, what he saw or even where he'd been. Is that right?"

"Essentially," he answered.

Then her focus settled on me. I've talked to people who have been on the receiving end of that glare. Most find it unsettling, at least unsettling. I talked to a guy once who admitted to me that he'd pissed himself when she did it to him. My defense against such a calamity? I'm her daughter. I have immunity of a sort. She never spanked me even though I tried to goad her into doing it. No, I had nothing to fear from her, but everything to gain *if I listened.* Well, I was going to.

She leaned forward and I smiled inwardly. It was an entirely unconscious tactic she used when she was younger. Okay, think tank top. Mom liked to wear them when she was younger. She'd lean forward and get whatever she wanted from whoever she was facing, man or woman. It never failed either. My inward smile got wider. *Oh, Mom. Give me a break here. I'm your daughter.* Well, that was all the proof I needed that it was never a practiced mechanism to get her way, but an unconscious tactic designed to draw her listener into her game.

"Baby...um, Evie?" she said without missing a beat. "You grew up with him. You understand his moods better than anyone here in Montana." Then she glanced at Mario and added, "No offense to you."

"None taken," he replied quickly. He was as eager to learn what she had on her mind as I was, as all of us were.

Then it fell on me again. "Evie? He wants to tell you something that a translation from Mario might not contain everything he wants to tell you." Then she squinted, tossed her beautifully dyed black hair over her shoulder and said, "My guess? Something medical. A question maybe. But it could be information pertinent only to you and not medical at all."

I smiled. "So, you're going with me to the hospital?"

"Absolutely," she said and smiled.

"Then I best get ready."

I excused myself, went to the shower and had every intention of taking a quick one. The shower door opened and I expected Mario. Nope, Maddy. She grabbed the shampoo bottle and made me laugh when she said, "Bend over, Mom." I did so while thinking of Quinn Riley and his escapades at the hospital. Maddy shampooed my hair and then I did hers. She washed me, I washed her and we had a good time. It got better when she grabbed the blow dyer and tried to dry my hair. It was a nice effort but I needed to finish it myself. Well, I dried both of our hair and then smiled at her and said, "That was fun."

Yep. Mario's daughter. She put her hands on her hips and said, "So, why don't we do it more often?"

"I promise we will from now on."

"And you also promise not to call me 'baby' and you still do. Is this promise like that one?"

"I'll try harder," I said rubbing her hair with a towel.

"Will you really do it or just keep promising?"

"I promise…" I stopped my in a fit laughter. Then I grabbed her, hugged her and said, "No promises. From now on? It's a standing date in the shower." Then I bent down to her and said, "Okay, *Maddy*?"

She giggled, I giggled and that was that last time that was going to happen for a while. And the reason had nothing to do with Alex.

Mom? You were *that* close.

Chapter 24

The first thing I did was call the hospital. I identified myself and then I spoke to the admitting nurse in the ER. She transferred the call to a doctor who turned out the be Quinn Riley. "Quinn? Don't joke and say you didn't assist on a heart transplant last night."

"Heart transplant? Everyone knows I don't have one."

I moaned. "Not yours. Peters."

"Ah, Alex Payne. Him. Yeah."

"And?"

"Resting comfortably."

"When can his family see him?"

"Anytime they want. But conscious? At least twelve hours."

"Will they be admitted at that hour. It will be nearly eight in the evening by then."

"Yes. I'll make plans. Anything for the woman who dropped her pants and bent over in the admin's office."

"Quinn…"

I could hear the laughter in his voice. "See ya at eight, Evie."

That gave everyone a chance to rest. We took them to the third floor and Travis hooked up Alex, Junior, with his third floor Playstation. It didn't matter that the boy was barely five and tired from his long trip. Travis settled in as though they had been best friends *forever*. Holley followed us and hugged me when we got to the top and said, "Don't worry about the kids. We'll be fine."

"What would I do with you," I said to her.

"Well, you could pay me more," she deadpanned.

"Oh, god," I said panicking. "How much?" Then the panic went straight to my heart and I gasped, "Oh, god, no! You're going to work for someone else! I'm knew it! I'm a bitch! I'll double your pay!"

She put her hands on either side of my face and said, "Evie? Joking. I'm joking." Then she shrugged and said, "But if you want to…"

"Just name a price," I said, my panic still at full alert.

"How about what I'm already working for? I love your kids and love living here. It's perfect."

I hugged her. "Oh, Jesus, Holley. You scared me to death. You're getting an immediate ten percent raise and I won't hear any arguments."

"Oh, God, Evie," she said. "You can't buy me. I thought we were friends."

Well, the crisis passed and Holley mixed easily with everyone.

Josh, Kristi and Ellie all decided to get some sleep before tonight, so they wouldn't be exhausted when we went to see Alex, um, Normie. Mom followed us downstairs because it was obvious she had something on her mind. If I had to guess, it had something to do with whatever Alex had on his mind. Maybe a clarification, maybe something else entirely. But it was obvious she wanted to talk to me.

We settled in the living room and Mom just collapsed onto the couch. I pulled an armchair to the other side of the coffee table and said, "Okay. What is it?"

She was tired and pushing herself. I'd seen her do this a million times when I was a kid. She ignored all of her physical symptoms and keep pushing until she had an answer. Okay, I learned a lot from her because I tend to be the same way. But I know her. She'll stay awake until whatever oddness is pushing at her is revealed one way or another. That attitude, that ability, got her to Congress and will make her the next senator from Maine. She's been campaigning and this side trip has put a dent in her schedule.

"I've been talking with North, the coroner back in Portland. I think you need to talk to him."

"About?" I prompted.

She frowned and said, "It's above me. I don't know. He thinks he has an insight into what's happening. The issue is that he asked me to keep this between him, me and the FBI. Pee Wee." Then she looked directly at me and said, "Just call him. Tell him I told you to do it and he'll talk to you."

"Okay," I said. "What else. And don't give any crap that there isn't anything."

She smirked and said, "Your mother should spank you more often." Then she took a deep breath and said as she shook her head, "I don't know, Evie. That's as blunt as I can make it. There is something in the air and I can't put my finger on it."

Hunches. Mom was big on hunches when I was a kid. It drove me crazy because I saw no way to verify anything that she did. It took Mario one summer day to make obvious that her hunches usually had a point in fact if only in her mind. He gave at least a dozen examples and asked me to pick them apart. I couldn't. Ever since? I've been a convert to her hunches. In fact, I've gone all the way to calling them educated guesses.

"Okay, in what areas? Give me a ballpark to play in."

She sighed, draped her hair behind her ear and said, "Causality."

"In what sense?"

"You read those autopsies. Did you get any hints that any of those kids had something in common besides football?"

"You're implying that football isn't the common thread. I never thought so." Then I shrugged. "And so?"

She covered her face with her hands and yawned. "Just keep your mind open. Please?" she said looking up at me. "Something stinks and I can't find the source. And don't forget to call North."

"I will and I will," I replied. "Now let me get you to bed."

She leaned across the coffee table and said, "Promise me that Alex won't die."

"A doctor I talked to said he's resting comfortably."

She reached out and took my hands. "You talk to him. You promise? Something's rotten and I can't place it. Please, Evie? This is your area, medicine. You have friends in the profession. Talk to them. Figure it out."

Everything seemed calm. Nothing felt wrong either. While technically nothing was, everything that was going to happen was already in motion. But being a doctor means seeing things that can't be seen, dealing with things that are invisible to the naked eyes and making connections between elements of fact that are so disparate as to be on separate continents. Nothing was going to make sense. Period. And me? I was going to be frantic because events were about to hit close to home.

Very close.

It was as though I'd lived my entire life for this moment.

I took Mom upstairs and showed her into a bedroom I'd made just for her. There were pictures of her on the walls of when she was younger. There was even one of my father, Brian Sixkiller, hanging right next to Brad. Mom smiled at both of them and touched Brian's picture. "So long, Babe. So very long. I hope you're waiting for me."

It seemed odd, that little speech delivered to her dead husband. But I know she's dreamed of him over the years. I know there is still some sort of connection between them. If that sounds a bit spooky, I apologize. But I believe her when she tells me that she dreams of a certain Indian riding a horse at full gallop across the plains. I believe her when she says that the horse is riding toward her. I believe her when she says the rider dismounts and approaches her with a broad smile. I believe her when she says she always wakens at that point.

I got her into bed, kissed her goodnight and went downstairs to call the coroner back in Portland.

The circle was closing.

Almost closed.

Almost.

Chapter 25

I found Aidan Hall slumped in a chair in the resident's lounge. He was talking to Quinn Riley. Both of them looked like they been ridden hard and put away wet. That meant Quinn assisted Dr. Hall. I was at the medical center while everyone else was either sleeping or resting. All of them put in a long night and longer day.

"Good morning, Doctor…whatever," Hall said wearily.

I settled into a chair opposite him and said, "You could always call me Evie."

"And how would I explain that to my wife," he joked, still weary.

"How's the patient," I asked, cutting straight to the chase.

"A lot more active than we would like," he said looking down at the cheap table. Then he looked up at me and said, "Tell me you don't know Agent Barbara Reese of the FBI."

"She's an acquaintance of my mother…"

"…who was here last night," he interjected. "What the hell is this, Evie. They had their own frigging heart surgeon with them, a guy from New York. He did the operation and then flew out. I never even knew his name. Quinn and I did nothing more than assist him and were instructed by Agent Reese not to engage the doctor in conversation." He leaned across the table and repeated it. "What the hell is this, Evie?"

Stay in character. That would be Mom's advice. Advice? Hell, orders. She might be a kitten at home, but she's a tigress professionally. So, what was my answer? *The truth. Tell them the truth.* "Aidan? Quinn? They're trying to find the source of an extremely virulent form of cancer. There are eight kids, all between the ages of fifteen and twenty-two who have died from it, all within two weeks of the first diagnosis. Skin cancer. That's what is going on."

"Which is the same speech you gave me," Quinn said, his voice nearing anger. "How does skin cancer turn into a government conspiracy to give a heart to a person who was declared legally dead not a week ago?"

Aidan glanced back toward the operating room and said, "And that person was extremely active before he went into surgery." Stabbing his finger directly at me, he sneered, "And he specifically asked for you when he woke up after surgery. Furthermore, he didn't ask about his wife, children and grandchild. He asked about you. I'm supposed to deliver you to him as soon as you show up, not when he is healthy enough to see visitors."

The man I knew as Alex Payne was not the man they were describing to me. The man I knew as Alex Payne doted on his wife and children. His grandchild? He never thought he would have kids, much less grandkids, so this was unlike anything I knew about him. *Except. He turned into a first-class investigator after Mom sold him her business. Hell, he was already a good investigator before that ever happened. In fact, Mom wouldn't have sold it to him at all unless he was good at it.* So, what did this mean? As near as I could tell, Alex had something he needed to tell me and not my mother, something medical that he could only trust with me. He didn't know either Aidan or Quinn. He knew me and could trust me. But what was it?

"And now?" I asked. "Is this my fault? Are you blaming me for all this?" I looked at Quinn and said, "You know everything I do. And neither one us cares all that much. Our jobs are the same: heal the sick. Period. I have no stomach for intrigue and that's what this feels like. I'm a doctor, just like you." Then I turned to Aidan and said imploringly, "Don't treat me like the enemy. I'm no different than you. And the only difference between me and your patient? I'm trying to heal the sick while he's trying to find the sick in our society. We're no different than opposite sides of the same coin."

Aidan said, still weary, "And you want to see him?"

"What danger will it put him in?"

"Risk of rejection, risk of respiratory system compromise, immune system collapse and any other thing you care to name." Then his look got angry. "And furthermore? His original condition was brought about by steroid abuse. And David Ryan? Was a tested user of steroids. You just dumped a boatload of steroids into the system of a man who had a history of abusing them. What will that do to him? I don't know, but I wouldn't bet on a positive outcome."

It was a risk I was willing to take. Had been willing to take. Alex lived clean for over twenty-five years, then this. But the consequences of not using David's heart was death. Alex was dead without that transplant. But HGH has been identified as a cause of enlarged hearts where the patient died. That meant, Alex might die from a surgery meant to save his life.

But.

Ellie kept Alex on a strict diet since they married. Heck, from before they married. She kept to it with him and passed the diet to her children. What's that mean? *Alex? Other than your heart failing, the rest of your body was in shape. You had the lowest cholesterol readings of anyone I'd ever tested. And blood pressure, heart rate and every other indicator of good health were all in your favor. Her diet healed your liver, your kidney and kept your heart rate at normal levels for twenty years.* Given that, the only organ that could have failed was his heart. *And the steroids in his body because of the heart transplant won't hurt him otherwise.*

"You're serious?" I asked Aidan. "The levels of HGH in his body was a low level exposure. Yes, HGH can enlarge the heart, but not at the levels that were present in David Ryan's body. In fact, stopping the administration of the drug can reverse damage done by its administration." Then I frowned. "But you know all this. Getting David Ryan's heart with a dose of HGH in it can't hurt him. It might even add some muscle mass to his heart that wasn't already there."

Aidan spat, "Add muscle mass! Are you serious? It adds nothing but definition. You want muscle mass? Use steroids, not HGH. I'm not convinced that, given his condition, we didn't perform an operation that might not do him more harm than good." Then he stabbed his finger at me again and spat, "And you know it!"

Step back. It's done anyway. I sighed, bowed my head and said, "Can I see him?"

"Yeah," he said, his voice tilting toward disgust. "Why not? But I'm still not convinced I didn't participate in a legal murder."

We all got up and headed toward the ICU. None of us spoke as we walked through the ward toward the room where Alex was recuperating from a heart operation. The ICU his was in was a clean room. An infection now would be fatal. I donned all the clean clothes necessary to go inside. Both Aidan and Quinn stayed outside and watched from beyond the window.

Given his monitor readings, I thought he was unconscious. His heart rate was slow and his blood pressure was barely normal. I went to his bedside and stood there for maybe fifteen seconds when every reading started to increase nominally. Concern began to grip me like a ill-fitting glove. Then his eyes fluttered open and he looked up at me. What? Twelve hours on the other side of a heart transplant? And he was struggling to speak to me? Okay. Maybe that's the ex-football player, or the man that loves to compete, but when it was obvious he wanted to say something and was having difficulty, I bent down to his mouth and heard what he wanted to tell me. "Warren Trick."

And he was out.

My initial reaction? *Oh, this is going to be fun.*

It wasn't.

Chapter 26

Kalispell, Montana, has one AM radio station in town. KAMT. At one time it played what my mother affectionately calls "classic rock". It wasn't classic when the station played it. It was current. That was easily forty years ago. Then it became an easy listening station, an all-news format station, a progressive rock station, a country station and then sat idle for nearly five years until Warren Trick happened by. This was fifteen years ago. Then Warren Trick bought the property – including the transmission towers – at an auction and settled in to hate everyone that didn't agree with him.

Warren Trick has a bigger audience than you'd think. Painting himself "to the right of Hitler, to the right of all those people that put down Jews, to the right of the people who believe that liberals are little more than ill-advised heathens, I am the person you need to make this world stop smelling the way it does." That's Warren Trick.

The towers are between Ashley Creek and Airport Road. The station itself is on Airport Road opposite the baseball diamonds at Begg Park. The sign over the door reads "Tricks Lair. You Won't Be The Same". There's a lady in the lobby of the station. Well, lady is a stretch. She has a razor blade in her eyebrow and her pink Mohawk goes from ear-to-ear rather than from front-to-back. She has huge white circles painted around her eyes and fingernails so long that you wonder how she holds a pencil or…does anything intimate in the bathroom. She calls herself "Spite" but I'd never win a bet on whether it's the name she was born with. It could be.

"You better have business here," she said out of the corner of her mouth.

"Do you always look stupid or did I win a prize?" I said. That's pure Grandpa. He loved messing with people that assumed they were in charge. "Never speak in anything but a total *non sequitor*" he'd say. It took years for me to understand what he meant. This was one of those times.

"Lady?" she said. "I'm about to call a cop."

I pointed at a bank of pictures on the wall behind me. They were all of Warren Trick. "Wow. Porky Pig, Bugs Bunny and the Rockettes. That's a cool montage."

She picked up the phone as though to dial. I leaned over the counter that separated us and held my nose. "Oh, gross. Don't you smell that?"

"I know you," she said and predictably put down the phone. "You're that California doctor. Hogkiller or something."

I motioned toward her side-to-side Mohawk. "That would make a bad scalp. Now a blue one? That has possibilities." Then I smiled and said, "Yep. You'd make a great blue hair."

"What do you want?"

"To accuse Warren Trick of being a sane voice to sane people, to ask him why the entire country hasn't embraced him and how we can accomplished that."

"Wait here," she said. She left her desk and disappeared into a room that had a red light in it. She spoke to someone by leaning through the doorway and talking as though I was infectious and wanted to give her listener time to escape. The person to whom she spoke must have responded because the woman nodded. Then she looked back over her shoulder at me and said, "That California doctor." She listened more and then nodded. Then to me, she said, "Hey? You want on the air?"

I clasped my hands to my bosom and exclaimed, "Oh, really? With the Trickster? Oh, be still my beating heart."

Spite looked back in the room and said something. Then to me, "Lift the lid and come back here."

The counter ended in one of those flanged lifts. I raised it and went to where she was holding open the door. I whispered to her, "You know what would look great?" Then without waiting for an answer, I said, "A hook through your cheek on which you could hang baby diapers. Then no one would wonder where the smell is coming from."

She gave me a look that was supposed to intimidate me. It didn't. I smiled at her and wiggled my fingers in her direction as I approached a booth that had a blinking red light in it. The woman sitting in the booth was Warren's call screener. She nodded toward the door and I went inside. "My name is Rachel Wells," she said.

"Evie," I replied.

"Doctor…" she said with a leading question mark in her voice.

"Sixkiller-Collins Collins. The inbred cretin from California."

"Ah," she said neutrally. "Al Livingston."

Al Livingston was the sheriff/coroner in Flathead County before Al Hastings. Thompson was killings gays and lesbians from Canada and I tracked him down. It almost destroyed my ability to be a doctor because Thompson shot himself in my presence and I did not try to stop him. If anything, I encouraged him to do it and he did. I survived him and what he did to himself only because Woody, Travis' best friend, was hit by a car in front of our house. I went into automatic mode and Woody survived intact. His parents treat us to dinner on occasion. But Rachel.

Unlike the female out front who called herself Spite, Rachel looked positively normal. Sparkling blond hair cut to shoulder length, a nice smile, blue eyes that caught every stray bit of light and a voice that sounded a bit too much like Lauren Bacall. I hated her immediately.

"Yes," I said just as neutrally.

"You want to see Warren?"

"Yes."

"Why?"

"We're compatriots. I want to hug him and proclaim him King of America." She looked like she swallowed a worm. It was possible she agreed with what I'd said but didn't think I was serious. I wasn't. I smiled and tossed in, "I love his views on racial harmony and can't wait to engage him in conversation about the health care bill that's in the House."

She glanced at the clock next to her desk and spoke into the headphone she wore. "Ten seconds, Warren," she said evenly. She watched him through the glass. She counted off on her fingers, "Three, two…" and then mouthed, "One."

Trick was back from a commercial. As soon as they were live, he leaned into the microphone and said, "And socialism. We're heading headlong into an economic straightjacket that will ruin our country within a generation. You'll be fighting in the streets, shooting your neighbors for food, boarding up your windows against the mobs outside. Comments? Please call and share your stories." Then he stabbed a button on a console in front of him and said, "And speaking of callers? This is Steve. What's up, my friend?"

Without even acknowledging his host, the man named Steve started in with, "No one should be allowed to vote unless he owns property. That gives you a stake in society and the right to be heard. If you get welfare from government, you shouldn't be allowed to do anything."

"Anything else, my friend?"

"And queers should be shot. They should be put up against a wall and shot point-blank in the head."

And it went like that. One hate-filled call after another. Rachel allowed me to watch as Warren worked his callers. In fact, every caller was an excuse to rant about whatever subject was at hand – and they were numerous. From abortion – I think he was against it – to foreign affairs, to taxation, to immigration, to public works, to education, to military affairs, to any subject you can name – with the exception of one. Health care. He didn't touch the subject at all. The longer I watched, the more I became convinced that Rachel wasn't forwarding any calls about health care to the good Mister Trick. Which meant I was going to be on the radio for the first time in my life.

They went to a commercial break and Warren turned to Rachel and said, "Is she ready?"

"Untouched and virginal," Rachel replied.

Then he looked at me and said, "Would you care to discuss your profession with me on the radio?"

"Sure," I said smiling.

What followed was a crash course about how on-the-air radio worked. It wasn't hard to understand and when they came back from commercial, I was wearing headphones and waiting for Trick to pull one.

He did. Right off.

What happened, however, was not what he planned.

Not at all.

Chapter 27

Rachel counted off, "Three, two," and then mouthed, "one."

Warren turned on me. Literally. "Folks? We have in the studio the murderer of our coroner, Al Livingston. No, she didn't pull the trigger on Al's life, but she didn't try to stop him either. That makes her complicit in his death, and thus a murderess." He wasn't smiling and had no intention of apologizing or acting as though he was anything other than serious. "She likes to be called Doctor Six, as in Six Six Six. If I have to tell you that's the sign of the devil, then you haven't been paying attention." Then he leveled his first question at me. "Doctor Six Six Six, why haven't you turned yourself in for the murder of Al Livingston?"

Well, golly. Wasn't this going to be fun? I had two choices here. I could play his game and try – unsuccessfully – to defend myself. Or I could change the subject and talk about why I was here and not somewhere else. I folded my hands and said to him, "Mr. Trick? Have you ever seen anyone die of skin cancer? Melanoma?"

I can't say he didn't try to steer me back on a course of hatred. "Doctor Six Six Six? Please, one subject at a time. Why haven't…"

And I interrupted him. "No? Didn't think so. It starts as a hairy mole. Maybe one side of it doesn't match the other. And there's hair growing out of it. But it's pretty small, so you discount it. Then? Two weeks later you're dead. And three or four days before that? They put you in a medically induced coma because the pain is so excruciating that they consider it humane. The problem with that? When they induce the coma, you know you're never going to wake up again. You know you're dead. Your body might last a few more days, but anything you might have accomplished is gone." Then, despite the fact we were on radio and no one could see the gesture, I pointed at him and finished with, "In fact, it's possible that when they induced that coma that you were no longer capable of thinking in the first person, possible because the cancer was probably eating at your brain. Anything that made you unique was gone before the coma settled you into the long road to death."

He sneered and said, "We aren't chasing death here, Doctor Six Six Six..."

"Does the name Danny Hardiman mean anything to you?" I said interrupting him again.

Chasing death. Maybe he wasn't, but I was. With Alex out of the picture, the medical mystery surrounding Danny Hardiman's death fell to me. While I felt awful about all the deaths since Danny's, I was going to let Chief Adams and his band of yes men do their jobs. Danny Hardiman's death was in my hands. But Warren Trick? I watched him closely as I asked that question. Did the name mean anything to him? Based on his minor wince, my opinion was that it did.

"I am aware that a boy by that name died of cancer recently." Then he resorted to the tried and true. He said, "And how does his death, however tragic, have anything to do with your callous treatment of Al Livingston? You were complicit in his death and you should turn yourself over the state police for prosecution."

"Danny Hardiman," I replied, not allowing myself to be reeled in by his net, "did not kill himself. Quite unlike Al Livingston." Then I added, "If Livingston was such a man, such a hero, why did he kill himself. I'm a girl, a doctor, I abhor weapons, I was no threat to him because he had the gun, so how could I have been a threat? Danny Hardiman? What chance did he have? And why did he have to die that way? And why aren't you upset that a teenager died of skin cancer the way he did? Why are you standing on a stump cheering for a man who admitted to being a murderer – and was not upset over it – and not over a boy who had no chance to live? Why, Warren? Why doesn't this upset you?"

He punched a button on the console and said, "Caller? What would you like to tell the doctor?"

I glanced at Rachel. She was expressionless.

The caller said, "You're a whore." Then he rattled off a long line of invectives that made me smile as he went on the prove his point to his own satisfaction.

When he ran down, I asked, "Do you even know what I look like?"

Warren leaned into the microphone and said, "She married her uncle. That makes her children inbred."

That ensured that the next half dozen calls were all of the same type: that spit hatred in all the typical ways and never stopped to ask the question, "Are you related by blood?" I'm convinced that Warren knew I was not. He allowed the long string of vitriol to continue through two commercial breaks. During each of them, he left the studio and went into the screener's room. To Rachel, he punched his fist as though making an emphatic point. It wasn't hard to see that he wanted all the calls to be of the same type. That didn't bother me. What did was the reason Alex sent me here in the first place. Why did he? Why was I here?

Warren came back into the room, sat down and said into the microphone, "We're here with Doctor Evangeline Monica Sixkiller-Collins Collins. Doctor Six Six Six. She's famous for murdering Al Livingston, marrying her uncle and having two inbred children. Caller? Say hello to a true degenerate."

It got so bad that I interrupted the caller and said, "Are you having trouble with Jimson weed again?"

Predictably, he went into a tirade that included, "That evil weed that destroys our youth and how can accuse me of smoking it?"

"I didn't," I smiled into the microphone. "I accused you of using jimson weed, probably to help with your bedwetting."

The caller started screaming. I don't think he was saying anything, just screaming. I looked at Warren and he was concentrating on his headphones. Then he glanced at Rachel and she nodded imperceptibly. If I read it right, the string was going to get longer. The calls would all be of a type and I'd be accused of everything including the kidnap and murder of the Lindberg baby. It did and I was.

I was on the air for about an hour, his last guest in fact. He didn't bother to shake my hand and I thought I was leaving with nothing. I'd taunted him, was insulting to his callers and he didn't blink an eye about anything I'd said. I began to feel that Alex was hallucinating or maybe even talking to me with the effects of a drug.

I left the studio and Rachel offered her hand me. I clasped it and felt something tickling my palm. She'd passed me a note. She said merely, "Thank you for your time. I hope you can come back and be a guest another time. You did well out there."

"It wasn't hard," I said. "I don't care what people think of me. I want to practice medicine. That's all. If Warren came down with a serious illness that I could help treat, I'd do it because the stuff he spouts is meaningless to me. You too, Rachel. Sickness doesn't know politics. It knows people."

"Well, please," she said. "It was an interesting hour, one of the best we've had lately."

I smiled. "Next time? I'll call."

When I left the station, I had two basic problems. One was Alex. Why did he send me there? Nothing happened at all. And two? The note passed to me by Rachel. I kept it rolled inside my hand until I got into the Highlander and then read it. "Midnight under the Stillwater overpass on the 93. Pls."

While I could think of a dozen reasons not to go, I knew I was going to. I drove to the office, saw as many patients as I could, all while thinking about tonight at midnight. It was sufficiently cloak and dagger that I wondered about the meeting, but decided to go because it wasn't that far from home.

What I didn't count on was fairly basic: that stupid meeting with Warren Trick didn't leave me with two problems, it left me with three. The third one? That wasn't going to be divulged until tonight. Midnight. The hour of goblins, witches, the undead and the uncertain.

One of them was going to meet me at midnight tonight and reveal the third problem Warren Trick had left for me. Oddly, I wasn't worried.

I think I should have been.

Chapter 28

The last thing I did before going to that meeting was visit Alex. He was conscious and I wanted to ask him a few questions. I know better than to stress him because there is a whole panoply of problems that could arise if he got agitated. Ellie was all smiles because his condition was improving. Josh and Kristi were so happy that if I didn't know better, I swear their moods were drug induced. Mom was with Mario, but Holley didn't know where they went. It didn't matter. I wasn't worried about them.

Quinn Riley was on duty in the ER. He called the ICU and asked if I could visit "the patient". No one was calling him Alex – or Normie for that matter. He was "the patient". I thought it was cute. It was like ignoring the eight-hundred pound gorilla who was sipping wine in the corner. Cute. Real. I was *ordered* not to cause any duress, stress or inadvertently cause his blood pressure to spike. I was asked to smile a lot. No. I was *ordered* to smile a lot. It didn't matter that I was wearing a moon suit because he was in a iso unit.

A standing order was that only one person at a time could be with him. Ellie kissed me on the cheek and looked as happy as I've ever seen her. Then she hugged me and said, "Thank you, Evie. Thank you so very much." It wasn't hard to hug her even inside the suits we wore.

Ellie left. She shed the suit and remained on watch outside the sliding glass door that formed one side of the decon room.

"Hey," I said to him easily. That's when the first signs of trouble started. His blood pressure readings started to spike and I knew he could be in trouble unless I defused whatever was causing it. I took his hand said, "Hey, dude. Don't worry. I've already seen him and nothing happened."

"Evie…" he started to say, then stopped and closed his eyes.

"I'll repeat, Alex. Nothing happened. Well, he knew the story of me and Mario, so I'm the biggest degenerate in the western world. And his callers? Jesus. Where does he get them?"

"I'm sorry," he said weakly.

"I'm not," I replied as upbeat as I could. "I love the mangy bastard. Always have."

"Let him do this," he said. It sounded like begging.

"Sure," I said. "I'm not cut out to be a spy."

"Please?" he said. "Let Mario do this?"

I let go of his hand, put both of mine over my heart and said, "Promise. Mario is the spy and I'm the doctor."

A nurse came into the room and said nothing but said it so loudly that they probably heard it back in Portland. She was monitoring his vitals, but watching his condition. His blood pressure was still a little high and his pulse was a bit rapid. Something was wrong and he wasn't telling me. I thought it was obvious. Did he know that he was hooked up to a primitive lie detector? Did he know I could infer a whole range of assumptions from the readings?

I took his hand again and said with a smile I hoped showed in my eyes, "Please, big guy. Don't worry about me. I'm fine. No one is following me and no one going to either. I'm a country doctor."

The nurse was watching me as his readings remained higher than she wanted them to be. Finally, she said, "I need to ask you to leave, doctor."

I squeezed his hand and said, "Relax. I'll be back in the morning to check on you. If you behave yourself, I'll let you jump out of a closet and scare me." It was old behavior. Alex and Mario taught me self-defense all those years ago and he knew no one could sneak up me. Still, he was worried and I wouldn't find out today.

I leaned down and said, "Alex? Please, don't worry about me. I'll be fine."

He whispered, "But you don't know what they want."

"Do you?"

"No," he said weakly, almost silently.

"I'll talk to Mario. I'll tell him you want him to do that side of this. Okay?"

"Please, Evie? Stay out of it?"

"Sure," I said and meant it. "I've got kids and they need me. With Mario? It's just sex." Then I laughed and said, "Thank god."

When I got out of the suit and outside with Ellie, she was visibly nervous. "He's worried about me, Ellie," I said. "The biggest thing you can do is reassure him I'm not in danger. I've got my practice and my family. That's where I'm going to be until something happens that needs my attention. Mario can do the skulking and that nonsense. I'll wait until my expertise is needed. Can you please make sure he believes that?"

Ellie is a smart lady. She asked, "Is it?"

"Yes," I answered as truthfully as I could.

We hugged and then fell into small talk. Josh was fine, but Kristi was her favorite. Little APayne was cute, but Kristi still carried that particular bug with her in endearing quantities. No, don't got here. Ellie loved Josh as much as she loved Kristi, but Kristi was the one who went places with her, shopping, lunch and such. Maybe Maddy would do all those things with me one day. I can only hope.

If you guessed I was holding a grand lie, you are correct. I was going to make the rendezvous with Rachel Wells. It didn't matter that it was under a bridge on a river. It didn't matter that I didn't know Rachel Wells at all. Nothing mattered but Alex and what he asked me to do. Something out there was killing young people and doing it in the most gruesome way possible. If he was involved in this, then I was going to use all my expertise in medicine to figure it out.

However, I was about to step into a situation that I could not have anticipated. Had I been able? I can't say I would have done things differently because Alex Payne deserves everything I can give him. Period. There are no alternatives here. He didn't even have to ask. Indeed, he asked me to step down and let my husband do it. The truth was that I was going to. After tonight, I was out of the spy business. And not because I didn't want to help Alex. I did. I felt that the best way to help him was to concentrate on medicine, on the side of the investigation that was going to discover what sort of bug it was and then figure out how to treat it. That's what I was going to do.

But, like the say. The best laid plans and all. And you know what happens to them.

It was about to happen to me.

Chapter 29

I had time to spend with my family, but I didn't. I went into my upstairs office and began reading through all those autopsy results and findings. I read through everything I had and did it maybe a dozen times. I got nothing out of it but the reaffirmation of a diagnosis of skin cancer. Every case came down to that. And no, I'm not arguing that the diagnosis was wrong. I'm saying that the diagnosis was consistent in every case. The disease took the same course each time and the treatments didn't do anything to slow down its progress.

I heard a noise at the door and saw that it was Maddy. I was tired, grumpy and frustrated from seeing the same things in the same places time after time. I wanted to tell her to leave me alone, but couldn't. This wasn't her issue. It was mine and I couldn't throw it at her.

"Hi, baby," I said miserably. Yep. I'd totally forgotten. I sighed and said, "I mean, hi, Maddy."

"I just wanted to say goodnight, Mommy," she said uncertainly behind a wad of fingers she had stuffed in her mouth.

"Well, come in, baby," I said again. Then grimaced and said, "I mean, Maddy."

She came in tentatively and that hurt a bit. I can think of a million times that I was afraid of my mother. No, not because she'd hurt me, not physically anyway, but because she'd bark and get short-tempered. No, she rarely got that way, but the fear was always there. Even though I love my mother, I swore my children wouldn't be afraid of me and here my youngest daughter was showing every sign of being just that way. I held out my arms to her and said, "Come on. Jump in my lap."

She did and carried with her the exuberance that she carries with her everywhere. She saw the autopsy reports and asked, "What are they?"

"Doctor stuff," I said, not wanting to tell her that they described a horrific death to a kid not much older than her.

"Mom," she said sounding perturbed. All that was missing were fists held against her hips and a head tilted just *so*. "I wasn't born yesterday."

"Patient files," I said hugging her. "They tell me the name of the patient and what was wrong with him when he saw a doctor." That was putting it as mildly as I could tell it.

"What was wrong with him?" she asked.

"Skin rash," I said. *Please, Maddy. Don't be curious. Not now. I don't want to inflict this on you.*

"Is he okay?" she asked, her voice full of wonder.

Never lie to your children. No one had to teach me that; it was common sense. Now? I think I had to. Danny Hardiman was dead, but Maddy didn't need to know that. I took a deep breath and said, "Yes. It went away."

She didn't speak for a long time, several seconds anyway. It bothered me because she kept staring at the sheaves of paper in front of her. she pointed to a line on the report and said, "That word is Daniel. I know because there's a boy in our class by that name. Daniel Kingman. Is that his name? Daniel?"

"Yes."

She pointed to his last name and said, "And what does that say?"

"Hardiman. It's his last name."

She slowly slid out of my lap and I know I'd screwed up.

"You lied, Mommy. That boy died because everyone says so. He died and you lied to me."

Mom? Now I know how you felt. Miserable. You gave battle to every sort of degenerate and yet I had the power to weaken your knees. Just like you, I had the urge to yell at my daughter, and yet I couldn't. She stood in the doorway to my office in full and unyielding judgment of me and I was helpless even to defend myself. In the end, I yielded to her unwavering and complete power over me. "You want the truth?"

"Yes, Mommy."

"Then come back over here, crawl into my lap and I'll give it to you."

She's the second iteration of Melodie Chang. People said I was just like her and I didn't agree for a long time. Years. Now Madsion

Sixkiller-Collins is the second version of my mother. As she climbed back into my lap, I smiled at her, wrapped my arms around her and said, "I'm sorry, Maddy. I won't do that again."

"I've heard that before, Mom."

"This time I promise, Baby."

"See?"

I dropped my forehead into her hair and smiled because either tears or anger were very near. I took a deep breath and said, "Don't lose faith in me. Please?" Just like my mother said to me years ago.

"Why did he die, Mommy?" she asked with a little voice that finally betrayed her age.

"He caught a disease called cancer."

"What's that?"

My kneejerk reaction was to call it, "A rash." I couldn't though. She was at the age when skin rashes were annoying and mostly nonthreatening. If I slipped and called it that, she'd worry about dying every time her skin turned red or itched. I considered my answer and said, "There are a lot of different types of cancer. The kind that killed Danny Hardiman was rare. Only seven other people ever caught it. It gets into your body and causes your organs to stop working." Lord, that was putting a spin on it that made me wince. "But like I said, only seven other people in the whole word ever caught it and the youngest one was a lot older than you. You don't have to worry about it."

She looked down at the autopsy report on one of the victims, a kid named Vince Myers. She pointed to a word and tried to sound it out. "Ma…malign…I don't know that word."

"Malignant. It's a word that means harming your body."

"Like when I have a cold?"

I smiled. "Well, not exactly. A cold doesn't change your body, just makes you feel bad. A malignant disease is a lot worse."

"And I don't have a…malign…that kind of disease?"

"No," I responded and hugged her tighter. "Please don't worry about it, Maddy. Please?"

"Do you know about Avian bird flu?" she asked with her brown eyes huge and trusting.

"I know that it's called H5N1 and that it's difficult for humans to catch."

"Really?" she asked.

I smiled. "Really. No lie this time."

"I know," she said smiling. "You don't lie about medicine. Except when Danny Hardiman dies." Then she tapped the autopsy report in front of her and asked, "Can I have a cell phone?"

Aha. The little rascal wound me up tighter than a spring and then sprung her trap. "Nope," I said. "But I'll make you a deal."

"What kind of…deal?"

"The next time you catch me in a lie? I'll buy you one. Your choice."

She smiled and squealed, "Oh, Mom! I'll have one before school starts!"

"We'll see," I said and carried her to her bedroom.

It was the perfect way for my daughter to end her day with me. It focused me, gave me strength and was going to make my night easier to handle. That didn't mean it was going to be successful, just that it was going to be easier to face. I tucked in Maddy, then went to check on Travis and he was already asleep. Ellie and her family was still at the hospital and Mom and Mario were just out. That left Holly.

"Oh, I'm fine," she said covering her phone with one hand and waving goodbye with the other.

That left Rachel.

Oddly, I wasn't worried. That was going to come later. Well, not *that* much later.

I wiggled my fingers at Holly as I left.

And never considered that unless everything went perfectly, that I'd never see any of them again.

As they say, ignorance. It's bliss.

Ask me, I know that one.

Chapter 30

No moon. I didn't notice, though, until I was at the bridge that spanned the Stillwater River. Okay, it isn't much of a river. It's more of a stream. But the bridge was made to look like it spanned the Mississippi. I parked on the northbound side nearest the bridge and saw no one else, not even traffic. It was eleven-fifty-three. I was early. And there was no moon. Nervous. I was nervous. Nervous but ready. I was wearing a black turtleneck with black pants. My disguise outfit. Or camouflage outfit. Whatever. I was trying to blend in. Not be seen. It was probably going to be impossible as long as I sat in the car. I got out.

I stopped and looked across the street. Did they know the house over there was Mario's school? One he operated with Cayn? It would have been reassuring to see a light on over there, but none were. *Dude? I could have used some backup.* Actually, it didn't matter. I was prepared all along to do this by myself. *Alex? You better appreciate this.* I closed the car door and looked at the dark ground on the other side. Not even a parked car. What was I supposed to do? Not knowing, I walked around the car and waited on the passenger side of the Highlander.

It didn't take long for a car to cruise to a slow stop on the other side of the bridge. It was impossible to tell if she was alone. It was too dark to see anyone at all inside whatever she was driving. I don't know those things. Mario does. All I saw was a single person exit it when the driver's door opened. It remained opened long enough for me to see an empty passenger seat. She was alone, too. Actually, I was making an assumption it was her. It was so dark, it could have been anyone. Warren, maybe.

"Rachel?" I called out.

The voice that called back was hers, but it was full of paranoid fear. "Oh, fuck! Shut up! Just meet me under the under the bridge."

She hurried to the side of the road and disappeared in the brush along the road that led down to the stream. Look, I can't call it a river. I've seen the Androscoggin in Maine and *that's* a river. This is the water that named the street I live on: Stillwater *Loop*. If it was a real river, I'd live on Stillwater *River* Loop. It's a stream that gave it's name to the loop that describes our street. But the question became simple: should I follow her? The even simpler answer was yes. I should. So I did.

There's a first time for everything. This was the first time I'd ever been under a bridge. As I edged my way through the dense foliage that marked the border between the road and the river, I resisted the urge to curse. Thank you, Maddy, very much. Instead, I tried to be a quiet as I could. I had no idea why that would even be necessary. I keep saying it: I'm a doctor and not a cop. Or a soldier. Yes. I was nervous.

As dark as it was up on the road, it was even darker under the bridge. Even though there was no brush under the bridge, it was hard to see her. Only the cement wall behind her made it possible to make her out as a dark figure against a slightly lighter background. As my eyes slowly adjusted to the darkness, I saw her pull her purse across her body from right to left where it came to rest against her left hip bone. The Ilium.

"Um, Doctor Six?" she said.

"I'm here," I said.

"Um, are you alone?" she asked with the frightened voice of a child.

"Yes," I answered.

"Um, is anyone else over there?"

"No, it's just me."

"Oh," she said. "That's good, I suppose."

"What brings me here?" I asked.

"Um, well," she said uncertainly. "I…um…need to tell you something."

From the way she sounded, her blood pressure was probably elevated, she was probably short of breath, her heart was probably racing and her concentration would be almost nonexistent. I was describing a panic attack and not taking my diagnosis to the next level: I wasn't extrapolating it into real life. I was in danger and was playing the part of the ER doctor who practiced medicine within the safes confines of the Emergency Room of a larger hospital. "Exactly what?" I asked *stupidly*.

"Um, are you sure you haven't seen anyone on that side?" she asked with such disjointed diction that I'm surprised I didn't see it at all.

"No," I answered. "I came alone."

"Um, and you didn't see anyone over there?"

Okay, she was telling me what was going to happen and I didn't see it through the medical definitions I was replaying through my mind. Not the least of them was Nyctophobia, or the fear of dark places. Maybe I was guilty of projection, of projecting my own anxiety onto her and seeing the result before me on the other side of the narrow stream. Anything was possible.

"No," I said again. "It's just me. Why am I here?"

She opened the flap on her purse. I saw it as a dim movement in the dark.

"Well, Warren said…" and she looked down at her purse. Then her right hand went into it and she said, "Um, he said that everyone is getting sick on purpose."

"Everyone?" I said. "Can you be a little more precise."

Jesus. She was having a first class anxiety attack and I was asking her to be a bit more precise. It was like asking a drowning person to be a bit more coordinated in their movements. Worse? Why was she reaching into her purse? And why had she drawn it over her body into the position it rested? These were all clues based on family history, but you'd swear my family history was of the Ozzie and Harriet variety, not the one I got from growing up in Clan Collins.

"Um, you know," she said fumbling loudly with her purse and making small mewing sounds. "That cancer stuff. He said…oh, damn…he said that it was on purpose."

"How?" I asked.

She said something about her parents not being married and the fumbling got louder. Then I saw what I took to be a compact. She was taking it from her purse and then dropped it. I took a step forward and said, "Are you okay? I can come over there and we can sit."

Her face came up and she said, "Could you? Could you come over here?" Then she gestured at the water and said, "You'll get wet and stuff."

"That's okay," I said and began to look for stones and stepping places to cross the shallow stream. It was dark, the stepping stones nearly invisible, so I got wet. I stepped into ankle-deep water several times and even stumbled once as I crossed the stream. That just guaranteed that my hands were wet by the time I got to the other side. Yes, Rachel was still fumbling in her purse and, no, I didn't see it. I saw a young girl who was having an anxiety attack and didn't see causation until I saw the gun. Even then, I didn't see it until the barrel was waving about my face like a golf ball looking for the hole. And then? "Oh, I can't believe it," I said wearily. "Tell me you aren't going to shoot me over that miserable man."

She was so scared that I don't believe she *could* have shot me. The bullet would have hit anything but me. The bridge above us, the abutments on either side of us, the walls on either side of the stream, anything but me. She was clearly terrified. "You...you're going to spoil everything," she said as she tried to hold the gun steady.

"Explain that," I said.

"They're *supposed* to die!" she positively screamed. "But it's not killing them fast enough. They're supposed to die in a few days, not two weeks!"

One of the symptoms of an anxiety attack are muscles spasms. That was my worst fear. She could shoot me without meaning to. Of course, another symptom is diarrhea. That was the symptom that hit her when someone walked up behind her, stripped the gun from her hand and walked her to wall that was to her left by putting a hand to her throat and forcing her backward. Who? Well, Christ. My mother. Melodie Chang.

The smell hit her first. "Oh, please," she said, her voice full of contempt. "Tell me you didn't?"

"Oh, god," Rachel said, her voice ranging all the way to petrified. "She's going to kill me."

That's when I noticed the latex gloves. I grew up thinking they were a way to hide fingerprints. It wasn't until I was ten or so that I read that they were used to maintain a sterile environment in an operating theater. But now? Mom wasn't performing an operation. Well, okay, okay. She was. *Her* kind. She was going to terrify Rachel to death just by being herself.

"Explain that, little girl," Mom said coldly.

Rachel's voice warbled as she said, "I can't."

Mom turned her head toward me but kept her eyes on Rachel. She put two fingers of her left hand to her carotid artery and said, "What happens if I press right here, daughter?"

"Mom!" I said panicking. "You could give her a stroke!"

Well, that was one extreme effect of what she asked. The other was mere unconsciousness. Naturally, I opted for the most radical end of the causative spectrum.

Mom looked at Rachel and said, "Then explain what you just said or the local ER will have to identify you by the crap you're carrying in your purse."

"He'll kill me!" she squealed.

"And exactly what do you think I'm going to do when I press right here?" she said putting her fingers to Rachel's carotid.

In medical terms, Rachel was under extreme stress and was on the verge of trauma. Well, you would be too if someone was holding a gun under your chin with one hand and had her first two fingers of her left pressed to your carotid artery. You'd be convinced that either method could kill you. It would count as torture in my book, but then I was a spasm from death just a minute before.

I nudged Mom away from her and stood facing Rachel. "Girl?" I said. "You better tell me what you know about what you said or you're going to need the ER to pick up your pieces." Mom tried to nudge me back, but I held my ground and even frowned at her. "Do you mind?"

"She wanted to kill you!"

"And she didn't," I said calmly. Then I looked back at Rachel and said, "You have three seconds to tell me what you know about that. Then I'm going to turn you over to my mother." I added, "And she has your gun."

"With your fingerprints on it," Mom said to her as nasty as she could manage.

Aside from the smell of Rachel's loose bowels, she was near to collapse. Despite being a medical practitioner and a mother, I could leave her like this. Still, I had to know what killed those boys. "Rachel? No one is going to hurt you. Just tell me so I can start a preventive program to recognize the symptoms when I see them."

"I don't know," she cried with tears flowing down her face. "All I heard was that they were supposed to die faster."

"Who said that?"

"Warren."

"And why?"

"I don't know," she cried. "I'm only here because I like my job as his producer."

"Where did he say it?"

"He was on the phone when he said it."

"On the air?"

"No, in his car. I was driving."

"To where?"

"Spokane."

"Why?"

"To meet a doctor."

"Who?"

"Some guy named…" and then she said it.

It never ceases to amaze me as to motivation. You think you know someone, and then you discover they've been harboring hatred toward you for years. No, the name she gave us meant nothing to me, but meant a lot to my mother. In her various professional guises, she'd met him many times – mostly as a PI. Members of Congress don't have many reasons to meet people like him. But when Rachel dropped that name? Mom actually sounded shocked and surprised. But what name? Who wanted those kids dead? Doctor John North, the coroner of Cumberland County, Maine.

I pressed my fingers to her carotid artery and she dropped like a rock. Then Mario dragged Spite from the bushes behind me and threw her with her girlfriend. "Man, I hate pink hair," he said.

Mom hugged me. "Damn, that was impressive. If you ever get tired of being a doctor, you can take up waterboarding for the Republican Party."

"Not the CIA?" I asked.

"Nah, they don't do that crap anymore."

"But Republicans do?"

"Yep. To a man."

Then I turned on Mario and said, "And what in hell have you been up to?"

He kissed me and said, "Watching a master at work."

"What are we going to do with them?"

And Mom ended the night. "Leave them here. Who are they going to tell? The cops? Give me a break. Warren Trick? He can deal with them."

And we went home. To the biggest and most horrific shock I'd had since I was eleven. It was upon me. The most horrific thing I'd ever faced. And I was going to feel unequal to the task when confronted with it.

I was going to fail.

It felt that way.

Chapter 31

The first thing Mom did after we got home was call Pee Wee. She told her what Rachel told me. Whatever Pee Wee said satisfied Mom because she smiled and said, "Yeah, well stop being named after an old Dodgers shortstop and I'll stop calling you Pee Wee."

Maybe my adrenalin rush caught up with me, but I was tired. Maybe my neurons were shorting out and I was having the mother of all aneurysms. Whatever. I was tired and was prepared to let Mom play cop again. She was built for it, adjusted easily to the demands placed upon her and found it easy to slide back into the persona of a member of Congress.

I kissed her and said, "I'm going to get some sleep."

"I'm going to hang down here with Mel," Mario said.

"Cool. See you later."

If only. If only my night had been blessed with sleep and not what was going to happen. If only. All I know is that I was ready for a bed that did not include high heels. I wanted sleep in as many hours as possible. Christ, I even settled for an old t-shirt instead of something that might arouse Mario. Sorry, dude.

I checked on the kids first and they were sound asleep. I went upstairs to the third floor in order to check on Ellie and her family. They were all asleep, too. That meant I was ready to settle in to bed.

Mom caught me on the way upstairs and said, "I know you're tired, but can I talk to you for a second?'

"Sure," I said. I got less sleep than this when I was a resident back in LA.

"Let me get out of these wet clothes and I'll join you in the den."

She was referring to our upstairs living room. My only issue was weariness. It was possible that I was going to be asleep before she got ready for bed herself. I sat down on one of the couches that faces the TV and waited. Mario showed up in a t-shirt and kissed my cheek.

"Stop it," I said giggling.

"Stop what?" he said kissing me again.

"That's your high heels kiss."

He kissed me again and said, "No, that was my high heels kiss." Then he kissed me yet again and said, "That was my oh-Jesus-I'm-so-horny-I'm-going-to-burst kiss."

I kissed him and said, "That's my dude-you're-chaste-tonight kiss."

He smiled in my face and said, "Wanna bet?"

That's when Mom walked back in wearing yet another t-shirt. You'd think that with as much money there is in the family that at least one of us could find something to wear to bed besides a t-shirt. Mom's was red and featured a gorilla typing on a keyboard. The caption was something out of Shakepeare and the gorilla saying, "Finally." Mario's was a Dodgers t-shirt. Mine was plain white. While Mario's fitted like a proper t-shirt, Mom and me were wearing ours over the shoulder.

"Baby?" she said and then dropped her head and said, "Fuck." The she looked at me and said, "Sorry, Evie. But what happened at the radio station today?"

I frowned and said, "How did you two know where I was?"

Mario burped and said, "Do you even know the capabilities of a G3 phone?"

I decided to be serious and maintain the high level of the discussion. "Huh?" I answered.

"With the proper aplet running on my phone, I can see anyone around me, where they are and even log into other common aps. In other words, your phone has built-in GPS capabilities and I've been tracking you." Then he frowned and said, "Is your phone ever turned off?"

I leaned toward him and said, "And how does that equate to knowing I'd be under the bridge at midnight?"

He smiled, kissed, my nose and said, "I called Warren. He told me."

I groaned. "He did *not* tell you I was going to be under that bridge at midnight."

"No," he said kissing my nose again. "He told me that you had business tonight at the hospital and then both Pinko the gay clown and Rachel what's-her-name left the station. Pinko went there first and was waiting. She has a G3 phone, too." Then he kissed my nose again and said, "She never turns hers off either. We figured Rachel would wind up wherever Pinko went, so we actually were following her and not you."

"And she told you what?"

"Nothing," he said shrugging. "I mean that girl was a bitch with a capital 24. She not only didn't say anything, but managed to invent a few words that she meant as descriptive nouns."

"So, I showed up at the bridge and you weren't surprised?"

He grimaced and said, "Not really."

"What happened at the station, Evie?" Mom asked again.

Mario kissed my nose.

"Nothing, Mom," I said shrugging the same way Mario did. "He did an interview that lasted through three commercial breaks, maneuvered at least three callers to call back under different names and used the whole thing to blast me. I mean, I expected it. He just kept hammering away at my basic filthy nature," I said kissing Mario back, "because I married my uncle and that's all that happened."

She sat back on couch and seemed disappointed somehow. "I expected something different than what happened."

"Could the name of John North be nothing more than a red herring?" I asked.

"Possibly. Pee Wee will find out."

"Then anything else?" I asked.

She looked tired, too. "No. Go on to bed. We're all tired."

That's when it happened. I got up to hug her. I think it took years before I realized the depth of my love for her. There was just too much angst in our past. I wanted my life and she wanted it, too. I mean, she wanted whatever I did and I thought she was trying to provide me with the life she wanted me to have. Well, all that nonsense washed away years ago. I love her and can't imagine that emotion not lasting forever.

But. I was about to find out that forever can be a matter of weeks. Why? Because as I hugged, I saw it. It was on her left shoulder just above her t-shirt. What was it? Cancer.

It shocked me completely. I stared at it and she felt my response and misinterpreted it. She wiggled out of my grasp and said, "What's wrong?"

Instead of answering, I physically turned her around and ripped away her shirt. She was struggling, covering herself and starting to react physically. I yelled, "Shut up, Mom!"

Maybe it was the tone of my voice, but she did.

But I stared at the fuzzy splotches on her left shoulder. Three of them. The largest one was no bigger than a peach and the other two were much smaller, but I saw something else. I saw a cancer entering her lymph nodes and spreading to her body, to her brain and ending in death. Hers.

I couldn't think. I was too tired, too erratic and too scared.

"Mom?" I said fearfully. "You've got three areas that might be cancer on your back."

She smiled tiredly and said, "Well, it looks like I'm going to be sleeping in the hospital tonight."

But me? I was shell-shocked. What if this version of that strain was the accelerated one that Rachel referred to? What if she was dead in two days? What if she slipped into a coma long before then and was gone?"

Tears rolled down my face and I hugged her.

And not for the last time, I hoped.

Chapter 32

Denial. Even as Mario drove us to the hospital, that was my frame of mind. *No. Not my mother.* More succinct than that I can't possibly be. Oh, crap. Despite all those years of being an intern, an ER doctor, then being in private practice, I fell apart. Succinct? How succinct is begging your mother not to die? Beyond that? I called her a bitch for catching the disease in the first place. In that respect, I don't think I fell far from the tree. But Mom? Well, to coin a phrase, fuck.

No, she was handling it a lot better than I was. She even talked about my father, Brian Sixkiller. He died from a heart condition when I was five. As many times as I've tried to conjure his face in my mind, I can't. And now my mother was talking about him like he was still alive. To her, maybe he was.

Which brings, I suppose, the subject of Brad Chang to the fore. He's been my father for as long as I can remember. Mom called him last night. Well, earlier this morning. He's in Pittsburgh on his latest book tour. He's dropping everything to come here. Yeah, here. She said I was her doctor and she would do whatever I said. Great, huh? I've wanted this responsibility since I was seven and now that I've got it, I'd gladly wish it upon someone else.

Kris Tice was the ER doctor that morning. Despite her workload, she pushed Mom to the head of line when I explained what was happening and what I'd discovered. I tried to compose myself, but it was hard and Kris saw it. "Evie?" she said eyeing me closely. "We'll take care of her. All of us. Relax."

But I hadn't actually said the words. They'd been lurking behind my eyes ever since I saw those fuzzy splotches on her shoulder. I didn't want to say them because I was afraid the process of vocalizing my fear might make them come true. But I had to. I had to say the words so that I could continue to operate in her best interest. With tears rolling down my face, I said, "What if she dies?" The mere act of asking it caused me to put my face in my hands and cry with shuddering intenseness. I couldn't face it, yet knew I had to.

Kris picked up my face and forced me to look at her. "She's alive right now, Evie. We're going to do everything we can to make sure she stays that way."

Okay, I know better. I know how the disease – melanoma – progresses and I know her chances. What no one knew was how and why the disease progressed as fast as it did. When I left there? I was going to search for Warren Trick myself. Rachel dropped so many hints that he knew what was happening and why that I wasn't going to wait for the stupid police to start an investigation. I was going to start my own. Okay, okay. Mario was going to do it and I was going to help him. First, though, was the preliminary diagnosis on Mom. I owed it to her to be a precise as possible – my breakdown notwithstanding.

The first thing they were going to do was a biopsy. Since this particular strain of melanoma was fierce – and that particular form of cancer was aggressive anyway – the first thing Kris wanted to do was make sure they were dealing with cancer and not some other disease. Still, the first thing they did was consult with the hospital oncologist, a doctor named Barry Strait.

While Kris was busy consulting with Dr. Strait, I went to see Mom. It was close to two o'clock in the morning, but she was still awake. From the look in her eyes, I'd say she was thinking about her condition. Maybe she was talking to my father. Maybe she was making peace with her life. I don't know. What I knew was that she blinked away all those private thoughts when she saw me. Then she smiled. "You've been crying."

Hadn't *she*? Well, no. She'd do that when Brad got here. "Yeah, sorry," I said. Then I tried to get serious. "Mom? Don't worry. We'll beat this."

She might be the definition of the eternal optimist. Growing up, there was always a crisis to handle. Given the nature of her business – being a PI – there was always one to handle, too. We were her greatest fear. Her family. Us. Everything she did professionally was to protect us from them.

She reached up and touched my cheek. "I'm sure you'll do everything in your power. In that sense? I'm not worried."

That meant that something did worry her and it wasn't a very hard thing to guess. Mortality. She was scared to die. All of us are. "Mom?" I said taking her hand. "You promise me that you'll talk to Dad?"

"Oh, yes," she said smiling. "I will most definitely talk to Brad."

I didn't want to leave her bedside. I wanted every last minute I could get with her. Forget Rachel, Spite and even Warren Trick. Forget John North and everything they represented. I wanted time with my mother and I wasn't sorry at all. I suppose that's another way of saying that I wouldn't have left at all unless two things hadn't happened.

First, Kris came in and said, "Doctor Strait wants your input on the biopsy and then cytokine therapy."

I squeezed Mom's hand and said, "Don't go away, you hear?"

"Promise," she said.

The second thing wasn't going to happen until I was done with Doctor Strait. He was outside the door to the iso unit when I exited it. I didn't know how he'd managed to get there so fast, but I was glad to see him. I extended my hand and said, "Thank you for being here.?"

He took it and said, "Let's save the pleasantries for when your mother is well."

He outlined right there what he wanted to do. They already had a small piece of the tumor and were in the process of a biopsy. Cytokine therapy tries to heighten the effects of the immune system. He outlined that as the next step if the biopsy came back positive.

"Your know about the Hardiman case?" I asked.

"Of it."

That brought the subject of SARMs to mind. Their original object was to add muscle mass to cancer victims. In each of the previous eight cases, SARMs were the preferred method of treatment after the primary one failed. In five of the eight previous cases, cytokine was the first treatment given. In the other three, chemotherapy was administered to limbs that had been isolated from the rest of the body by a tourniquet. If you sensed that I wasn't convinced that either treatment was going to work, then you guessed right. The fact that *Alex Payne* had fronted their use to me was a red flag now. As a doctor, Alex was a good librarian. Whatever.

But what prompted that recommendation? And why didn't it work? On the surface it seemed like good therapy, a good idea. Patients suffering from a disease of the skin could use the added muscle mass. Treatment for the disease would debilitate them and the drugs would serve to strengthen their body. They hadn't. In fact, I could extrapolate from the data that they hastened the disease. Why?

"I'd rather that you didn't use SARMs in this case or steroid-bases therapies either. In the Hardiman, and others that I am aware of, neither of those therapies worked. I don't know what's different about this strain, but something is. Maybe something antiangiogenic?" I had hope that a drug like that might help. They inhibit the growth of new vessels that tumors need to grow and propagate. If we could limit the size and location of the three tumors, we might be able to stop the disease and handle it.

He nodded and said, "That might work. Where will you be?"

Kris smirked and said, "Sleeping in the resident dorm."

"Is that a problem?" I asked.

"Not at all," she said. "There's more space than we need anyway."

That was when Mario popped up and provided the second impetus to what was going to happen. To that point, he was nothing more than a background figure. He had no expertise in medicine past band-aids and knew it. So, he listened while I discussed Mom's treatment with people who were qualified to help me. Well, damn. Barry was more qualified than I was. He was only agreeing with my recommendations.

Anyway, when I headed back to where my mother was fighting for her life, he stopped me and said, "You've never been a wallflower, Evie. Don't start now."

"And what does that mean?" I snapped.

"You're going to spend all your time watching your mother die. You're going to wring your hands and then fall into grief when it happens. I hate the word proactive because it's overused and misused. But in this case?" he said nodding toward Mom's room, "I think it's warranted."

"And what would you have me do?"

"Help me find out who's behind this and then end it."

"And if my mother dies while I'm running around Montana looking for spooks and spies?"

He took a deep breath and said, "Then I lose the best sex life in the western United States."

Damn, but I wanted to claw out his eyes. I wanted to use every pejorative in the dictionary and invent some new ones. He was going to prevent me from being with my mother. One of the issues, however, was Mom. She was his sister. What he was telling me was simple: he was going to forego whatever time his sister had left in this world to find whatever was killing her. I knew he loved her because our common past was full of countless examples and reasons. But he came to one solid conclusion: his sister was in good hands and he needed me to help him do this. Whatever this was.

I put my face in his and growled, "Sex life? What sex life? You just find an answer or me and you are going to have trouble."

He knows me better than I'd like to admit. Why do I say that now? Because I was asleep in the passenger seat before we got home.

I dreamed of Indians and didn't know why.

Chapter 33

How Mario knew Pee Wee's phone number is beyond me but he knew it. Knowing Alex, probably from him. "Hey, Reese?" he said on his side of the conversation. "Anything on North?"

We were sitting in the parking lot of the radio station. Mario was alert, but I was still groggy from getting only four and a half hours of sleep. Maybe my days as a resident were farther behind me than I thought. I yawned and Mario took his right hand and tweaked my left nipple. I smacked him. He smiled. Damn man. Then I smiled. *Okay. I get it. You're trying to keep me awake and alert. I appreciate the thought.* I sipped at the coffee from the driving cup.

"Yeah, well you keep looking for him because that bastard is involved in this and you were the one that organized this fiasco." Then he dropped into listening. After a few seconds, he said, "Well, it isn't your sister laying in a hospital room wondering how many days she has left before she goes into a coma and never awakes. You fucking remember that Reese." Then he hung up.

"Nothing, huh?" I asked.

"He's not in Portland and his present location is unknown. Unquote."

"That figures," I commiserated.

He touched my cheek and said tenderly, "I'm sorry you didn't get much sleep. But I figured this was important."

"You figured right. Now what's my role?"

"Stay beautiful and keep yourself focused as a doctor while I'll play spy."

"I can stay focused as a doctor but the rest is iffy."

I put my hand to his and closed my eyes as he said, "I still remember you. You were four and I was five. There was something different about you. And now? Even after twenty-nine years? You're still the most breathtaking woman I have ever seen."

I don't think I tell him enough, so I held his hand tight to my cheek and said, "Mario? I love you now more than I did then and I think it was pretty intense when we were kids. Please don't lose faith in me."

It felt that way. I was doing everything wrong. People died just because I visited them. That was why David Ryan's heart was beating inside Alex Payne's chest. I paid his family a visit to ask about steroids and who sold them to him and now he's dead. They were all dead simply because I was looking for them. Dyan Hardiman, too. All of them simply because I had a medical mystery on my hands and was following my own personal itch. They'd be alive if I wasn't this way.

"I can see it," he said. "You're blaming yourself for what happened. Consider this please: how many other kids would be dead without you trying to find out why? And what is the object here? Why kill all those people that way?"

Without knowing it, he'd just named the reason this was happening. Well, to be truthful, I didn't realize it either. I was drinking in every last ounce of Mario Collins that I could get. Still, I couldn't have seen the reason even if Mario hadn't been trying to reassure me that my role in this was both justified and justifiable.

"Maybe we do what we came here to do."

"Wouldn't hurt."

I forced myself to smile. "And that is?"

"Foraging for information."

"And my job is to be beautiful and medically relevant?"

"Yep."

"Let's go."

The parking lot in which we parked had one car besides ours in it. It was an old Ford pickup and looked as used as reclaimed motor oil. And no, I don't know what that is.

Anyway, we went into the station and Spite wasn't there. It was a man, a kid. A year or two on either side of twenty, my guess was twenty-one. A nice little brush-up was as much effort as he gave his hair. He hadn't shaved, but then it wouldn't have been noticeable anyway. I don't know what not being able to grow a beard does to men in male circles, but I didn't care either.

As Mario engaged him in conversation, I watched the young man. His answers to Mario's questions indicated depression of some type. He looked tired, winced several times as Mario talked with him, his muscles twiched and he seemed tired. I nudged Mario out the way and said, "Excuse me. My name is Doctor Collins. Can I ask you a question?"

"Sure?" he answered, his eyes losing their focus for a moment.

"Have you ever been tested for multiple sclerosis?"

He tried to remain still, but failed. "Um. No? Why?"

"Because you show some symptoms of the disease. At the least, you need an MRI that could help eliminate other conditions. A blood test, too."

"Are you the one that was on the air yesterday with Warren?"

"Yes."

"Um? Is this him?" he asked, twitching visibly.

"My uncle? Yes."

"And you're not related to him by blood?"

"No. Otherwise? Who would give us a marriage license?"

"You're married?"

Mario smiled and nudged me. "He just called Travis a bastard." Then he shrugged and said, "Well, when the Giants win…"

I gave him my coldest stare and said, "Do you mind?"

He moaned and closed his eyes and he said, "Oh, god. I love it when you get bossy."

"Pig," I added. But I was smiling, too. When I turned back to the kid, I said, "Whether or not we're married, practicing incest or are the nicest people you ever met has nothing to do with your condition. Go to the hospital and see the ER doctor on duty. Tell them I sent you and you'll be tested. Then do whatever they tell you."

"Warren said it's nothing more than a muscle twitch."

I could cite statistics to him concerning the disease, but said merely, "The average lifespan of a non-treated person is eleven years after the onset of symptoms – and you already have some. They can clarify your condition and help you. Even if you don't have MS, you can get help for whatever it is. Please go, get tested and help yourself." Then I looked at him squarely and said, "And helping yourself seems to be what Warren is all about. If he doesn't agree you should get tested? Then you have to be suspicious about anything else he says."

A bell sounded somewhere and he said, "Excuse me. That's my signal for the network news."

As Mario watched the kid hurry into the control room, he whistled and said, "Damn. An ass like that and she's smart, too." Then he looked at me and said, "Maybe we should get married. Who cares if I'm your uncle?"

"I thought Travis wasn't a bastard?"

"Well, the Dodgers lost yesterday, so…"

I suppressed a giggle, looked down and said, "When we get home…"

"Ooh, a threat."

The kid came back out and looked nervous despite his condition. It was difficult to unwrap the symptoms, but that's how I read him. In short? He was different before he went into the control room. His nervous twitches were still there, but there was something else in the wind as well. He looked around the room and finally asked me, "Is MS genetic?"

"Unknown," I replied honestly.

"But it's possible?"

"Yes."

He started muttering to himself. The only word I heard was "kids". I reached across the narrow counter and put my hand on his forearm. "You have a girlfriend?"

He nodded, but made it look miserable.

"And she likes you despite everything she sees?"

He shrugged, but nodded.

"Then tell her what I said and make a decision with her about children. Don't cut her out of the decision because if she's with you and sees this stuff, then all the twitches and spasms in the world won't matter to her. You matter more than they do. Just talk to her."

"But, what if…"

I smiled and said, "Talk to her. Make the decision jointly. Don't cut her out of it."

He looked at me, then Mario. "You're here because Spite and Rachel aren't, huh?"

Mario nodded once and said, "Yeah."

"And Warren made you look foolish," he said to me.

I smiled. "Well, he tried."

"There are people who think he succeeded."

"And there are those who think he missed by a wide margin. I've been on the receiving end of stuff like that for so long that it no longer bothers me. My job is to help people, not belittle and humiliate them."

He looked down at the counter, his shoulder jerking mildly just once. He glanced at Mario but said nothing to either of us. Mario began to ask a question, but his face came up and he said to me, "You don't even know my name."

"MS doesn't have a name."

"I could be anyone. I could be putting on an act."

"I'm not giving you anything but advice. True, I think you should take it, but if not? Well, sooner or later, the truth will come out. Either you're in trouble medically or you'll threaten us in some obscure way and feel superior to us. Truth?" I said leaning down toward his face. "I've been threatened before. By professionals. You can't say anything that will scare me. So unless you have something to tell us, we're going to leave."

He remained, head down, silent. I turned to leave and heard him say, "My name is Greg."

"My name is Evie and this is Mario."

"Will you be my doctor?"

"Come to my office in a week and yes."

"Why a week?"

"Because Warren is doing something with cancer that has infected my mother. Unless I find an answer, she'll be dead in a week."

He started to write something on a pad of paper. I stopped him and said, "No notes. Just tell me."

It was an address.

"It's the only place I know outside of the station when he stays."

"So, he should be here?"

"An hour ago. And Spite and Rachel, too. No one has called and I'm running the place by myself. If he doesn't show up by noon, by airtime? I don't know what I'll do."

"Want some advice?"

"Please."

"Go home and watch TV."

"By my job…"

"Is pretty much over," I said. "Why?" I shook my head and said, "No idea. It just feels that way."

"Do you have an office?"

"Right across from the medical center. Ask the ER doctors and they'll point you in my direction."

"Thanks." He said finally.

"Stand up straight," I said. When he did, I looked at him and saw several signs that he might have MS. The issue were those tests. That was the only way he was going to know. If he had it? Well, doctors could help. Without them? Ten years. Maybe eleven. And those were averages. It could be less. "Get those tests, Gary. Go over there and tell them I sent you."

"Thank you, Doctor…"

"Six," I said smiling.

"Well, thank you. I'll do that. Honest."

We left.

Mario murmured, "Lake Mary Ronan."

Gary gave us an address, but it meant nothing to me. Was the lake even in Montana? If so, where? So, I asked. "Where is it?"

"Just west of Flathead Lake. Not far."

"I can hear it. What?"

"The village of Lake Mary Ronan is on the northern end of the lake. That's the address he gave us. If Warren Trick wants to be inaccessible to people, that would be a good place. I'm going to need to find the address."

I smacked him. "You mean 'we' are going to need to find the address."

He smirked. "Well, I'm going to use a computer mapping program, but you can sit in my lap if you want to."

I pushed him toward the Hummer. "Just go."

He grinned. "So the answer is no?"

Despite my anxiety about my mother, I grinned and said, "Maybe."

"Cool."

I was in a for a long night.

Very.

Chapter 34

Mom was in pain. Worse, the tumor now covered her entire right shoulder and licked down her back to below her shoulder blade. In the ten hours since I'd last seen her, they had grown in size by several hundred percent.

Quinn said, "She's been refusing sedation until she sees you." He was on duty, but wasn't the attending physician. That was Barry, Doctor Strait.

Strait said, "She's being difficult, Doctor. Please make her understand that we're only trying to help."

Biting my lip, I said, "Sure."

Entering to where she lay was excruciating. I could see the pain in her eyes. Yes, she was trying to mask it, but when you've spent your entire life looking for the smallest problems in your mother, you come to recognize the signs. She was being brave for both of us. For me because she didn't want me to worry. Well, I would and did. But for herself because that was the way she lived her life. She ignored pain and dealt with life and not death. Obviously, this was not going to change the way she lived.

"Mom?" I said smiling. "You've been misbehaving again. You have to let them help you."

She winced but tried to mask the pain she felt. But I knew where it hurt and how much. The pain was considerable. If it stayed that way, she would handle it. But it wasn't and she wouldn't be able. "What do you hear from Barbara?" she asked.

"Nothing. Mario's talked with her twice and she hasn't returned either of his calls with anything. I have to assume we're in this by ourselves." I took her hand and looked down at her. She was hurting and I was seven again. This time? Her pain was real and – like then – I had no answers. Unlike then, she was going to die unless I found an answer somewhere, somehow. Alone? Despite everyone who was trying to help,

I felt that way. My self-proclaimed job had always been to keep her alive and now I was failing at my calling.

She turned her face away from me. In that instant, I saw fear. I can't say she's been fearless because that's not true. She feared for us, her family. Her reaction was always a bit beyond. Just beyond. She found the strength somewhere to keep all of us on track and ready for life. She did that for us. For me. She allowed a rich brat from Maine to grow up with something besides money. She did that. She helped all of us find a path and explore it. Yes, I've heard the family gossip that she came to be that way because of Grandpa Jack. There was nothing she wouldn't do for him and the reason has always been obvious. Why her? What did she do to deserve being adopted by him? What toss of cosmic dice found the two of them needing each other the day they found themselves facing each other on The Prom back home? And now? The little girl who was afraid that her mother was going to die from the aspirins she took for a headache was really going to die and she had no idea how to stop it? *Don't you dare cry. She'll haunt you forever if you do. She expects you to do everything in your power to help her. Crying doesn't help.*

"Hey?" I said to her. "I'm over here."

"Sorry," she said. Then she squeezed my hand and said, "Call her! Call Barbara yourself! She knows something! Call her!"

"Mom?" I said with disappointment in my blood. "The coroner? North? He's involved in this. I got that from a third party."

I think it is possible to find yourself at a point in your life when you begin to question every decision you ever made. You find yourself wondering if the cascade of failure started with the way you raised your oldest daughter. You find yourself wondering why you followed the path you did. You question everything about your life because it put you *here*. That's what I saw on her face when I broached the news about John North. No, I didn't know him. She did. But then I think she knows everyone back home – and not because she's their congresswoman. She made it her business to know them, to know her neighbors. But something in her eyes screamed a betrayal so fundamental that I believe she began to die right there. She saw a decision somewhere, one that she made and saw it as so flawed and wrong that it challenged everything that followed it. I also knew her well enough to know that she wasn't going to tell me what it was. It was going to fall to me to find an answer for this. In that sense, my life hadn't changed. My motivation had. I had to find the answer that put John North at odds with her.

She sighed and began to die. I saw it in her eyes. The spark I'd always seen in them was gone. No, please. Don't misunderstand. The disease was killing her. That's not what I mean or meant. Before I mentioned North? She would have died defiantly. Now? Death might have been a godsend.

Well, no. Goddammit, no. I looked down at her and did something most unprofessional. "Mother? I am not done with you yet. Don't you dare die!" But she didn't care. Something was gone and I didn't think it would ever come back.

"Evie?" she said with defeat in her voice. "Please tell Doctor Strait I'm ready to be sedated."

"Mother…"

"Please?"

It was the first step toward death. The pain would eventually become so intense that they would induce a coma to help her. The theory was simple: eliminate her pain by making her unconscious and then cure whatever is wrong with her. But everyone knew. She had just admitted there was nothing we could do. She was going to die and I was helpless to stop it.

And she refused to look at me.

It hurt more than anything I'd ever endured. Every time I viewed her life with the calm and deliberate voice of reason, she swamped me. She led her life as though nothing could stop her. The stories about her on the hill back home – Munjoy Hill to outsiders – are legend. The one that no one believes is The Kiss. Her best friend, Paula Watkins, was dying in a Portland hospital. There was nothing they could do. That's what the doctors admitted by their actions. But not Mom. She knew that Paula had an aversion to being kissed by a woman. No, not a homosexual aversion, but one that maintained she could only kiss her husband *like that*. So, Mom leaned over her hospital bed and gave her the best kiss she could deliver. Tongue included. The medical staff was astounded when Paula began to come back. When she recovered, Paula asked simply, "Why? I can't die until I know why you did that?" And like me, Mom told her best friend, "Because I'm not done with you yet."

And now there was nothing left. There were no more miracles. She was going to die and not because I wasn't going to kiss her. There were no magic bullets or spells or wands or heroes that were going to pull a rabbit out of a hat anywhere. She was going to die.

And that was a medical fact, a medical guarantee.

It was hard to leave her bedside. I tried talking to her, being reasonable, being unreasonable, being a bitch, being a daughter, being her little girl again. Nothing helped. She wouldn't look at me. She preferred death to whatever life held beyond that bed. She wanted to die and I couldn't make her tell me why.

It wasn't hard to beat down the obvious guesses. She had an affair with him. No. That wasn't it. Mom had that affair once in her life and John North wasn't it. It was long ago and had nothing to do with whatever this was.

Dad was there.

I don't know where he'd been but he was there and he held me as I cried. I mumbled something about John North and he said quietly, "Oh, fuck."

So I looked at him and begged, "What, Dad? Please tell me. What is it about him?"

He looked at me sadly. "You realize that she's the sixtieth vote?"

"No…" I said not understanding.

"The sixtieth Senate vote. She's independent but will vote with them, the Democrats."

"And North?"

"He runs her campaign committee."

"But," I said turning back to where Mom lay. "How does that translate into what I saw in there?"

Brad Chang is my father. He is everything a little girl needed in one. He was supportive when I needed him to be, strict when necessary and always understanding. But now? His wife, my mother, was dying and he needed something from me, a piece of reassurance that I didn't have, advice I could not give, life that wasn't in my power to grant. All I did was cry. And he held me. And I never got an answer about John

North, about why her shock went to suicidal lengths. At least he held me. In that sense, we was stronger than me.

I didn't have the strength to continue.

Had Mario not dragged me out of the hospital, I would have stayed there and watched her die. Mario? Thank you. That is not something I want to watch.

I'm a coward, I think.

Chapter 35

The perfect father, the perfect son had devolved to the perfect husband. The rich kid from Maine had the perfect fucking life and the perfect fucking husband was going to rub her face in it.

We drove south on 93 all the way to Dayton, which is on the western shore of Flathead Lake. Not ten miles from Lake Mary Ronan, we were headed for a showdown with the man who broke my mother's will to live. I remained silent as Mario drove the Hummer south. I'd like to say I was despondent – well, I was - but I was thinking about her condition, the cancer that was eating her and what could be done to slow down and defeat the disease. Nothing came to mind.

Once In Dayton, he got onto Lake Mary Ronan Highway and pulled off on the shoulder once the small town was behind us.

"Evie?" he said, his voice even and full of a confidence I didn't feel. "I need you to be focused and you're not. She's your mother, but she's my sister, too. She isn't dead and we owe her our best effort while that is still true."

"I know," I said miserably. "I just can't believe it."

"What do you expect out here?" he asked. "What do you expect to do?"

That was simple. "Reason with him. I don't carry a gun, never have and never will. I'm proud of the fact that I've dedicated my life to keeping people alive. Him? North? He's dealt with death in his job as coroner. But why this? "I'm not built to swarm that house with a SWAT team and wouldn't even if I was. I want to know why. That's all. If that's not good enough, then leave me here and go do this by yourself."

It was an empty bluff and both us knew it. He doesn't like guns any more than I do. He wouldn't leave me here, but wouldn't stay here either. He was going to allow me to confront the man that murdered my mother.

"He'll kill you," he said.

"I doubt that. I can't prove anything against him. Hear-say evidence isn't admissible and that's all I've got."

"You're going to ask him how he did it. At that point? You'll be a primary witness. He'll have no choice but to kill you."

Well, no. I've seen his special madness in others. I'll plead with him to *know* and he won't tell me. He'll smile with a false superiority and tell me to go home and finish watching my mother die. Maybe he'll tell me the reason he doesn't like her, but he won't be stupid enough to break discipline. He'll stand ten feet tall and look down upon me as a mortal not worth his time. In that sense? I'd get a reason he hated my mother, but not an admission that he was responsible for her death. He'll look at me and know that I'd never get the final answer to how he did it, what the mechanism was, but would gladly tell me that he hated her with enough venom to kill her.

"Mario?" I said feeling empty. It was an old emotion, one I've carried since Al Livingston took his own life in front me and I did nothing to talk him out of it. "He'll let us leave. He'll tell me why he hates Mom, and then smile. He won't even tell me how that bug got into her system. He'll make me go back to the hospital and watch Mom die."

"You're betting your life," he said.

"And yours," I answered. "Are you willing to take the chance that I'm right? Besides, what worse could he do to me than to make me watch Mom die?"

He gripped the steering wheel and looked up the road. "When Mom and Dad were murdered? That was worst day of my life." Then he looked at me and said, "And you know how I lived before they adopted me." Then he hit the steering with the palms of his hands and said, "And I've tried, Evie! I've tried to be above that sort of violence, but this? He's going to kill my sister!"

I put my left hand on his right forearm and said, "And our children? You'd condemn Travis and Madison to live without parents?"

"It's hard is all I'm saying. I understand your point-of-view, but it's hard to see myself in that room facing him and just let him go."

You can't be with someone as long as I've been with him and not *know*. It was in his eyes, written on his face and in the way his mouth curled downward. It was in his hair, the way he moved his head, the way he used words and how he was taking the time with me to explain himself. He had a plan, something that was already in the works. We were here and not on the road because he needed to tell me about it. We were here and not on the road because he knew I couldn't abide secrets, not now. "What is it?" I asked suspiciously. "Who else is going to be there besides you and me?"

"Norm Houser, a couple of state cops and Cayn. The state guys have jurisdiction."

My next question would have been, "When did you arrange all this?" before I could ask it, though, I realized that he'd had so much time to do this that I'm surprised it took me this long to realize it. That left me with my fallback position. "No one gets killed, dammit."

"Even North?"

"Especially him," I said. "I only want answers, not his life."

"He took Melodie's."

"And you know what Ghandi said."

"Yeah. An eye for an eye leaves the whole world blind. It doesn't make it any easier."

I wiggled his hand free from the steering wheel, held it and said, "So, that's why we're here. You want me to talk you out of simple vengeance."

There were tears in his dark eyes as he turned to face me. "I don't think you can. Okay, it's my sister. But it could be Travis or Madison."

"Or Wanda or Norma or any of them. That doesn't make it right and you know it." I gripped his hand tighter and said, "I'm a doctor, not a killer. And you're a man trying to teach children right from wrong. How could you go back to that school with a death on your hands?"

"They'd understand," he said harshly. "Hell, they'd expect it."

"And that makes it right? I thought your job with them was to teach a better way, not the same old one that got us here in the first place. And don't forget their parents. They put those kids in your school because they expect something different than the usual revenge killings. They expect wisdom."

"Then why does it feel like cowardice?" he asked as the tears broke free and rolled down his face.

The same question I asked myself not that long ago. I felt like a coward when I forced myself from the hospital to be *here* doing this. "Wow, a couple of cowards out to change the world." I kissed his cheek and said, "Who woulda thunk it?"

And we stared at each other as traffic passed us on the road. I wiped his tears and said, "I know it's hard, but are our convictions nothing but words? Vengeance is easy. Peace is tougher."

"Would Melodie agree?"

"You know better."

"She killed many times as a PI."

"And tried to teach us what you're trying to teach those kids. Moral convictions are hard. Or should be. Preach vengeance and you'll have a large following. But no one will remember them. Teach peace and people might listen."

"Yeah," he snickered. "Right before they kill you."

"But at least your life meant something. All those people following blindly? Who will remember them?"

"So, you're doing this for fame?"

"I'm doing this because it's how I feel." Then I kissed his nose and said, "And you know it."

He leaned over the center console and hugged me. "Thank you, Evie. Thank you for making it right."

"And Houser? Does he agree with us?"

"Nope and you know it, too."

"Then let's end this peacefully and make his type redundant."

I smiled and said, "I don't think that's how Wanda sees him."

He laughed. "She sees him without pants."

"Let's go protect him from himself."

I'd like to say that this started the rest of my life, but I'd be wrong. It started the rest of Mom's life.

Please…

No…

But we went anyway.

Chapter 36

The town of Lake Mary Ronan doesn't qualify as one. A village? A wide spot in the road? Whatever. Warren Trick's home was on the western flank of the mountain that bordered the north side of the lake. Nothing was beyond it but forest. As a place for a showdown, it was perfect. The nearest building was at least a mile away. The Gunfight at the OK Corral could erupt out here and no one would hear it.

"Where's Norm?" I asked.

"In the hills on the back side of the house."

"Let's try to keep him there."

The road that led up to Trick's home was a single lane of asphalt. I tried to visualize it in winter, but couldn't. Who would come up here to plow the road? Knowing it was irrelevant to why we were here made it unnecessary to wonder about. It made the rest of the property similarly irrelevant. We were there to see John North, not wonder how he got his driveway plowed.

There were half a dozen cars in the lot that faced his home. They were the usual types of vehicles you would expect in the mountains. Four-wheel drive pickup, SUVs and one Lexus Hybrid. If any of them had a Maine license plate on it, I didn't notice. Mario parked next to a Ford Escape.

The weather was nice. The sky was high, blue and endless. It was why I moved here in the first place. Los Angeles was too crowded, too spoiled and too much. This place, minus people like John North, was paradise. Wanda asked me once why I didn't move back to Maine. The answer was easy. I can't fail there. My family won't allow it. I'd be their doctor and practice safe medicine. It was why I went to Compton in the first place. I knew I'd see a side of medicine I wouldn't see in Portland. Yes, Portland can be violent. This is, after all, America. Violence is our national pastime. We fight the war on drugs, on cancer, on poverty, on terrorism and each other every day of our lives. No, I was looking for someplace new, someplace where there was a tradeoff between lifestyle and the violence that has become America. Montana is perfect and I can't see myself moving from here.

We got out of the Hummer and I stood by the side of it while Mario walked around the back and came up behind me and wrapped his arms around me. Heaven. If it exists, that's what it feels like, like his arms around me. It isn't celestial, ethereal, but as real as his arms. I can only hope that he feels the same way.

"God, I'd love this," he said.

Okay. Maybe he does. I let the moment linger under the wide porch that wrapped around the front of the building.

"Let's do this," he said at last.

"Okay," I said and kissed him. Then I said with a smile, "I hope that's what you meant."

"Nothing else," he said and then kissed me back.

As kids, we traded silly kisses. As we grew slowly older, we wondered what a real kiss would entail, what it be like. It wasn't until after I was raped at sixteen that I knew what it was, what a kiss was. It was protection and promise and shelter and love and understanding and an offer to help each other forever. It was that and so much more. A true kiss, I came to believe, entailed exchanging pieces of ourselves with the other. I know he gave me a piece of himself the first time he ever kissed me. I think the reverse was true as well. You trade places for a bit. You become helpless in that moment, helpless and stronger than life, helpless and able to leap tall buildings. You become immortal if only for a little while. And then? In front of that house? I felt like I could do anything.

"Husband?" I said. "Let's rock."

He grinned and said, "Dang. I was just getting the hang of country and western."

"A thing for which I'll have to talk to Wanda."

We walked up the steps hand-in-hand and Mario knocked. There was no doorbell.

After a few nervous moments, Rachel Wells opened the door. A hovering presence behind her turned out to be Spite. She held the gun. Rachel looked scared. "Come in," she said fearfully, her eyes darting all over. You didn't have to be a doctor to recognize the stress she felt.

Everything was made to look heavy and masculine. The head of a buck over a fireplace punctuated it.

"In here," Spite said, a bruise marring her cheek.

Rachel had a black eye, her left. The eye was totally closed. She walked with a limp.

We were led to a nicely furnished kitchen. Then we were directed down a flight of nice steps into a basement. Everyone was there. North, Trick and another man I didn't recognize. Trick doubled his fist and punched Rachel in the stomach. She dropped to her knees and then started retching. He said to Spite, "When she gets up? Punch her again and again and again." Then he punched her in the stomach despite the gun she held. God knows what kept the gun from going off, but it didn't. Her hand should have flexed against the trigger and the gun should have discharged. Then I saw it. *It isn't loaded. They don't trust her.* Punching her was nothing more than letting us know where the power lay in this room.

"All I want from you, North, is an answer. Why my mother? What did she do to you to deserve to die like that?"

Mario held my hand.

North's appearance hadn't changed. He was still gray. His hair, his clothes, the way he spoke. It was designed to highlight the fact that his life was colorless. Even his gray eyes looked lifeless.

Mario said to the second man, "You're Paul Fields."

He smiled and it looked successful. "At your service," he said with a short bow.

Then Mario said, "You planned this in Canada. When Melodie insisted on no cell phones, it worked into your plan precisely. With no phones and record of phone calls, none of this could be traced to you."

Odd. I've never mentioned Paul Fields to him. There was no point. He's Canadian and as such, had no point in this mess. It made Deborah Hollis' role that much more prominent. Fields was nothing more than a spy. Hollis was a doctor. If North was behind this and Canadians were involved, then Hollis was a prime player. But did it matter? Knowing wouldn't save Mom's life. She was going to die. That much was a scientific fact. All I wanted was out of here so I could be with her at the end.

"Just tell us why, North," I said. "My mother did nothing to you."

The gray men of the world live in the shadows where they are neither dead nor alive. They blend into whatever backgrounds in which they find themselves. Or? What was the name of the coroner who did the autopsy on anyone you can name? Your aunt? Your father? A movie star? Coroners do their job in the gray places, in the shadows that are neither black nor total. They operate silently and leave few traces. No, I don't hate them. They merely are necessary for what they do for us. They clear suspicious deaths and find answers for those that need them. No, not cops. I mean families and people who want to know what happened to their loved one. And that was the niche that John North filled with silent precision. He found answers for us.

I don't think the gray people are eloquent. If so, they wouldn't be gray. They'd stand out from their background and you would remember them. Having said that, North tried to stand out from the crowd. The sneer he wore on his face was palpable enough, but wasn't enough to answer my question. "She was a bitch," he said, his voice trying to add depth to his issue. It didn't.

I laughed. "Mom didn't become a bitch overnight. It took years," I said rolling my eyes.

Mario high-fived me.

"You know what I mean!" he yelled.

"No I don't," I said and meant it. "Mom treated everyone the same and most of them didn't try to kill her." I rolled my eyes again and said, "And *those* times were years ago. I mean, no one tried to kill her in…Jesus…fifteen years? So, what did she do to you that makes her death the only answer?"

"She…" and he stopped himself. We were at the bottom of the stairs. North and the rest of them were arrayed around us. He produced a gun from inside his coat and pointed it at me. "Move over there," he said indicating a spot by the wall opposite the stairs.

I held my purse in front of me as we crossed the room. I'd say I was scared, but I wasn't. Well, not for me. I wanted to be there before Mom died. I wanted to say everything that was in my heart to say.

Mario was to my right as North crossed the room to face us, me. He held his gun out at Mario and said, "Don't move. If you do? I swear…"

Then he punched me in the stomach with his right hand. I sank to the floor and Mario knelt with me as I did. North said something I didn't pay attention to and the basement emptied of everyone except us. Then I heard a deadbolt slide and a door latch shut and didn't need to ask what door it was. We were locked in the basement and I had no idea why.

Meanwhile, my mother was nearing death.

As my breath began to return, Mario whispered in my ear, "Let me know when you can talk."

I nodded and took a few gasping breaths. Then I looked up at him and nodded.

He reached for my purse and opened it. He pointed at something and it took a long moment before I realized what it was. The blinking red light betrayed it as some sort of bug. I mouthed, "Transmitter?"

"Yes," he answered the same way.

"Bastard," I mouthed back. Then I bit his ear and whispered, "You couldn't just tell me?"

He pretended to bite my nose and whispered, "I just did."

Then I started to cry. It seemed like the best way to hold onto my role as hostage. But you remember I said I wasn't a spy? Well, as events were going to prove, I wasn't. Mario was.

Mad? Oh, god. That man is *always* ahead of me. I'm busy seeing holistic approaches to health and he's busy plotting the perfect crime – or rescue as it were.

As I cried, he held me and tried hard not to laugh. I didn't think we were in danger. Neither did he.

Well….

Things kinda got spooky.

Real fast.

Chapter 37

We were sitting on the bottom step of the stairs that led back to the kitchen above us. There were no other doors. The only windows were narrow slits at ground level that looked out on the mountains beyond. Naturally, Mario put it succinctly.

"Well, this is another fine mess you've gotten us into."

I smiled and look at the floor between my knees. "Should I be scared?"

"Nah. No future in it."

"Why did they lock the door? If a punch in the stomach is their greatest threat, I can live with it."

He turned and looked back at the door. "They're waiting for someone."

"Hollis," I said.

"Probably."

"That means she's en route."

He turned back to me and said, "Well, she is now. They probably called her when we showed up."

I looked in my purse and said, "Hmm. Radio transmitter and cell phone. I can't believe they let us keep them."

I reached for the phone and he said, "Don't bother. There's probably a white noise generator in the house somewhere."

"Then why would the transmitter work?"

He looked embarrassed. "It probably doesn't now that I think of it."

"Great," I said.

He misunderstood my dejection. It was obvious when he started to apologize. "I'm sorry, Evie…"

"No," I said to him. "That means that Norm and the boys outside will go into full cowboy mode and start shooting." I leaned into him and said, "I don't want anyone killed. Understand?"

"Golly," he answered with a smile. "I'd never die and piss you off."

"Good thing," I said.

That left the basement and finding a way out of it. It didn't take long for us to realize that the door above us was it. We couldn't even breakout the window slits because they were made of some type of unbreakable glass or plastic. It was just us.

"Wanna mess around?" he said.

"How come to you it's 'messing around' and to me it's 'making love'?"

"So, no?"

I hugged him. "If we die down here, I'm probably going to regret passing on the offer."

He kissed my cheek. "Well, you're on top in that case. The cement floor and all."

It was odd. We sat there talking like we were on a date. We were lighthearted and in a good mood. You would never have thought that our lives were in danger. Worse was when Norm Houser showed his face in one of the window slits. Mario jumped up immediately and went to the window where he was trying to say something. I pushed Mario aside and wrote backwards on the glass with a lipstick, "NO GUNS! WE'RE FINE!" We probably weren't, but my demand for no gunplay was an adamant one. I pointed at the words I wrote on the glass and mouthed, "I mean it!"

He didn't look convinced but nodded and ran back into the hills beyond the house, the forest swallowing him entirely.

About ten minutes later, we heard the sound of a car out front. A single door closed and my guess was that Debbie Hollis was here. We waited, looking at the ceiling as we heard people walk around. Still, minutes passed, but nothing happened. Then we smelled smoke. It didn't take long before we saw it curling up under the door at the top of the stairs.

Both of us turned when someone started rapping on the window. It was Norm and he was trying to break the glass. That's when a sound at the other end of the room caught our attention. Someone had unbolted the door at the top of the stairs. We heard people running across the floor upstairs, so maybe it was as simple as a house fire.

Mario shouted in the glass as Norm listened, "The door's unlocked! We're leaving that way!"

Norm shouted something from his side and darted off. We turned toward the stairs and carefully approached the smoke coming from under the door.

"It can flash if there's a lot of flame," he said. "I'll be careful with the door."

"My hero," I said squeezing his hand.

"That does it," he said reaching for the doorknob when we got to the top of the stairs. "You're on the bottom."

"Brute," I said as he reached for the door.

The smoke spilled into our faces as he cracked the door just a little. No flames, though. I took that as a good sign. Mario pulled open the door a bit more and both of us saw flames on the other side of the kitchen. The stove maybe. If so, maybe a propane leak started the fire. Mario pulled open the door farther and we saw a growing inferno on the wall opposite us. The front door was to our right. Another door led out back, but the entire wall was in flames. We turned right and headed through the burning house.

We were coughing before we got through the kitchen. Mario stopped me and peered into the rustic living room. The wall that connected the kitchen to the living room was aflame as well. The flames burned and snapped around us as we stepped into the living room. We still saw no one. It was likely they had all fled.

"Damn, I don't like this," Mario said peeling off his shirt. Then he handed it to me and said, "Put that over nose and mouth."

I ripped it in half and said, "Ditto."

The fire was gaining in intensity but would take a few minutes more before it got to this side of the room. Smoke was rolling up the walls and most likely through the roof. The heat was considerable but not overwhelming yet. I didn't know how long we had before things got to that point, but I was totally willing to follow Mario's lead.

He leaned close to my ear and said loud enough to hear over the growing noise around us, "By the front door. You crouch on the left and I crouch on the right."

Well, why not? We moved across the room and dodged something that fell burning from the ceiling. A board of some type. That meant we had less time than we thought. We approached the open door and I immediately knelt to the left of it. Mario was crouched but then stood in the open door and remained standing for too long.

A shot rang out and he immediately reacted to a gunshot that hit him in the upper torso. It spun him around to his right and that meant the shot hit him on that side of his body. He went down hard on the floor near the door and I started screaming at him. "You stupid fool! Why did you do that!"

But I knew why. With that shot, they'd drawn first blood. It would justify what Norm and the others cops were going to do.

Still, it wasn't hard to ignore the growing gunfight out front. This one of my worst scenarios, one of my worst nightmares. As I turned him onto his back, I became dimly aware of another shot hitting the wall outside the door. It wasn't hard to ignore. Mario had my full attention. The grimace on his face scared me more than anything I'd ever felt…since my mother. Blood seeped from a wound in his shoulder. I rolled him onto his side and didn't see an exit wound. The bullet was still in him. That was better than an exit wound blowing a hole in his back.

I placed the ripped shirt against the wound and said as professionally as I could, "This isn't the best place to treat a gunshot wound. I need to get you out of the building before it collapses on us."

His grabbed my forearm but such little strength that is scared me. "Right here," he said. "They're shooting outside."

"And the goddamn building might fall on us!"

"Better to die in a fire than be killed by lunatic," he said as he winced.

And with what was I going to treat him? My medical bag was in the car, so I had to go outside anyway. "If I get killed, you better not remarry, especially not Wanda!"

His grip remained just strong enough to hold me for a moment. "Love you, Evie," he moaned.

"Hang on, dude," I said. "I'll be right back."

I looked outside and our car parked near the end of a line SUVs and hybrids. I was about to make a dash across the open ground when a gunshot sounded and I ducked back behind the wall. Two more shots sounded. I turned and looked at Mario and he was still conscious. He smiled but it held pain. *Dammit. He'll bleed to death.* That was enough motive for me. I ducked down and sprinted toward the car. I was carrying my purse and totally misjudged my coherence. I couldn't find my keys to open the door. That's when a huge pair of hands took my purse from me and said, "I really don't think you're going to need that." It was North. And he was holding a gun.

I didn't know fear until he put the barrel to my forehead and said, "You and your whole fucking family."

Then there was a shot.

And I was covered with blood.

Damn.

Chapter 38

I have seen too many people die. The first person I saw die was my rapist. Alex killed him. I was so scared when the shot fired that I froze and tried to determine if I was dead or not. It was that terrifying. This? Okay, I've seen a lot of death between when I was a sixteen-year-old rape victim and now. The worst deaths I saw were children back in LA. Most of them were victims of gunshots, drive-by's mostly. It took effort and stamina not to react to them. My job was to save them, not cry helplessly over them as they lay dying. But this? It was a death that saved my life. But who saved it? Norm Houser.

Maybe he knew the cruelest way to shoot a man. In the neck. You don't die quickly. You die from a combination of loss of blood and the inability to breathe. I watched North as his mouth moved in a futile attempt to draw air, watched as his legs lost strength and he dropped to his knees, his hands clutching his throat as his last breath remained forever out of reach. When he fell onto his face, he wasn't dead, but would never arise again either. I stood over him and asked, "Why, John? Why was this necessary? I came without a gun, without anything but a willingness to learn. Why was this necessary?" I knew I wouldn't get an answer, but didn't expect one anyway. He died with his face in the dirt.

Norm rushed to where I was standing and said, "Drop the tailgate, Evie." When I didn't move, but stared at North, he pushed me and said, "Now!" Then he hurried to the house and picked up Mario in his arms as I dropped the gate on the Hummer. My purse lay in the dirt next to North's head. Stuffing all my panic, I picked it up, found my keys and unlocked the door. My bag was on the passenger floorboard. For better or worse, I was ready to save Mario's life – or wish that North had been a second faster.

I donned my medical mask and looked at Mario. He was unconscious and bleeding profusely. If I couldn't stop the blood flow, he was dead. From the look, the bullet severed the axillary artery above the shoulder. Norm lay Mario on the tailgate and said, "I'll stay and keep them away from here."

There were gunshots behind and around me. It wasn't hard to ignore them. If I lost focus now, I'd spend the rest of my life wishing that one those stray rounds found me.

I carry a complete of tools that allow me to do my job wherever I am. That includes the scalpel with which I made an incision inside the wound. I used Bupivacaine as a local anesthetic and hoped the dosage I used was large enough.

"Norm?" I said. "Open that bottle of rubbing alcohol and pour a small amount into the wound."

It was going to hurt him, but it was necessary. When Norm poured the alcohol into the wound, Mario's entire body jerked against the pain. "Please hold him."

"Girl?" he said. "I can either be your bodyguard or your nurse."

I growled, "I won't need a bodyguard if he dies! Now, hold him!"

It was the worst operating theater in the world. Dust floated in the air, gunfire still sounded around me and my only thought was to find the severed artery, close it and hope the resulting infections from my ersatz operation were manageable in a hospital. Worse was doing the work of a nurse as well as managing everything else. As I sliced through muscle, I found the bullet and the severed artery. I desperately wanted someone to suction off all the blood in the wound, but knew that was impossible. The only fortunate aspect was that the artery wasn't shredded. If it had been, it's possible Mario would already be dead. It was possible that I was killing him anyway given the unsanitary conditions.

Frustrated with my lack of progress, I said sternly, "That suction bulb in my bag? Get it and draw out as much blood as you can."

Another gunshot startled me. It brought back the world and how scant my chances were here. Norm showed up and said quietly, "Show me where and how."

A tear rolled down my cheek.

"It's turkey gravy, Norm. Just put the bulb in the gravy bowl and suck out as much as you want."

"This is where I tell Mario you called him a turkey," he said, his voice still quiet and reassuring.

"Oh, damn," I said and began to fall into tears.

Norm held the bulb in one hand and carefully wiped away as many tears as he could as he said, "You're sweating up a storm, Doc. Just keep going. You're doing fine."

"And how the fuck would you know!" I barked. That made it worse and I withdrew my hands from the wound. "Oh, God," I said. "I'm sorry."

"Doc? I know it stressful, but he's a patient and this is what you do."

I took a deep breath and saw all that blood. No one was measuring his blood pressure, his heart rate or any vital signs at all. It was just me, a cop and the dirty tailgate of a Hummer. *And if you don't do this as best you can, Mario is dead while you stand and cry.* That put my resolve back on firm ground and I went back to work. How long did it take? I have no idea. Norm kept the bulb going and even found time to blot sweat off my forehead. Finally, I got the artery closed and then closed the wound with sixteen stitches and hoped I hadn't killed him antiseptically.

I backed away from Mario, slipped off my mask and stared stupidly at him. "Oh, my God," I said. I'd done everything wrong, done it against every rule of hygiene and medicine. "I'm sorry, Mario," I said. "Oh, my sweet God, I'm sorry."

Then I turned away from him and didn't know what to do. Literally, I was wandering around thinking of the damage I'd done to my husband. Then someone put his hands on my shoulders and said, "I drive. You're with Mario in the back. There's an evacuation helicopter down by the lake. Let's go."

Again, it was Norm.

I squatted in the back, all the seats collapsed and watched my husband die. He was pale from the loss of blood and unresponsive in every other way. I held his hand and he did not respond. "I'm sorry," I said again. "I knew better, but I did it anyway. I'm so sorry."

True to his word, the was an evac helicopter waiting. They took Mario from the Hummer and my only response was, "I'm going! I'm her husband!" No, not one of my better moments. Maybe I was so wrapped up in what I'd done to him that Evangeline Sixkiller-Collins Collins no longer existed and that was why I referred to myself as my husband and not his wife. Whatever.

They put an IV in him as they transported and called for blood when I stumbled through the scenario and how I'd operated on him. I looked at the man with the helmet and cried, "It was dirty."

"And if you hadn't?" he asked.

My mind never got that far. Ever. It stopped with the dirty tailgate, the unclean operating conditions and how I violated every precaution doctors set from themselves. I didn't save his life; I took it.

The ER doctor was Kris Tice. Wanda was there, too. They took over and I was glad. I'd done enough damage. They began a transfusion and started him on antibiotics. Maybe they could do it right. I'd done enough damage.

Finally, an ER nurse came to me and said, "Doctor? We need to talk about your mother."

And it had come full circle.

My mother was dead.

I went, numbly.

Chapter 39

She was thrashing in her bed, calling them horrid names and screeching at the top of her pain-filled lungs. She wasn't dead. Not yet. Dad was there and I was glad to see him. I hugged him and he looked scared. Maybe all of us were.

"How is he!" Mom shrieked.

A nurse said to me, "She won't allow us to sedate her. She heard about her brother and won't cooperate."

I went to her bedside and decided to be a daughter and not a crybaby. Oh, God. It was awful. The lesions that had started on her shoulder had gone up her neck and covered part of her face. It was probably in her hair, too. I can't imagine the pain. Still, she took my hand and screamed at me, "How is he! Is he dead! I won't die until I know he's okay!" All that meant was that she'd heard about Mario. Dad wouldn't have told her, but my mother had a way of learning things. Anyone could have told her. "You go and find him! You tell me that he's okay!" And she screamed, "Go!"

I was torn between them, between my mother and my husband. But Mom always got what she wanted, so I went.

He was in the ER being prepped for surgery. He was awake, however, and that was a good thing. Probably from the blood they gave him. Still, I was worried about the infections, but the medical staff knew about the conditions under which I operated on him. No one faulted me. Kris said, "He would have bled to death, Evie."

Despite all my knowledge of medicine and physiology, I asked the same question any wife would ask. "How do you feel?"

"Like someone shot me," he said painfully.

The monitors showed his vitals. Blood pressure, heart rate up, but otherwise, everything was within normal ranges. From what I saw, I thought his body was beginning to fight the inevitable infections from my stupid gamble.

Kris came up beside me and smiled down at him. "He's been flirting." Then he smiled at me and said, "I don't think he knows my status."

"Just be truthful, Kris."

"I think you saved his life, to be truthful. We're aware of your concern for the conditions on site and we're going to be feeding him a steady diet of antibiotics to make sure things don't get away from us. We're going to do an ultrasound on his shoulder, then an MRI if necessary. Don't worry. He'll be okay for you to abuse for years to come." Then she hugged me and said, "You did great, girlfriend." She hurried away because she had other patients to monitor.

I knew he was weak, in some pain and needed rest. I knew all that. Still, I think he's a better person than me. Why? Because he reached up and said, "It's Mel, huh?"

Based on what I saw, her condition, her spiking blood pressure, I could only nod.

"Will they let me see her?"

"Yes," I said. "I'll be a bitch otherwise."

His smile held some pain. It hurt my heart.

"Is she…"

"No."

"Will she?"

"Yes."

"Evie? I need to see her."

Arranging things wasn't difficult. They cleared the space in the ICU next to her bed and rolled him into it. He held my hand as they rolled his bed down the hallways. He was scared, not for himself, but for her. Melodie Chang had always been a part of his life and it was impossible to accept that she was going to die. It was cancer, inoperable and had very nearly completed its job.

Before we got into the ICU, he asked, "Is she…still Mel?"

"Yeah," I said with a broken heart.

"I love her, Evie. This can't be happening."

Just before we got to the ICU, he said, "Please, stop."

The orderly stopped the bed and I looked at him hopefully. "Alone, please?"

His name was Buck. He left with an understanding nod.

Mario was five when my grandfather bought him for three-hundred-sixty-two dollars and change. Sounds barbaric, right? Well, no. His birth mother was a crack addict and when grandpa walked into her home and saw how the boy was living, he swore that Mario would never hurt again. Even the state of Maine agreed with him. A worker went to her apartment and was as appalled as Grandpa had been. Mario has been a Collins ever since. As much as he revered and idolized grandpa, he worshipped my mother because she was the same as him – adopted. Save for Uncle Patrick, Grandma and Grandpa adopted six kids. But Melodie, my mother, was the first of all of them.

Maybe she set their roles, the ones that established that Clan Collins was better than yours, whoever you might be. That's the prevailing wisdom in the family and I agree with it – and not because she's my mother. I saw the things she did with her life and decided that someone had to be there to nurture and nurse her back to health. And now? She was going to die and there was nothing I could do but watch the train wreck.

"Have I failed her, Evie?" he asked as tears rolled from his eyes. "Has my life been something she would be proud of? I can't fail her, I can't."

She's had that effect on the entire family, even the parts that aren't related by blood. Take Uncle Alex, for example. Mario was feeling what everyone was feeling. I felt it. I had no doubt that Alex with his new heart felt it. I had no doubt that people in her district felt it, that colleagues in Congress felt it. Mom has that effect on people.

And now, it's gone, or soon will be.

His question was the one everyone was going to ask. Did I fail her? With as much strength as I could grasp, I said, "No. You haven't failed her. That school? Aunt Dora would be proud." Then I rolled my eyes and said, "Hell, she already is. I've talked to her and she wants to come out here and see it."

"She would love me anyway, Evie," he cried. "She wouldn't turn me away just because I failed."

"She isn't dead, Mario. Ask her. Just see her, talk to her and be with her. Right now? It's the best medicine you can give her."

And that was all we could say. The orderly rolled the bed into the ICU and positioned him next to his sister, my mother.

In his condition, he wasn't supposed to get out of bed. He was weak, was fighting infections and was under the effects of mild pain killers. In short, his condition was perfect for what was going to happen. Still, everyone fought him but me. It is said throughout the family that I have the best evil eye in the group. I used it on everyone that tried to steer him back to bed. Finally, Doctor Strait said, "I think he'll be fine. Or? What better place to rip out your IVs and collapse under the weight of exhaustion than a hospital." Everyone left him alone after that.

"Do you need to be alone, Doctor?" Strait asked.

"No."

Her condition caught Mario the same way it caught me. It was an ugly way to die, not one my mother ever thought she would endure. Okay, there are no noble ways to die. It just happens and nothing you can do can stop it. It's an express ride downhill. There are no hills and no morning. Your body follows the prime directive and you die. But this way? I've already said that I've seen too much death, but this was one I was never going to forget. In a world where we try to find some nobility, some purpose in death, this was a monstrous evil.

"Mel?" he said weakly. "I love you and I always will."

"Sister," she said weakly, painfully. "Not wife."

Even as she lay dying, she was better than us.

I looked into the hallway and the entire family was gathering. Aunt Dora, Aunt Tiffany, everyone. Their husbands, their wives, their children. And in front of them leading them? Her best friend, Paula Watkins. God alone knows what sort of rules she bent, who she vilified, what she said to allow them in here because there were dozens. They were here to watch The Queen die. All of them were in tears.

"Mel?" Mario said. "I've tried so hard. I've only wanted to be the best and now I find…"

And she stopped him. "Your example…has been…exemplary. Don't do this to yourself."

He touched her cheek and cried.

And me? They would insist that I was The Crown Princess. They would jostle and maneuver me into her place. And, by damn. I didn't want it. I wanted her, my mother and not a phantom, a ghost. I wanted my children to know her, to understand why she was great and wise. I wanted an active mother, an active grandmother, not a picture on a wall or a memory I could not pass along properly.

He bent down and placed a final kiss on her cheek. That's what it felt like. He was telling her goodbye. He said something to her that I did not hear. That was fine by me. It was private and meant to be that way. I would honor it.

But Mario has some of her in him. Meaning? My mother did not accept defeat. At least, not graciously. She screamed and fought and struggled until things were as she wanted them. And now? The world was going to win. Life was going to continue without her.

"Cancer, Evie?" Mario said to me. "How can this happen?"

Technically, it was easy. She was passed a carcinogen and the process began to act out its course. While I have no doubt that Debbie Hollis was the prime mover and designer of that particular carcinogen, all the hand-wringing, wailing and god-calling won't stop what was going to happen. It would continue until it squeezed the last breath from her. No, it was ugly and not a death someone like my mother should have to endure.

There are no shortcuts through science. I know that. I knew that the first time I saw a patient die under my care in an ER room. It was coarse, hard and unyielding. Death takes us and we can't look for a loophole to beat the process. We die. Even when a doctor knows the disease, he cannot change its prognosis. It's science, not wishful thinking.

But.

Mario looked at me and his heart was breaking. "Evie? Please. Do something."

I whispered to him, "It's cancer, Mario. She's in the final stages. Don't do this to her."

Then he said it. Oh, I don't think he believed it, but it was something a person in his position would say. Many surviving relatives have said such things. But the difference in this case was her doctor. Me. He said it to me and I began to read the fine print on the aspirin bottle *again*. What did he say

"What if it isn't cancer?"

Mario? After this? There is nothing I won't do for you. I'll even be on the bottom on a cold cement floor.

Yeah.

What if?

Chapter 40

Enter SARMs. Selective androgen receptor modulators. And steroids. None of the eight kids that died had used steroids. SARMs were experimental medicines that were supposed to be used to add muscle mass to cancer victims. The theory was that the added mass would help to fight the disease. Except. There have been studies that show large doses of SARMs can actually cause cancer. And there was the problem. All eight of those kids underwent SARM treatment as an early treatment option to fight the aggressiveness of the disease. And steroids? The doctors of those kids did not pursue steroids as a course of treatment. If I was right, then SARMs were used to spread the disease quicker than normal by adding muscle mass and then infecting the new tissues.

Mom said, "You're thinking, daughter."

"Mom?" I said, my mind a million miles away. "Shut the fuck up." Then I realized what I'd said and stopped thinking. "Oh, God," I said. "I'm sorry."

"Child?" she said, her voice struggling to be heard. "Tell me."

"You don't have cancer."

"Then...what..." and she was too weak to continue.

"I don't know."

'Then...think...somewhere...else..."

The doctor's lounge. I kissed Mario, Mom and Dad and ran down the hall toward the lounge. It isn't much, but it was quiet. There's a nice TV that is seldom turned on, some food in the form of crackers and water, two couches and a table. All I was able to do was pace.

Then Kris entered.

"Evie?" she said. "What's going on?"

"Kris? Do you trust me?"

"Of course. Now, what..."

"Then either help me or get out."

She crossed her arms and said, "I'm staying."

I crossed the room, took her biceps in my hands and said to her face, "Then convince me that my mother has cancer!"

"All the tests came back positive. Even a biopsy of the tissue."

"But what is the agent causing the cancer to spread as quickly as it does? What skin diseases spread that fast?"

"Actinic Keratosis."

"No. It wouldn't spread that fast?"

Her eyes widened and she said, "Melanoma, Evie!"

"Spreads quickly, but not this fast."

"Evie..."

I screamed, "Get out!"

"Psoriasis," she counted, not giving an inch.

My immediate reaction was, "No!" Then I said, "But, maybe."

"Are you kidding? Psoriasis doesn't do that!"

"Then something else!"

"Skin tags!"

I stopped and thought about it. Then, "No. Their spread isn't as dramatic as we've seen."

"Are you fucking crazy?" she said again. "Every test..."

"And what do all those victims have in common? They were treated with an experimental regimen of SARMs because no other treatment was found to be effective! We're giving medicine to cancer patients that actually add tissue into which the disease can spread!"

She leaned into me and said, "Atopic dermatitis."

"Affects mostly children."

"But can..."

I leaned into her and screamed, "Something else!"

"Eczema!"

It stopped me. Could it be? the first symptom, however, is usually itching. Had any of them complained of such a thing? "Fuck. No. None of them itched."

"Yes, they did. All of them did."

"Not as a primary symptom." Then she screamed back, "And every one of them tested positive for cancer!"

"It's not cancer!" I screamed back.

"Well, it isn't lupus either!" she yelled.

Both of us started laughing.

"What else?"

"Ehlers-Danlos syndrome," she said.

"None of them had loose skin! And my mother kept in shape! You should see the crowds when she jogs!"

"If she was my age, she'd be my lesbian partner!" Then she screamed, "Heat rash!"

"In Maine or Montana during football season!" I screamed back. "No!"

"Marfan syndrome!"

"Get serious!" I yelled back.

"I am serious!"

"Then what else?"

"Reynaud's!" she screamed.

"Affects the fingers and toes and you know it!"

"I also know skin cancer when I see it!"

"No wonder you're a lesbian! You're as stupid as a Texan!"

"I was born…"

"I know where you were born! What else, lesbo!"

"Scleroderma, hetero!"

"Starts with scar tissue! Where did you go to medical school? JC Penney!"

And then…

She said, "Hives!"

I tried to find a way around it.

Then Kris screamed, "Are you fucking serious!"

"Convince me I'm not!"

"Look at her! that is not what hives look like!"

"And you don't look like a lesbian!"

"And what does a lesbian look like!"

I was on track and nothing was going to knock me off it. "Convince me, you ugly lesbian hag! Convince me it isn't hives that has been altered and adjusted to look like cancer!"

"How is that even possible!"

"I'll ask Debbie Hollis the next time I see her!"

"Who!"

"The designer of this bug!"

"How would she make hives carry cancer tags and footprints?"

"Has the way you treated her been successful? Has her condition been helped in any way by the cancer treatments you're giving her!"

"No...but..."

Then we looked at each other and screamed in unison, "Antihistamines!" Then we screamed even higher, "In massive doses!"

"Knock holes in it," I said with a totally panic-stricken voice.

"We still can't account for the test results."

"And AIDs tests are always one hundred per cent positive?"

"You can't just dismiss them, Evie!"

We were so close to having an answer. So close.

"Dammit, Kris," I said. "Don't stop prematurely!"

"That's why I'm a lesbian! Women are never premature!"

We giggled.

Then.

"Carbuncles!"

Then.

"The same antibiotics that we're treating Mario with!"

Then I kissed her because I was so giddy, so happy and so eager to run back to Mom's room.

She stopped totally. "Um, Evie?"

"I'm sorry, Kris. I won't do that again."

"I hope not because I have the female version of having to sit down."

"Jesus, Kris. Don't tell me you're horny."

"Okay."

But we stared at each. "We could be giving her a treatment that won't do anything," I said.

"And the alternative is?"

"She dies anyway."

We turned toward the door and saw a line of four people standing there. Barry was one, Quinn Riley was another, Arthur Berrington was the third and Wanda Lansing was the fourth. They held up pieces of paper. 10, 8, 9, 10.

"Eight?" Kris said to Quinn.

"I didn't like your technique."

"Kris?" I said. "I have to hurry."

She pushed me. "Go."

"But I said…"

She put her hands on either side of my face and said, "Don't tell me you weren't working. Because otherwise, you're a bitch."

"But I was and I am."

She hugged me. "That was so cool that I never even heard the insults. I heard a doctor spurring to me to be better than I was. It was pure research. It was an exercise designed by a genius to get answers from a mortal. Damn, that was cool."

"So, you're not mad at me?"

"Mad? I'm practically in love with you."

We hugged and this when she said, "Go," it was gentle and sweet.

But I went with the stupidest diagnosis in the history of medicine. I was going to give a cancer patient antibiotics. It was asinine, wrong and was probably going to hasten her death. But with no other answers, I was committed to fighting an army with a slingshot.

If I stopped and gave it a second thought, I wouldn't do it at all.

I didn't stop.

I ran.

Chapter 41

Penicillin. Or a derivative. That's what I was thinking as I ran down the hall. I started a conversation with myself that included John North in it. I still had no answer for why he turned on my mother the way he did. But. *What one thing could he do to my mother that would cause eternal condemnation to her? Especially in this country.* Easy. A venereal disease. It hit me so hard that I stopped outside the ICU door and stared at Mom. It fit. If John North hated her that much, then he would kill her with a disease that only spreads through sexual intercourse. Syphilis. This super-bug would not only kill her, but color her supporters with its taint. In this country, it was the perfect way to smear an opponent. Not even Presidents are immune. *Debbie? You counted on me not being able to figure it out. Then you were going to announce your findings to the world. My mother caught syphilis and died from it.* The entire family was behind me. Literally. Only Dad was inside the ICU with her.

No one said anything to me as I stepped into the room. Brad saw me and looked hopeful. His black hair is streaked with gray. Mom's is still jet black and sparkles as though there are stars in it and her hair is the night sky. Okay, that makes her vain because black hair at her age is a scientific improbability. Okay, *okay.* She maintains the color of her hair through artificial devices. She colors it.

"Brad?" I said. "I think I know what's wrong with her."

Mom's breathing was labored.

"What is it? What's wrong with her?"

"She has syphilis."

"This is syphilis?" he said looking at Mom.

"Dad? I need your permission to start her on a round of penicillin."

"How long will she live if you don't?"

"A few hours."

"Okay."

The hospital got their signed release, but Dad would have let me do it anyway. He trusted me and my judgment. I wish I trusted it as much as he did.

"It would help my concentration if everyone left."

"And not be here if she dies?"

"To be a phone call away when she regains consciousness."

"Can I have a moment with her?"

"Sure," and I walked into the hallway.

Of all my relatives, Aunt Tiffany is closest to my age. We were five years apart. She has four kids of her own and runs a very successful PI operation out of an abandoned movie theater in Riverside, California. Her husband, Bobby Serrano, specializes in hardware for them and is good at it. It's possible that Mario got the bug he dropped in my purse from him. Possible? Likely.

"You look like shit," she said to me.

"You look like a runway model," I replied.

"Thanks."

"That wasn't a compliment," I answered.

"Didn't think so."

We watched as Dad talked to her. The lesions were advancing all over her body. I always thought that Mom's smile was a great one, but I wondered if I would ever see it again. I don't know what he said to her, and I'd never ask either. It was private and meant to be that way. When he finished talking to her, there were tears in his eyes that broke free and rolled unashamedly down his cheeks. Finally, he put her hand down and came out of the room. "Evie?" he said.

"Yes, Dad?"

"If it doesn't work? Just tell me that she went to sleep."

I hugged him and said nothing but, "Okay."

Aunt Tiffany led him and everyone else away and left me alone with her. That didn't last. Doctor Strait showed up. I expected an argument from him, but got none. He knew what I was doing and wasn't going to stop me. If I was wrong? Then the treatment was harmless anyway. Of course, when I stopped all the other treatments? He could have objected right there, but everyone knew her condition was terminal anyway. It was a last-ditch effort to stop the disease and maybe even reverse its course.

A nurse brought the drugs into the room in an IV bag and hung it on a hook above her bed.

"Any objections, Doctor?"

"No," he said. "Lots of reservations, but no objections."

It was a huge dose, larger than any I'd ever administered. I thought it was necessary due to the advanced stage of the disease. The only gamble I took was stopping the medication that kept her unconscious. There are any number of medical reasons why I did that, but the most basic one was that I wanted to hear her voice in some way one more time. Selfish. Okay, it's not a good way to practice medicine, but she isn't your mother either.

Strait extended his hand and said, "Good luck."

"Thank you."

And it was just me. Well, and her. I stood watching her for an eternity. She didn't move for the longest of times. Then she moaned softly and I knew the pain medication was wearing off. I sat down in the nearest chair and tried hard not to cry. As I struggled with my emotions, every old bit of home came back to bite me, hard.

It started with a tantrum I had at her expense when I was eleven. Mom wasn't strict enough and I felt I was walking all over her. So, I did the one thing that would prompt a reaction. I ran away. I still remember the night she went looking for me. We wound up in the neighborhood outside her office. I can still her voice as she begged to come home. She recounted a story I do not and cannot remember. I was allergic to the baby formula they were feeding me as an infant. She thought she was the worst mother in the world because it caused me such suffering. I can still remember the questions that night, still remember the pain in her voice when she asked, "How could I do something like that? And how could I not try to make your life happier after that?"

Mom? You gave me the best life of any kid who ever lived. You encouraged me, made me want to do more than other kids my age. You took the time to find out what interested me and what didn't. Then you challenged me to live up to my standards. Then you told me to have fun.

And then you told me that being in love with my uncle wasn't a bad thing. And then you told me why. I sat up in the chair crying openly.

Watching her in that bed was hard and made more difficult by her soft moans. It brought another unwelcome memory. *You were kidnapped by hoodlums who only wanted you to kill a little girl. Gina. They wanted her to kill Gina.* The reasons are not important now. It was Mom's reaction to those demands that proved to me how special she was. *They tied you to a chair and injected you with the best heroin they could find. They needed a junkie. They needed someone to do what they said and that was their mechanism. And you were totally willing to kill whoever was on their list. Until you saw that it was Gina.* Gina was four when that happened. She rescued that child all while fighting the biggest monkey in the world. *You wanted nothing more than another fix. Instead, you turned to me and showed me why greatness is earned. You turned to your family and got the help in the form of an eleven-year-old daughter who simply lay down with you on your bed. You still call yourself a junkie, but you have never fallen to the temptations that clawed at you every day of your life.*

Then I did the one thing that I saw as unimaginably cruel. I fell asleep in the chair and dreamed about Indians again. There was one that smiled as he rode by me on a horse. I smiled at him, waved and called out, "Will I see you again?"

"No time soon," he said.

The dream began to break up around me. The face of the Indian lingered in my mind long after it vanished into the fog from which it came. I didn't have to wonder. I'd been dreaming about my real father, Brian Sixkiller.

But there was a noise there that didn't belong. It was out-of-place on the prairie and startled me into wakefulness. It was a voice that invaded my dream, one that I recognized, one that nourished me when I was a baby, one that I recognized as it nursed me, one that took special pride that *I* was her child. Mother.

"Do you sleep through all your patient consultations?" she asked with a weak voice.

I jumped straight and caught myself before I was thrown out of the ICU for breaking every protocol they ever instituted. "Mom!" I cried instead.

I'd been asleep for hours when she wakened. That alone marked an improvement in her condition because she should have been dead. The lesions were starting to shrink and disappear, too. I didn't even have to check the monitors to know her vital signs were better. Okay, while I didn't have to, I did. But happy? There are really no words for it.

"Are you going to tell me what you did to me?" she asked as though she was fighting sleep.

"Yeah. I gave you a large dose of penicillin to combat your latest case of syphilis."

"Latest?" she asked with her trademark smile.

I took her hand and held it tightly. It was the best medicine I ever got. Then I told her what I had done and why I had come to that particular conclusion about her disease. She listened, yawned once but stayed alert enough to say at the end, "And you want to know why he did this?"

"No," I answered. "I don't care why. You're alive and that's all I want."

She squeezed my hand and asked, "And if I had been the doctor and you the patient? Would you not want to know what led to this attack on you?"

Bluntly, she was telling me that there was an overreaching reason for this attack. Okay, I already knew a lot of the motives. It would shred her credibility with voters, would destroy any coalition of congressmen she built and would sidetrack the country with sideshows rather than force it to come to terms with a crumbling economy. Her voice in the next Senate would be the one that broke the logjam.

"Damn, Mom," I said weakly. "I'm sorry."

"No, child," she replied. "You are not sorry. You are very able and you're going to do something extraordinary."

I smiled. "Really?"

"Yes."

And she told me what I was going to do. And I agreed to do it. No, not because it was extraordinary, but because I knew that she was right and it needed to be done.

I smiled and asked, "Do I have any leeway in how I accomplish it?"

"Well, you did save my life. I suppose that means I should allow it."

"There's a 'but' in there somewhere, Mom."

"If you do it wrong, I'm going to punish you."

"You never could press that button," I said smiling down at her.

"Well, make sure you cover all the bases, daughter."

I leaned down, hugged her and was thankful it wasn't for the last time.

Then I went to the waiting room and broke the news to the family.

Aunt Paula? I don't know how you do it, but the hospital didn't even blink when every person in the waiting room exploded into cheers.

I went back to where Mario was recovering from minor surgery to repair some sloppy work done by his doctor. Otherwise, he was fine. The infections that I started by doing the operation on the tailgate of a Hummer were minor and the drugs took care of them. When I told him what had happened, he broke his stitches in his exuberance and a nurse had to redo them. Then he looked up at me and said, "Lord, I wouldn't miss this for the world."

Well, his doctor got the last word.

"You're staying here until all signs of infection are gone."

He smiled. "You're on the bottom."

"I'll let you know how it comes out."

It wasn't going to take long.

Thankfully.

Chapter 42

"And you're sure you have the authority to do this?" I asked Barbara Reese.

"I can put her in a place will make the Black Hole of Calcutta looked like Club Med," she replied. "The question, Doctor, is do you have the intestinal fortitude to do it?"

"Guts?" I said.

She shrugged. "You say potato."

And that was it.

Deborah Hollis was being held in the Flathead County Jail by recommendation of FBI Agent Barbara Reese through the local DA, a man named Randy Barnovich. Had that not been true, I would not have been involved and my mother would not have gotten an end to a personal nightmare. But I'm getting ahead myself.

Barbara and I saw Debbie the day after my mother told me the truth about John North. I didn't have to believe her, but I did. No, it has nothing to do with the old adage that "she would never lie to me". Well, she wouldn't but that's neither here nor there. Debbie Hollis was going to reaffirm everything Mom told me or else Pee Wee would follow through on her threat. Yes, America is *that* kind of place now. And, no, I don't especially like it. But that, too, is neither here nor there.

Debbie looked defiant and angry when we entered her cell. You heard right. The meeting was not held in the visitors center; it was conducted in a place that would be a constant reminder of her status. She was a prisoner.

"Inmate Hollis," Pee Wee said only to reaffirm that fact. "My name is Barbara Reese and I'm here to offer you a deal. If you accept it, you will be returned to Canada and they can do whatever they wish with you. No records will be turned over to Canadian authorities."

I was next to her as she spoke. I knew what Pee Wee was going to offer her and I had very mixed feeling over it. But. It was what and how Mom wanted things settled.

Hollis stared at Pee Wee for a moment before she said with a shrug, "Okay. What's the deal?"

"Peace," she said flatly. Then nothing.

Deborah Hollis was a cipher in the play that starred both my mother and John North. My part was destined to be one of a walk-on, a bit player no one would remember expect trivia buffs. Doctor Evangeline Monica Sixkiller-Collins Collins. She was called Doctor Six by everyone that knew her. And then my name would slip away as though it had become invisible and unpronounceable. But cipher or not, Debbie was interested in self-preservation. She looked up at Pee Wee and said, "Okay. I'm listening."

"There will be an announcement tonight from the Billings Office of the FBI. It will announce the death of Congresswoman Chang's campaign chairman, Doctor John North. His death will be described as a hunting accident. All accounts of the story will support that claim. Your part in killing her will not become public." Then she added for effect, "Unless you decline the offer."

"Why?" she said. "Everyone here knows that North tried to kill her and that I provided the means that would destroy her political career. I could agree to your deal and then double-cross you."

"The reason you will not double-cross us is because you were the shooter that killed Dr. North. That's one reason. The second reason is the rather unfortunate accident that would befall you should you decide that peace isn't enough."

"North hated her," she said.

"And he had a wife, three kids and four grandchildren that had no idea," I said to her.

"His hatred had no basis in fact and will have the effect of destroying his family if it becomes known," Pee Wee said to her.

"And still…"

"And a story to the effect that Congresswoman Chang's campaign chairman died in a hunting accident will air on the radio tomorrow morning. It will prompt the FBI to make their announcement. Warren Pick will describe the accident in detail because he was a witness to it. If you see Mr. Pick ever again? You will suffer an accident. Ms.

Hollis? It would be best if you behaved yourself, practice good medicine and loved your neighbor as you would have him love you."

"No charges for any of us and all because North had a family?"

Ah, the gunfight. I'd forgotten about the gunfight. Other than North himself, the most virulent hatred in that group was Spite, the pink-haired lopsided-wearing Mohawk girl from the station. The only two people who died that day were North himself and her. Officer Houser killed both of them. Coach Horn turned out to be another minor player named Peter. His motive? He needed the money. Period. And Bernie Ryan? Was in debt and had a drug habit. Did drugs kill his son? Maybe. My guess? A rather big gun killed his son.

When I described the events of the day to my mother, she listened and I could hear the wheels turning. She's been in Washington DC long enough to have turned cynical, but what she proposed to me proved that there is still hope for us. That conversation led me here to be a part of an offer that I hoped Debbie Hollis would accept.

"Yes," Pee Wee said.

"Can I think about it?" she asked.

"No," Pee Wee said and turned to leave.

It wasn't my part to be included in that scene to convince her. That would come later. But then? I felt sorry for her because she was escaping without consequences and Americans are big on them. We believe in an eye-for-an-eye. We believe in retribution. We believe in righteous anger. But this? Deborah Hollis was being offered absolution by the only person with the power to grant it. My mother. She's seen enough violence in her life to make this offer both decent and genuine. But. I couldn't believe it.

"You need time to think?" I said incredulously. "You're being offered the rest of your life and you need to think about it? You don't even know her and yet you tried to kill her. She should want your head on a plate. Instead, she's offering you a chance to think about life and how to live the rest of yours." To that point I hadn't considered her motive for being involved. When I saw her tears, it became obvious. "Loving a man who would commit murder is as heinous as pulling the trigger yourself. You need to think? Grab a fishing pole and head into the arctic north where life is reduced to its minimums. Go there and find whatever solace is there for you to find. Go there and ask yourself if Melodie Chang's life was worth a lifetime with the man who murdered her. Ask yourself why he would kill her and then turn his back on his entire family. Not only would he kill Mrs. Chang, but his own family as well. Think, Ms. Hollis? Think about death by lethal injection. Think about the footsteps coming for you outside the cell where you can do little but wait for them. Think about it, Ms. Hollis? You don't appear to be a fool, but then looks can be deceiving." Then I turned to go.

Her voice, weak with the emotion of the moment, squeaked, "Okay. I'll do it. But can I meet her?"

"I'll ask."

"And who are you that you should be here now?"

Pee Wee turned back to her and said, "She is the last condition you will face. You can do it or not. It doesn't matter to me." Then she looked at me and smiled. "Yes, yes. I know. It matters to you." Then she looked back at Debbie and said, "You will send your research to Doctor Barry Strait and the two of you will publish your findings jointly. You can do whatever you wish with it. No one will object if you opt out of the process and bury your work. That is a decision you will face with him, Doctor Strait."

"That process doesn't include her," Debbie said to Barbara.

She smiled for the first time and said, "Ms. Hollis? Meet Doctor Six, Congresswoman Chang's oldest daughter."

Debbie looked up at me and I wasn't certain who I was looking at. A murderess? A plot hatching? Insanity breaking out? Her face was that clouded. While looking at me, she said to Barbara, "Then I have a condition of my own. I want to talk to the doctor alone."

Pee Wee looked at me and asked, "Any objections?"

"No."

A guard let her out and it was just us, the woman who tried to kill my mother and her oldest daughter, the one who swore she would always be there to tend her wounds and make her whole again.

"Do you have any ID?" she asked.

I showed her my driver's license, Mario's picture and then showed her my kids. "That's us, my family."

"He told me you would figure it out," she said. "And if you tell that FBI person? Then I'll accept a bullet in the back of the head gladly. This is between you and me. I'll accept whatever terms she suggests, but you have to accept this one."

Justice in this country is a business. We like business and like our leaders to act that way. Winners win and losers are never heard from again. More, winners make their own rules. They hack and slash their way through the financial world they devised and then proclaim victory when all their opponents have less than they do. We admire men who act that way. We shower them with adulation and then quickly forget them as losers when they cross one too many line. But this? This was the ultimate loser defining and proclaiming her own rules. This was one of the vanquished deciding that the game had been unfair and *these* were the rules. All I had to do was agree with her.

I turned toward the cell door and smiled. *Lady? I wouldn't miss this for the world.*

I turned back and said, "Oh, hell yes. In a heartbeat."

"Really?" she said as though she didn't believe me.

"Momma didn't raise any fools." No, she surely didn't – and only she had the power to say no.

No, I wouldn't miss this for the world.

Chapter 43

Damn, she looked better. The lesions were fading away and she was no longer in pain. I knew that before I ever saw her. She was laughing and the nurses were laughing with her. She was probably telling dirty jokes again.

Her face lit up when I walked in to the room. Paula, Dad, Mario and Alex were all there and from the giggles, I'd say that Mom was the butt of a joke sprung by Paula.

"Baby!" she squealed. Then she put her face in her hands and screamed. "I'm sorry! I won't do it again, Evie."

"Oh, yada yada," I said. "And stop lying to your children."

Mario's arm was in a sling, Alex was in a wheel chair and Paula was dressed like a doctor. She even had a stethoscope hanging from her neck. There were more nurses in her room than patients, too. And three doctors. If someone somewhere else in the hospital needed help, they were in trouble. It wasn't hard to smile.

She looked at me seriously and said, "Is it over?"

"Nope," I said. "There is still one step left."

She frowned and tried to look fierce. "What?"

I went to her bedside, nudged Dad out of the way and said, "The rumor I hear is that The Great White Puritan is going to be your campaign manager."

Mom looked at Paula and said, "Who else? Especially now?"

Paula was the one who suggested that North become her manager. I can't say she didn't mean well because she did. They been friends since before I was born. I grew up with Aunt Paula, Uncle Simon and their kids. I still see their oldest daughter, Regina, on occasion. Someday Dad is going to write a book about them, about Mom and Aunt Paula, and it will filed under fiction because no one will believe it. Well, they should believe it. Those two women share stuff that not even I know about. It's the stuff of wonder and there is nothing they could say that I wouldn't believe.

"Yep," Aunt Paula crowed. "I am here with my stethoscope in tow to bring life back to the Chang campaign." Then she did the worst Groucho Marx routine I'd ever seen and said, "And someone has to."

"That's great, Aunt Paula," I said. "Really."

And I meant it. But no one knew back then what I know now. Well, Mom knows. Mom knew. But she relented anyway because it was always in her character to do something like that. Aunt Paula knew the story, too, because there is nothing that one of them knows that the other doesn't. Together, they cooked up the best feel-good story in New England. Why? Because Mom *knew*. She knew how North felt about her and why. And she still let him run her campaign. She knew the risk she was taking and knew the consequences if she guessed wrong. Well, she did. Guess wrong, I mean. But there was one person in this story who had ultimate faith in our family – and none of us had ever met her. But, wow, isn't that putting the antibiotics before the disease.

Despite all that, there is one person who has always had the power of truth on her side. And, no, it isn't my mother. Or Aunt Paula. But again, I'm getting ahead of myself.

"Can either of you relate the story about John North? I mean, I want all the details and I know they're in this room."

"Why?" Aunt Paula asked suspiciously.

"Because I said so, Aunt Paula." Then I bowed and added, "Respectfully, of course." Then I looked at my mother and said, "Had you died? It is very possible I would not have known why. That is why I'm here. I want you to tell me why John North tried to kill you."

Mom sighed and said to Aunt Paula, "She deserves to know, kid."

"Why am I always the kid?" she asked.

"Because you're younger than me," she replied for the millionth time.

"Well?" I asked. "Am I going to be condemned to watch bad imitations of Laurel and Hardy or are you going to tell me?"

"North had a daughter named Marie," Mom said sadly. "She was their youngest at sixteen and had all the typical teenage angst. She ran away and landed in Aunt Dora's school. She was there for about a month ending about six months ago. North blamed me for what happened. Well, the family."

Page 234

"And what did?"

"Marie got pregnant and had abortion, an illegal one."

That meant the person who performed it wasn't licensed. Marie was lucky she didn't die. "And?" I prompted.

Mom said, "That was it. That's why she ran away from home. She was pregnant."

"That's it?" I said.

She shrugged and said, "Well, I could turn this into a he-said, she-said affair, but you know how much credibility that stuff has."

"So fast-forward. What happened?"

"She had an abortion."

"And he blamed you?"

"I was the easiest target."

"But Aunt Dora runs the school."

She smiled and said, "All she had was medical proof that Marie wasn't pregnant when she got to her school. Marie insisted on it. She didn't want the school to take the blame for something she did herself."

"She could have died," I sympathized.

"Which is the issue Marie wanted to bring into my campaign. I didn't only because the matter was private and deserved to stay that way."

"And North hated you anyway?" I asked, my credulity stretched.

"He knew I agreed with Marie. He knew that I support and always will support a woman's right to choose. It isn't religious; it's personal. It something you decide with those who are involved. The fact that North had no idea his daughter was pregnant was irrelevant. He was going to make her have it and raise it. She wouldn't even have been allowed to put it up for adoption."

"And yet you made him your campaign manager?"

And there it was. The Issue. I understood her reasoning and so did everyone else in the room. In fact, the rationale behind John North being asked to run Mom's campaign – even with no experience – probably eluded even North himself. In retrospect, the only reason he took the job was access. Access? Yes, to a whole horde of people who could direct him to people like Deborah Hollis.

And that left the last step.

But this was my mother. I could have taken the easy way, the *conservative* way out of the box by saying no. But I couldn't. No to what? To the people in the hallway. There were two of them and they were listening to my mother explain why she made an enemy into a campaign manager. One of them was already convinced. The other? Well, let's just say the jury was out on that person.

It was up to me to arrange this meeting and I had. The rest was going to be up to them. I went to the door and said, "It's all yours."

And Aunt Dora walked into the room with Deborah Hollis.

As they say in show business, the final curtain was going up.

Chapter 44

Aunt Dora is letting her flaming red hair burn out. Strands of gray are filling in to replace what used to be the reddest hair this side of Shangri-la. It's also shorter than it used to be. Gone are the days when boys would fall hopelessly in love with her just because she tossed her hair back. She wasn't the attraction, however. Debbie was.

She'd heard Mom's explanation for hiring John North. Now, she was going to decide if the fairy tale was true, or if her life was condemned to be short-lived and expected to be that way. I know where my own prejudice set down and it was with her – and not just because I'm a doctor and will always side with life. I sided with her because our family has seen too much madness and this was entirely within the realm of possibility for it to do something like this. Or put another way, it was akin to John Kennedy taking as a confidant Lee Harvey Oswald.

Debbie stood at the end of the bed and stared at Mom. Then, she began slowly, "I tried to kill you. And yet, here I am. Why?"

Lord, but Mom could have appealed to her status as a patient, to her physical weakness and bowed out. But she didn't. She isn't shy and hasn't been ever since she approached Grandpa on the Prom all those years ago. She looked at Debbie and said, "What would you have gained by my death?"

"A man."

"Really? That's your definition of one?"

"He said he loved me."

"He probably said the same thing to his wife."

"You're saying he used me."

"No. I'm saying that he probably said the same thing to you that he said to his wife. He wouldn't be the first man to act that way. He won't be the last."

"You're trying hard not to blame me," Debbie said.

Mom looked at Paula, then at me and replied, "Okay, you're guilty of trying to kill me. I guess my people are better than yours. Does that satisfy the Neolithic beast inside you?"

"I could try again."

"You would need a reason."

"Maybe you'll give me one I haven't thought of yet."

"And maybe you'll get so mad that the only answer is lunch."

"That sounds too much like Pollyanna," Debbie said.

"You'd rather I got angry and called you're a bitch for trying to use John North to kill me. Okay, I'm not too happy about that, but the best answer is the obvious one. If we become friends, the worst thing you'll do to me is return a sweater dirty to me."

She turned and looked at me. "I could kill her."

Mario giggled and said, "Right. Lady? Better people than you have tried."

She stamped her foot and said angrily, "I'm serious and you people aren't! I'm the fox in the henhouse! I'm the one that you don't want your son to bring to dinner! I'm the woman in red!"

I don't think it fell to me. Not really. Dad had a better answer and I'm convinced he was going to throw the ghost of Vince Tamuglio on the pile. He was Mom's Mistake. He was the one that could have destroyed the family. He was The Other Man. I don't know all the reasons it happened, but I know that Mom and Dad learned all their lessons and applied them. Maybe Debbie would have been moved by an example from Mom's own past. But this didn't happen in Portland, Maine. It happened here in Montana, in Kalispell and I'm convinced there was a reason. Me. It happened here because someone knew I lived here and knew I was the eldest daughter of Melodie Chang. If that was true, then it was up to me to play my part in this drama.

"Nicely done, Deb," I said. "The woman in red? Why don't you call yourself Mata Hari and save all of us the trouble of wondering what you're talking about." Then *I* stamped my foot. "You aren't here because this was the only place you could find Melodie Chang. She's accessible to anyone who wants to talk to her. You're here because of me, because you wanted some proof that Marie was wrong and I was your foil. You were betting that the distance from Portland to Kalispell was far enough to make me less attentive, less able and less willing to do this. You were betting that mother and daughter, that father and daughter carried with them their own term limits." I stabbed my finger at my mother and said, "Or did it escape you that I was chasing these answers long before *she* showed up here! I didn't do for her anything I wouldn't have done for you! And you tried to kill her! If you want something, don't use me as a reason to fail because I didn't and don't. I succeed every day of my life – and she's responsible for it! She encouraged me to chase life instead of death! She's responsible for me agreeing to let you in to see her! She's evidence of a better answer for us! She's proof that we can work together!" Then I took a step toward her and practically screamed, "Even those who try to kill us! She's proof that the best answers are usually the most obvious ones!"

I'm glad that I don't put much stock in body English. Why? Because she turned her back on us. She did not, however, leave. She stood at the glass door and looked out, looked away from us. If asked, I would have said what I thought she was thinking. Maybe she was plotting how to get past the non-existent security inside the hospital. It could have been anything. Then she turned around and said, "Okay, then here's my condition. Take it or not." She took a deep breath and looked at Aunt Paula. "I want to work with her on your campaign. I want first hand looks at what your family looks like and how it works. That's my condition."

Paula tsk-tsked and said, "Boy, Lacy's gonna be pissed." Then she extended her hand toward Debbie and said, "Any salary demands?"

Debbie looked confused. "That's it?"

Paula threw her hands in the air and said, "Well, okay. What's your favorite color?"

"What?"

She repeated it.

"Blue."

"Then you're hired."

"I tried to kill your boss!" she screamed.

"Boss?" Paula growled. "Boss! That woman is nothing more than my figurehead! She doesn't shit until I tell her to! Boss! I've been picking up her crap for thirty years…"

"Thirty-five," Mom interrupted.

"...and *you* aren't going to change that fact! Boss," she said, her temper fading. "I can't believe she called you my boss."

Debbie looked at me and asked, "Are they always this way?"

I smiled. "Just don't make that mistake again."

Mom insisted on a hug. She said it was better than a handshake.

As promised, Warren Trick went on the air the next morning and made his tragic announcement. He was helped by his new on-air assistant, Rachel Wells. Again, as specified, the FBI office in Billings, Montana, corroborated the story of John North's death. It was called a tragic accident and no one ever heard otherwise. No one missed Spite, not even her family. They figured she overdosed somewhere in LA. No one bothered to check either.

And life went on Kalispell, Montana.

Until one night two weeks later.

It really didn't end until that night.

Epilogue

We were in the middle of our infrequently frequent poker game when the doorbell rang. Since I was a player and not a playboy bunny, Wanda yelled, "I got it!" She was wearing a red bunny costume with black heels. It didn't do a thing for me, but it cost Norm three straight hands because he couldn't concentrate on his cards.

She opened the door on…my mother. She was wearing a coat, as were all the others. Paula, Debbie and Alex were with them. Better yet? They were all healthy, even Alex.

I bounced up and ran to the door. Life had settled down into its grinding routine and Mom was a pleasant break from it.

"I've heard about your poker games," she said.

"Well," I replied. "We don't have them as often as we'd like."

Kris was there, too. She was dressed in green and she was sitting in Norma's lap. Yep, *that* Norma. My PA Norma, my Physician's Assistant Norma. Who knew?

Cayn was upstairs with the kids, and their number included Janet Hardiman. She was still having some bad days, but Cayn was taking care of her. Given enough time, I think she'll be okay. Cayn has already said that he's going to discuss her parents with her as times passes. Also, I was in contact with Regina Ryan. She misses David, but has met and come to like Alex.

That's when life finally got back to normal. "Well," Mom said. "Let's get back to the game. Just ignore me because I'm a servant of the people." And she removed her coat and revealed herself to be dressed in a black bunny costume and black platform boots.

Wanda stared and then started to cry. "All this work to get into this thing and then The Queen shows up and…" she couldn't continue.

Yep. Everyone stared. Even Kris and Norma.

Quinn Riley was struck speechless – and that was a thing I would have placed bets upon.

Aidan Hall asked Mario, "Does she need a doctor?"

"Nope. Grew her own."

"Damn," he said. "I would surely like to give her a physical."

But the night was perfect. Everyone had a good time and no one complained about losing at cards. At the end of the night, Mom got me alone upstairs in our bedroom and hugged me tightly. "I never thanked you, baby. I thought I was going to die and I only wanted to see you one more time. And Alex? He's speechless. He thought he was going to have to come here and do the investigative work by himself. Then you not only finished it but got him a new heart. Baby? I am so very proud of you."

And we cried together. It was, perhaps, the best day of my life.

Well, maybe that's why I'm proud to be a Collins and not someone else. I believed everything I said to Debbie Hollis and always will. Something in the way I was raised, about the way all of the Collins kids got raised, worked its gentle magic and left us just a bit readier to chase life than almost anyone I've ever known.

Hey, it sure beats chasing death.

Trust me on that one.

www.ingramcontent.com/pod-product-compliance
Lightning Source LLC
LaVergne TN
LVHW010200070526
838199LV00062B/4436